CHANGO'S FIRE

Also by Ernesto Quiñonez

Bodega Dreams

CHANGO'S FIRE

A NOVEL

Ernesto Quiñonez

HARPER ● PERENNIAL

NEW YORK ● LONDON ● TORONTO ● SYDNEY

HARPER ● PERENNIAL

A hardcover edition of this book was published in 2004 by Rayo, an imprint of HarperCollins Publishers.

CHANGO'S FIRE. Copyright © 2004 by Ernesto Quiñonez. All rights reserved. Printed in the United States of America. No part of this book may be used or reproduced in any manner whatsoever without written permission except in the case of brief quotations embodied in critical articles and reviews. For information, address HarperCollins Publishers, 195 Broadway, New York, NY 10007.

HarperCollins books may be purchased for educational, business, or sales promotional use. For information, please e-mail the Special Markets Department at SPsales@harpercollins.com.

First Harper Perennial edition published 2005.

Designed by Renato Stanisic

The Library of Congress has catalogued the hardcover edition as follows:

Quiñonez, Ernesto.
    Chango's fire : a novel / Ernesto Quiñonez.—1st ed.
        p. cm.
    ISBN 978-0-06-056459-9
    1. Difference (Psychology)—Fiction. 2. Hispanic Americans—Fiction.
3. New York (N.Y.)—Fiction. 4. Gentrification—Fiction.
5. Neighborhood—Fiction. 6. Arson—Fiction. I. Title.

PS3567.U3618C47   2004
8-13'.54—dc22   2004046721

ISBN 978-0-06-056564-0 (pbk.)

        16 17 18 19   DIX/RRD 10 9

Anna

You must concede that this Bronx slum and others
in Brooklyn and Manhattan are unrepairable.
They are beyond rebuilding, tinkering and restoring.
They must be leveled to the ground.

Robert Moses, New York City master builder, 1974

CONTENTS

CONTENTS

Book I

A FILING OF COMPLAINTS

Complaint #1

The house I'm about to set on fire stands alone on a hill.

In this Westchester darkness, it resembles a lonely house Hopper might paint. A driveway wide enough for a truck. A lawn with trees and wide-open space you can picture Kennedy kids playing touch football—their smiles perfect, the knees of their khakis stained with grass. No ocean though, but a wooden porch does wrap itself around the house as if hugging it. Large windows and spacious bedrooms, an American house new immigrants dream of. The type of house America promises can be yours if you work hard, save your pennies and salute the flag.

I open the screen door, punch in the alarm code and I'm in. It's my house, really. The owner doesn't want it. It's my house for these precious few minutes. I can indulge myself in snooping through someone else's life. Walk through wooden floors that I hope to inhabit someday.

When I was first hired, I used to enter these houses with my tin gallons filled with kerosene and quickly set to work at wetting the beds, couches and curtains. Light it all up with a flick of a match and quickly take off. Now I look around, wondering why, besides the money, does this person want his house taken out? I pace around. I pick up pictures, stare at the loved ones. I see childhood secrets that were never known to me, secrets of horses and country homes, of summer vacations. I open drawers. Sift through clothes. Read the spines of books and try to find clues about this person's life. Once I burned a house where an entire set of cheerleader outfits sat in an attic closet, nicely folded. Was his wife the coach? Did he kill these girls? Who knows?

I walk around. This house is beautiful but the furniture is out-dated, the lamps, doors and closets have old, yellow glows. In the living room, there's a television with knobs, a stereo with a turntable. Nailed to the wall is a black rotary telephone that hangs like an extinct breed. In the kitchen, there is not so much as a toaster. The wooden chairs in the dining room are chipped, and the walls are crowded with portraits of Catholic saints, of fruits and landscapes. But it is the faded sunflower curtains and dead plants by the windows that pretty much indicates an old woman lived here. Now that she's been put away, or is dead, this house seems to be used only as storage space, like a huge empty room where broken toys or unused objects from a previous life or a failed marriage sit lifeless. There's sadness in this house. It feels like its children deserted it many years ago and not so much as even cared to look back. Not a single tear. All around, everything carries such sorrow. A darkness attaches itself to the walls, as if no light had ever shone, even when tiny feet ran around these floors. There's a sense of neglected space in these halls. I'm stepping on unwanted family history. Nothing in this house has been deemed worthy to be saved or treasured. Everything has been condemned to be erased by fire.

But I can't really say for sure what happened here years ago that has made this house so bleak. But bleak it is. And now that the last of the old folks are gone, their grown children will light a match to unwanted memories. The house gets lit, the neighborhood stays the same color, and the property gets rebuilt with funneled insurance money.

Just as well. It's not my house, nor my memories. Even less, it's not my place to ask.

I don't ask.

I never ask.

The people I work for don't know me. I only deal with Eddie, and Eddie deals with them, and I don't know who they deal with or how the insurance is fixed, all I know is that the bread gets passed around in that order. Me getting the last of the crumbs.

I've been working for Eddie for some time now. The crumbs I get are large enough that I mortgaged an apartment floor in this old, battered, three-story walk-up. On the first floor, my friend Maritza has set up her crazy church, and the second floor is owned by a white woman I barely know. Though she seems nice, she rarely makes eye contact and is always on the go. She leaves the building early in the morning and I can usually hear her come back late at night when I'm reading in bed. She doesn't spend much time in her house or on fixing up her floor like I do.

I've been upgrading my floor slowly, because it's so goddamn expensive. But I'm happy there. At times and for no reason, I go outside and cross the street and stare at my building. I smile. See the third floor? I own it, I tell myself. I see the windows a little crooked, not exactly fitting in their frames. Got to fix that. I smile. I see the

paint chipping on all sides. Got to fix that. I like the gray shadow my
building casts when the sun hits it from the west side of 103rd Street
and Lexington Avenue, and how it's sandwiched between Papelito's
botanica and a barber shop. I tell myself, I've come a long way from
the clubhouse I built as a little kid. I had gathered refrigerator boxes,
painted them, cut open windows and doors, and placed my clubhouse on a vacant lot full of rats, charred bricks and thrown-out diapers. I called it the Brown House, home to the president of Spanish
Harlem.

What I was too young to know back then was that it was during
the decade of my childhood that my future boss, Eddie, and guys like
him were hired. Eddie burned down half of El Barrio and most of the
South Bronx. He got a cut of the insurance money from the property
owners, including the city, which was also in on it by cutting down
half of the fire services in neighborhoods like mine. It was a free-for-
all. Everyone was on the take. Everyone saw it coming. As the influx
of Puerto Ricans in the fifties and sixties became more intense, many
Italians sold their businesses and split town. Many Jews followed
suit, as did the Irish real estate owners who witnessed the neighborhood shift to a darker color and, most of them, turned to people like
Eddie.

Spanish Harlem was worthless property in the seventies and
early eighties. Many property owners burned their own buildings
down and handed the new immigrants a neighborhood filled with
hollow walls and vacant lots. Urban Swiss cheese. The city would
then place many of us in the projects, creating Latino reservations.
These city blocks, full of project buildings on each corner, were built
not so much to house us as to corral us. To keep us in one place. We
were being slowly but surely relocated, as many who owned real estate burned the neighborhood, collected the insurance, sat on the di-
lapidated property and waited for better days.

Today, the wait is over, Spanish Harlem's burned out buildings are gold mines. Many of the same landlords who burned their tenements are now rebuilding. Empowerment zoning has changed the face of the neighborhood. Chain stores rise like monsters from a lake. Gap. Starbucks. Blockbuster Video. Old Navy. Like the new Berlin, El Barrio is being rebuilt from its ashes. The rents are absurdly high, and it breaks my heart, because Spanish Harlem had always been a springboard. A place where immigrants came to better themselves and, when they had reached the next plateau, they'd leave traces of their culture, a bit of themselves behind, and move on. A melting pot of past success stories—Dutch, Jews, Irish, Italians. When it came our turn to inherit these blocks, East Harlem was still a magical neighborhood made up of families dreaming of their sons hiring the men their fathers worked for. Dreaming of their daughters sleeping in the houses their mothers cleaned. And then, the bottom fell out. Yet Eddie sticks around, he grows old, seeing the neighborhood change, and he laughs, "Wha' for? Who can afford these rents? Better when the city let it burn."

Eddie has a son. I actually knew his son first, Trompo Loco, Crazy Top. He's this wonderful guy I grew up with. He was never the brightest of people, probably borderline slow. But there's a beauty to him. An imperfect beauty, like one you can detect when looking for shells at Orchard Beach. A happiness you feel when finding a shell that's chipped yet it has markings like you've never seen before. Trompo Loco is like that. He is really skinny, making him look taller than he really is. Trompo Loco is so skinny that he would have been nicknamed Flaco, except that when he gets mad he starts twirling himself round and round until he falls to the ground. Sometimes he passes out from the dizziness. He's done this since we were kids, and because back then we all played with wooden tops, he got the name Trompo Loco. I always felt bad for him, because all the kids from the block would make fun of him. "Yo, retardo," they'd say, "why you gotta look so stupid?" Though at times—and this I hate to admit—to prove myself to the other kids, I made fun of him as well. But later on I was always defending Trompo Loco and trying to keep others from picking on him. I didn't know what was happening in his house but I knew it was something really awful, because he'd rather be outside, where all the kids made fun of him, than go upstairs. We became friends and he'd spend a lot of time in my house. So much time that my parents would bring him to church with us. It was at church that I found out the truth about Trompo Loco's crazy mother. I then understood why he'd rather be ridiculed by the kids outside than be upstairs with a woman who yelled threats to him and to herself. It was also at church that I heard the rumors that this big Italian guy was Trompo Loco's father. How that man had driven Trompo Loco's mother crazy. Then one day Trompo Loco took me to 118th Street and Pleasant Avenue, the last remnants of the Italian part of East Harlem. From a distance, Trompo Loco pointed at this coffee shop on the corner. I saw this tall man who first helped this old Latin woman and her shopping cart cross the street before he himself went inside the coffee shop. It was the first time I saw Eddie. Years later I wasn't just looking out for his illegitimate son. I was working for him.

When I started working for Eddie and was ready to set my first house on fire, he came along. He told me I was a JAFO, Just Another Fucking Observer, to stay out of his way and watch. "These new houses? Ga'bage. You can burn them with firecrackers." And he spilled kerosene all over the bedrooms, like he was about to mop the floors and was getting them ready. "But you know mattresses are fire eaters. The very thing we sleep on is a box of matches." I saw Eddie take no delight in setting fires; I did see youth and longing in his eyes when he talked about his early days. "In the old days now those houses were made to withstand air raids."

That first time, when I was being schooled, I spotted a Rolex watch on top of a dresser. My heart jumped and I was about to grab it and put it in my pocket. Eddie caught my eye. "Never take anything," he said, "never even take the ice cream from the fridge. The adjuster is going to look for every valuable thing in this house, and it better be burned. You know, it's gotta look good. I have people working for me, but it gotta look good. It's my name at the end of the day." And Eddie spilled more kerosene all over the floors. I asked Eddie if the firemen would know that this was deliberate. Eddie didn't answer me. I never asked him again. I learned that first day, you never ask. So I just listened.

"Each fire, Julio, has its own life, its own personality," he said to me that first time, as we watched the house burning at a distance, us safely inside his parked car. "Depending on building design, material and how clean your kerosene is, the fire will burn at its own pace, the smoke will take its own color and smell." I noticed that night that Eddie was not obsessed by fire. He saw no beauty in the flames. "Most fires are nasty, Julio. As soon as they reach a certain growth, they are like children that you can't control, or never wanted. They pretty much become an avalanche of flames and you can't take them back or stop them, Julio. So, know what you are doing before it's too late."

Like Eddie, I'm not obsessed by fire. But I have no problems with what I do.

My conscience is clean with God and men. I burn buildings, just like Eddie, and I burn them for the same reason, the money. But the

person whose house I'm burning knows I'm coming. He even gave
Eddie the keys and alarm code. And I don't know how Eddie does it,
how he fixes it with the insurance company, all I know is everyone
gets paid and my job is to light that house up.

Tonight, right before I set this house in Westchester ablaze, I call
Eddie. I want to make sure this is the right address; even though
I'm already inside, I check to make sure. I don't want to burn the
wrong place.

"All right," Eddie says over the phone, "read me the address
back."

I read it back to him.

"Yeah, that's the one. Read me the alarm code."

I read that back, too.

"You're set. Go wet the bed."

I tell Eddie this is my last job, that I'm quitting after this one.
That I'll work at the demolition site but that's it. I don't hear anything, so I repeat that this is my last job.

"How's your friend?" Eddie always refers to his son as my friend.

I tell Eddie, Trompo Loco is fine.

"Good, good. Keep an eye out for him, okay? But keep him away
from my coffee shop."

I always do, right? Then I say it again, that this is my last job.

"Are you taking him to church?"

I remind Eddie that I don't go to church anymore.

"Is he at least reading his Bible?"

"Yes," I say, and "did you hear me, Eddie, this is my last job."

"Are you getting married or something?"

"No," I say, "what's that got to do with it?"

Eddie hangs up.

I sigh and get to work.

I walk up the stairs and drench a bedroom, splashing some kerosene on the curtains. I do the other bedroom, where I hear a strange noise. Like someone or something crying. I get nervous. This house is supposed to be empty. I look for the source. I calm down some when I find under one bed a scared cat. He's afraid and wailing. I stomp my feet on the floor and, like a frightened mouse, the cat runs to the other side of the room. I chase after him and he runs down the stairs. I get a good glimpse and I see it's a beautiful Russian blue, I think it's a boy. His eyes are gray and he is too thin. The poor cat must not have eaten for days, living on mice, roaches, or whatever he could find in this house, and drinking water from the toilet bowl.

Not my problem.

It's just a cat.

I walk back down the stairs, pouring kerosene on the carpet. I take out my lighter. As soon as the lighter flame kisses the wet steps, the sound is one of thunder, and the fire quickly shoots up, running up the steps like a man possessed. The same possessed man who in the gospels asked Christ, It is not yet time to take us Son of Man? Because every time I start a fire, I think of my religious upbringing. I remember all the yelling, healing and anointing, and those sermons where the word of God was never "love" or "light" but "fire." Tongues of fire. And His angry presence was evident around a neighborhood that kept burning night after night. So often that the fires were disregarded and the people branded as sinners. In the news, we were being punished for being junkies, thieves, whores and murderers. The evidence of God's wrath was the blocks upon blocks of burned buildings we supposedly brought on ourselves. In my church it was a sign, these fires that consumed Spanish Harlem, the South Bronx, Harlem, Bed-Sty, you name the ghetto, it was being lit up. It was a sign, a pox on our houses, these fires were evidence of prophecy, of fulfillment, of . . . "The Truth."

But the truth was, it was just a guy like me, who had set those fires. A schmuck like me who had been paid by a local city politician or a slumlord. Each and every one of them a poverty czar.

Outside.

I see the house is wet in flames, not an inch of it is dry from fire. I start my car and I drive out, toward the highway. I hear that wailing sound again, the same one I heard in the bedroom. I look back and see the crying cat curled up in a ball in the back seat. I had left one car window open, and when the cat ran out of the house, he must have hopped in my car. At first I brake, and I'm ready to open the back door and shoo it away, but I'm too tired to pull over. I have to be at the site in the morning, then school, and I'm sure Mami would love it if I brought home a crying cat.

So I drive away.

When I reach the highway, the New York City skyline parades all its beauty across the Hudson River. The cat jumps to the front seat like he wants to take in those glorious lights. He sits there staring, and I wonder how the city looks to a cat. Because New York City does different things to different people, even creatures. I started building my own private New York the second I came of age. When New York City was filthy and broken and, in my mind, holy. The city left its mark on me, like a fish hook that caught me, was yanked and scarred my flesh. That first image of a dirty, broken city burned in my nine-year-old eyes and memory. And no matter how much the skyline changed over the years, what towers fell, what new buildings rose, the changes have never supplanted the vision of when I first climbed up on that Spanish Harlem roof and gazed upon its bright lights. How up above on that roof, Spanish Harlem sang to a nine-year-old kid like our church choir, and the skyline shone so saintly there was no doubt I was, at that very moment, closer to God.

Now, years later, somewhere in that glorious mess of a city, I own an apartment. A real space, with walls, doors and locks. It is mine. I will not die paying rent.

And that's how it's going to stay.

"Right, cat?"

Complaint #2

I park the car and pick the cat up slowly and hesitantly, thinking he's going to scratch me. I start to like him, because he doesn't. The cat lets me pick him up as if he knew this was now going to be his home.

It's late, I'm tired, and I begin to walk toward my building. I spot the white girl who just moved in. She's ahead of me, dressed in black, and her waist is small and thin, like she could be snapped in half. She looks back and sees me carrying a cat. I know I must smell of plaster from work and of kerosene and smoke from the fire. She reaches the door before me and takes her keys out and opens it. I am about to thank her and go inside, when she turns around to face me. She has a polite expression laced with a bit of suspicion. The kind of look I've seen white people give to office janitors and delivery boys.

"Excuse me," she says, blocking the door. "Do you live here?"

"Yeah, I'm on the third floor," I say courteously. She becomes even more hesitant to move away.

"Really?" she smiles nervously. "Then you wouldn't mind ringing? I just need to be sure." She looks at the cat, thinking I'm homeless or something. "I don't want to let anyone I don't know in the building."

I want to turn street on her and just rip her to pieces. Listen white bitch, I don't have to prove I live here. I lived in this neighborhood years back, when this very block was burned and broken. So move out of the way and go back to that town in Middle America where you came from.

I would love to say that.

Instead I take a deep breath.

"It's past midnight," I sigh. "I don't want to wake my parents up."

Why am I being polite when, unlike her, I have history here?

"I've just never seen you before. These aren't rentals," she says, as if I don't know this. Then she starts digging her hand into her purse and keeps it there. Mace, I'm thinking, cell phone or something?

Truth is, I want to push her aside and walk inside my property. But I just stand there. I see how vulnerable and small her body is. How her blue-green eyes highlight the splash of freckles around her nose, mirrored by a bigger splash just above the V-neck of her shirt and around her breasts. I stare at her. I think about when I was growing up, when there were not too many white people in Spanish Harlem. You only saw white people when you went to work and clocked in, and usually they were your bosses. At school they were your teachers. On TV these white people were always doctors, lawyers and detectives. They lived in another part of the city, or were wealthy and lived in Dallas or ran a dynasty, and you knew you were not wanted there. You'd be arrested on the very spot where you had

set foot on their lawns. Now that I dealt with white people on a regular basis, and I never let them push me around, I stood my ground,
but somehow, in Spanish Harlem, I felt they were in my backyard.
On my lawn. I should be the one asking questions. But the other
voice tells me that if I show them politeness and education, it throws
them off. They expect the rude Latino from the street, and the truth
is that I am that, too. And, at times, I have a problem deciding which
face to put on.

"Please, can you ring?" she says again as a smile trails her last
word.

El Barrio was no longer my barrio, and the past seemed irretriev-
able. White people living on many blocks. Some had money, some
didn't, but we were supposed to leave them all alone. We were supposed to accept them moving into our neighborhoods, as opposed to
when blacks and Latinos started entering their suburbs. How they'd
stare at us with evil eyes. Tell their kids to stay away from our kids.
Made sure their daughters stayed away from our sons. They never
warmly welcomed us into the great American Dream.

"Could you please just ring?"

Give us your tired.

Your poor.

But not on my block.

Not in my suburb.

Not in my building.

"If you don't ring, I can't let you up."

And here, in Spanish Harlem, we were supposed to take the high
road. Like Christ, turn the other cheek. Welcome white people and
smile as greedy real estate brokers changed the name from Spanish
Harlem to Spa Ha, because El Barrio was not a cool, catchy name.
They needed a new name, something that would attract yuppies and
make them feel hip while they wear all that black.

All that black, just like the girl blocking me from home is wearing.

"Sure," I say to her, "I don't mind ringing," which I do, because I have to ring a lot and wake up my family.

"*Quien?*"

"*Pa', soy yo.*"

"*Coño*, don't you have keys?" my father grumbles over the intercom and she giggles with reassurance, now that she is sure I live there.

"Nice cat," she takes her hand out of her bag and holds the door for me to walk inside.

"Thanks," I say. I can smell the booze on her breath, and her cheeks are bubble-gum pink. She must have been out drinking late with her friends. Because with the influx of yuppies, bars are springing all over the neighborhood. It's actually brave of her to confront me. I wonder if she would have done it if she wasn't tipsy.

We walk inside the lobby, and I hear my father ring me up.

"You live with your parents?" We start walking up the creaky stairs.

I mutter, "Yeah well, even if I had the money, I'm never putting them in a home."

"Excuse me?" she says.

"Nothing," I say, wondering if I said that too loud. "Yeah, we help each other out."

She becomes really friendly and tells me that her name is Helen and that Manhattan is so expensive and how she always wanted to buy an apartment.

"My god, I don't know how much you paid, but even in *this* neighborhood, it's so goddamned expensive."

This neighborhood? This has been my home for three decades.

"Yeah, it's not a good neighborhood," I say.

"Do you know where there's a good, cheap place to eat around here?"

"La Fonda, it's good food and cheap. It's on 105th between Lexington and Third."

I say this nicely, but I know that if it was the other way around, if I moved into an all-white neighborhood, my neighbors wouldn't want me around. Even if I hit the lotto jackpot of a hundred million dollars, I'd still not be in their class. The board members of the luxurious Dakota building on 72nd and Central Park West wouldn't let me buy even if I could. I'd be rejected on the spot. It's not all about money. And I really wanted to do the same to Helen. Let this white girl know how it feels to be invisible and hated. Even feared.

"Go check it out, great Puerto Rican dishes," I say.

"Great," she says, smiling again, "want to get coffee at Starbucks sometime?"

"Sure," I say, thinking that I wouldn't be caught dead in that place.

"Bye." She then strokes the cat, "Bye cat," and opens the door to her floor. "I'm Helen, by the way," she says again.

"Julio," I say.

"Great," she says, closing the door.

I'm happy she's gone.

I walk upstairs and hold the cat with one hand while I fumble for the door key with the other. When I finally find it, my father opens the door.

"*Mira un gato?*" my father says, half asleep, "wha' you doing with a cat?"

"Sorry Pa'," I say as I kiss him hello. My father, who is getting old before his time because of all that work and fast living in his youth, groans at the cat.

"Not a mean cat," he says and takes the cat from my arms.

"I brought it for Ma'." And just then I hear Mom get up and walk toward the living room.

"*Mira*, it's late. Where's the *vi-va-poru? Quien ha visto el vi-va-poru?*" Mom is looking for the Vicks VapoRub. I laugh. Whatever linguists say about Spanglish being invented in the street is wrong. It was invented in the home. By our parents, who weren't born in America or didn't come as children. "Where's the *vi-va-poru?*" Our parents never had a chance to grasp the English language. They just worked and worked and worked. With no schooling, they made English their own. *Pichon* for pigeon, *rufo* for roof, and so on. It's a language of family, of home, not street.

Mom sees the cat and forgets about the medicine. "*Que lindo, de quien es ese gato?*"

"Ours," I say. Mom takes it from Pop's arms.

Hot potato with a cat.

"It's hungry and skinny," she says, then lifts its tail. "*Un macho.* Kaiser," she holds the cat up, "*te vamos a llamar Kaiser.*"

"No that's a terrible name," I protest, "that's not a cat name."

"Let's call him Hector Lavoe," my father says and we pay him no mind.

"Kaiser is a German king, Ma'."

"No it's not." She goes to the kitchen to pour the cat some milk. I follow her. The dishes are dirty. Mom looks at Pops and points at the dishes.

"You better start *dishwashando*," she says to Pops and then tells me, "Is not a German king," picks up a clean plate, "*ese nombre esta en la biblia.*" She takes the milk from the fridge, pours a plateful of milk, and places it on the floor.

"Kaiser?" I say. "I never read that name in the Bible."

The cat starts licking the milk clean, like it hasn't eaten in ten years.

"Well it's there, in the Book of Job," Mom says.

"How you spell that? *Cómo se escribe, Ma'*."

My father starts doing the dishes. This late, and he's doing the dishes. Why? Because like me, Pops can never say no to Mom.

"*No se*, but it's in the Bible." She strokes the cat as he drinks. "I've seen it. *Mira*, Trompo Loco was around looking for you."

"What he want?"

"*Nada*, I guess he just wanted to play. *Bendito*, Trompo Loco, he should just move in with us," Mom says to me, not looking up, admiring Kaiser licking his whiskers.

"Barretto, let's call the cat Barretto," my father says as he washes, "after Ray Barretto."

"You forget about those old musicians and just keep *dish-washando*," Mom tells him as she strokes the cat's fur.

Having both my parents up, I decide I might as well tell them that things are going to be tight.

"I quit my second job," I say, and Mom takes her eyes off the cat and embraces me. Her hair smells of almonds.

"*Gracias al Señor*," she says. "Now you'll be a full-time student?"

"No, I'll still have to work, at the construction site," I say. I know they had their suspicions about my second job, but they never asked me what it was. I see Pops start to nod and smile as he keeps washing. "I want to pay more attention to graduating next year. It's taken me seven years," I say.

"*Mijo*," Mom says, "now see, see," she says, pointing a finger at me, "now all you have to do is find a good girl, get married, have kids, come back to the Truth, *mira que el fin está cerca*."

"Ma', please," I say, and she gets a little embarrassed; because we had this discussion already, years ago when I broke away from the church.

"Look at what happened in September, those are signs, Julio. *Cristo viene y pronto.*"

"Whatever, Ma'." I'm not going to get into it with her.

"Then at least get married, let Christ come back and at least find you married. *Mira, que hay una blanquita, muy linda que se mudó aquí.*" Mom whispers about our new neighbor. "She seems nice."

"Ma', please. You sound like Papelito."

"Oh no, not that man," Mom shoots the wall a dirty look, "that *pato es hijo del Diablo.*"

"I like him, Ma,' and Pentecostals have their little weird shit, too—"

"Don't curse, Julio. Every time you curse the Devil takes a little piece of you."

"If that were true, Ma'," I say, "there would be no Puerto Ricans. Come on, Ma'."

She calms down. "'*Ta bien*, he's your friend. But why don't you make that *blanquita* your friend, too?"

I stay quiet.

"The thing is, those *blanquitas* don't clean their houses," Mom says. "We may never be rich but we will always be clean. Our cup may be small but it will never leak. These women dress nice but their apartments are a mess. But I hope you find someone soon. You're almost thirty."

"Jesus never got married," I say. "I'm just following in his footsteps."

"You're so funny today," she smirks, and I await another of her favorite expressions. "Did you swallow clown for lunch?"

"Yes," I say, "how did you know?"

"All I'm saying Julio, is I can pray *al Señor.*" Mom shrugs, looking at me, "I can pray that you'll get married, see the signs and come back to truth."

"Keep praying, Ma'," I say, *"al Señor y al doctor chino."*

"Mira cuidado," she says, knowing I'm making fun of her praying. *"Cuidado.* You can't talk to me like that, I carried you for nine months. So you can't talk to me like that. Nine months I carried you."

"Oh yeah, Ma'," I say and lift her up, "well I'm going to carry you for nine minutes."

"She's heavy," Pops says, "like nine seconds is all you gonna make."

I put her down after she complains.

"Mira que sinvergüenzas los do'," she says, laughing.

My father cleans his last dish, wipes his hands dry on his shorts, and joins Mom, who is petting the cat again.

"Mira Julio," my father says, looking up at me, "I'm happy you're leaving that other job, too." His stare holds my eyes. I know what he means. "You did a good thing."

"Gracias, Pa'."

"But your mother's right, you should get married."

"You can't force marriage Pops."

"No you're right, you can't force it," he says.

Mom puts the cat on the floor and places her hands on her hips.

"Yes you can," she says to him.

"No you can't," Pops shakes his head.

"But if Julio was a girl, you'd then be forcing him to get married, *verdad*?"

"That's different. A woman is different."

"No it's not," she says.

"*Oh sí,*" he says.

"*Oh no, señor,*" she says.

"*Oh sí,*" he says, and I leave them arguing as Kaiser finishes his milk and starts sniffing around his new home.

I go get ready to shower. Maybe later get in a bit of studying for class tomorrow night. I leave my parents in the kitchen talking. My parents always talk in the kitchen. It's like their conference room. When I was a kid, the kitchen was always warm, even when there wasn't enough heat. I'd usually see my parents sitting at the table, with the oven door open, emitting its warmth at full blast as they argued, laughed, or just stared at the walls. The kitchen had food and water, and so it was the ideal room to discuss matters of survival, rent, family, God.

My parents had met during the glory years of salsa, when the neighborhood was full of people and not projects. My mom was the religious one, really. She loved singing hymns with that voice of hers that went high enough to break glass and low enough to make you shiver. My father, Angel Santana, could play the timbales like Puente. Okay I'm lying, no one could play like Puente, but my father came close. I have the tapes to prove it. My father played with the greats, though—Barretto, Blades, De Leon, Colon, Palmeri, Cuba, Feliciano, Pacheco, and "*el cantante de los cantantes,*" Lavoe. He was partying with Lavoe, when my father said, "*el Señor se me presentó.*" When the Lord appeared to him. Lavoe and Pops had shot up everything "*hasta gasolina,* and when we ran out of that, we cooked the Pepto-Bismol in the medicine cabinet and shot that up, too." Hector Lavoe was always late to his concerts, and many times it was because he was living it up with my father. All this hard living led Pops to fall into a deep depression. He stopped playing music and one day, while sitting alone in his apartment, ready to jump off the fire escape, my father asked God to give him a sign that He loved him. At that instant, he heard a knock on the door, and it was my mother, preaching with her fellow sisters, the Good News of Jehovah. Not only did he convert, he married Mom, who helped him kick the habit, and years later Pops even played his music at church.

They are a pair, those two. I love them dearly, and as insane as Mom can be and as wimpy as Pops gets, I never doubt their love for me and they never doubt mine for them.

Getting ready to shower, I hear my parents talk about helping me pay the mortgage. I hear my father regret how he threw his life away doing too many drugs. And that his disability check is nothing. Mom thanks the Lord for what we have and how her job at the hospital can help me pay the bills. They talk about fixing some of the bedrooms that are not fit for anyone to live in them. Especially the walls. What a mess. That will be expensive. Mom would rather have new wooden floors put in. That is expensive, too.

But they are happy. Especially now that I am doing the right thing. My parents aren't stupid. They know that I have done things God wouldn't approve of. But they never questioned me. And if I had told them, given them the choice, your son can be an arsonist and buy a place in five years or just work a nine-to-five job, go to church, and die paying rent?

I know what they would have said.

So I made my own choice.

Not just because I love this town but because I also know this town. And New York City, like the country it's in, is a place that promises you everything but gives you nothing. And those things that can't be worked for must be taken, conned, or traded for with bits of your soul and sometimes even the morals of your parents. In

America, it's where you end up that matters, not how you get there. As long as you get there, no one asks questions. You don't ask. You never ask. And if someone does ask how you got there? It's usually a harmless person who never got anything, never got out, died paying rent as he waited for God to deliver him.

Complaint #3

It's payday in America," the new boss, a small man with huge slumping shoulders, as if his arms weighed him down, hollers at the workers. "It's payday in my country and I want to hear English, Ennnnglish!"

Just a minute ago I was stripping the roof of a five-story walk-up groomed for renovation. It's one of five tenements lined up on 108th and First Avenue. They're beautiful buildings, one of the many that were set afire years ago and are finally being renovated.

Like the rest of the workers, I get in line to collect my pay.

We know this new boss is nothing like the old one. The other boss was kind and understanding. There is a nervous silence on the line. But I knew this about the job the minute Eddie offered it to me.

"James Steven Phillips," the new boss calls out and a worker walks happily to collect his check. The boss stares at him.

"*No habla* English?"

The Mexican worker just smiles at him.

"You tacos," the boss hands him his check, "are stupider than the niggers ever were."

I'm sandwiched between Antonio and a new worker, a real white guy, not a phantom but a white man of flesh and bones who keeps cursing under his breath.

The boss yells out another Anglo name, and another Mexican worker walks up to get his check. "No English, too?" The boss gives him the check. "Ah fuck it, at least you work, not still angry about the past."

On line, Antonio whispers to himself in Spanish, knowing I can hear it and understand him.

"I didn't come to this country to be an American. I came to work."

I don't answer Antonio. I just nod.

"Vincent Pennisi," Antonio's named is called. He goes to get his check. "A satellite dish for your house in Mexico. Pick up *Baywatch*. Learn English," the boss says, laughing, and behind me the white guy loses it. He barges to the front of the line.

"Mario DePuma!" he yells. "Just call my name and give me my fucking check!" the white guy demands.

The boss smirks at him.

"DePuma, right? Mario DePuma," the boss says, fumbling for the guy's check. When he finds it, he doesn't hand it over to him. "You must be a very important man, Mario DePuma. So important, you have to actually be here in the flesh."

Mario looks up, shrugging his shoulders in embarrassment.

"I got a parole officer with a hard-on, threatens to show up at any time, you know." Mario reaches behind his ear for a cigarette.

"So what you are telling me," the boss says, "you actually have to work, just like these tacos here?"

That right there tells me that whoever got Mario this job isn't anyone important, like Eddie. Mario is just a favor for someone's brother, cousin or nephew.

"Hey, I was told I would work for real. But I wasn't told it was gonna be with all these fucking Mexicans." Mario glows incandescent, you could see the green veins in his neck. "Since when do we work with Mexicans?"

I don't know how long Mario had been locked up, but he is Rip Van Winkle waking up in an East Harlem he is not familiar with. Undocumented workers and yuppies are the rage. Both groups live in boxes, apartments that had been cut up to make more units, charge more rent. Only yuppies don't have to worry about the INS knocking at any minute and kicking them out.

"But I don't really mind the Mexicans, I don't really fucking mind," Mario takes a drag, and when he speaks, clouds of smoke escape his mouth and nostrils, making him look like a newly fired-up chimney. "What I fucking hate is you treating me like one of them!"

Just then the real owners of those names start trickling in. They drive their cars by the construction site. Out-of-towners entering Spanish Harlem, nothing new these days. Some stay in their cars, some park. The Mexican workers hand their checks over to the owners of the names, the owners of those social security numbers. And the owners of the names hand the Mexicans cash.

It's all profit, really. These union jobs pay sixteen dollars an hour, the Mexican is given five, the owner of the name takes eleven. The undocumented worker is making more money than he ever imagined, the average wage in Mexico being four bucks a day, other parts of Latin America even less. The owner of the name, the member of the union, can spend his days doing other things or nothing, the buildings gets gutted, later renovated, yuppies rent them, and everyone is happy. So everyone keeps quiet. No one asks. You don't ask. You never ask.

When I told Eddie to help me find a real job, with benefits and union, Eddie offered me this job. He told me I didn't have to show up, just get an illegal alien to front for me. They don't complain, he said to me. Besides, demolition work is brainless work, you're tearing down walls and roofs, any idiot can do that. Put your American citizenship to work, he said. It's the way New York City was built. I should relax, Puerto Ricans already put in their time, let some other sucker group build the country. He said it as if Puerto Ricans were now part of the American Dream, as if we had arrived, just because we seemed to be in more movies these days.

Still, as long as I show up, it's legitimate work, and there are very few genuine aspects in my life. So I show up and work, because I want as much legitimacy as I can get away with.

"Julio Santana," the boss calls my name and I walk over to get my check.

"You're one of Eddie's fire bugs, right?"

"No," I say, because I would never admit that to anyone.

"No? Don't fuck with me, the only check with a Spanish name? Don't fuck with me."

"Don't know what you talking about," I say for no good reason. The boss knows I'm lying.

"Listen, Julio, don't take offense when I play around with these Mexicans, okay? I mean, I don't know if you're Mexican. But I do know you must be an American cuz you got a social and all. And tell Eddie that I said hello, okay?"

"If I see him, I'll tell him."

"Yeah, George, tell him Georgie says hello and this is all yours," he says, handing me my check. He looks at the Mexicans trading in their checks for cash to the real owners of the names. SUV after SUV, the true owners of their American identity.

"I tell you, Julio, one day those Mexicans are going to catch hell from the blacks, like the blacks caught it from the whites."

"Why's that?" I fold my check, put it in my back pocket.

"Because it's not that blacks won't work really, I say niggers are lazy but that's not really true. They just won't work for peanuts, like the tacos here. So, when they see Mexicans working for shit wages they'll get angrier than they already are, because now they have no bargaining power at all."

"What makes you think the blacks will come after the Mexicans and not the whites who are using the Mexicans?" I say, looking at both parties. The undocumented workers counting their bills and their contemporary slave masters driving away with their weekly checks for doing nothing but being Americans. Both parties happy, for now.

"Because when you Porto Ricans showed up in Spanish Harlem," the boss says, "we took it out on you and not on the Jews or Irish, or whoever the fuck was running the show."

The boss looks at the workers happily counting their money, exchanging laughter, sun in their faces.

"Okay let's go," the boss rains on them. "I want you working on those buildings like you were the ones who were going to live in them." He laughs.

The boss heads back to the trailer, knowing the workers didn't understand what he said, but he's happy because he can yell at them at any time of the day and whenever he wants.

I get ready to go back to work, stripping decades-old tar off the roof. Back inside the building, there is dampness and a smell of wet wood, plaster and old paint. I climb up to the roof, and Antonio starts talking to me in Spanish as I prepare the air hose for the jack.

"*Mano*, what do you do with your money?"

"I put it away," I say, though it's none of his biz.

"You know there is talk you are homesexual," Antonio says, laughing.

"Who's saying it?" I ask, not really happy to know this.

"Everybody. We all have families back home, and you who live here freely do not. Your friend, the *santero*, is gay."

"Maybe I don't want to get married. Maybe I like being alone. And the *santero* you're talking about, yeah he's gay," I say in Spanish. "But he's my friend not yours."

"I am just asking, *mano*, just asking." Antonio steps back a bit, like he is excusing himself. "Still," he says in Spanish, "you always keep to yourself and never talk to nobody. In my country a man like you is always a homosexual."

"Okay," I say. "Good."

"I mean, I wish I was like you," Antonio says in Spanish, "only not a homosexual."

"Yeah, why's that?" I say, not wanting to cut him off, but I'm ready to crank up the jack and start cutting up the tar from the roof.

"What money I would make, *mano*," he says, rubbing thumb and forefinger together, as though he is starting a fire in his hand, "what money, if I had no wife, no children, no debt. I would be a big man and then I would buy a big house and then a big—"

I start the jack and begin cutting the roof's tar.

Antonio's face slams shuts like a storefront gate. I have insulted him but I don't care. I don't really know him and he has no bearing on how I live my life. Antonio curses something at me but I don't pay him any mind.

Cutting up tar, I ask myself what is with this marriage thing? Why is it so important, as if being alone is worthless? Mom and Pops, now this guy? Please. I don't exactly like my life the way it is, but it's better than some people's. Yes I'd like to meet a nice girl, have nice children. Problem is, my recent past isn't all that nice. What will I say to her when she asks me how I managed to buy an apartment? What do you do for a living? I'd have to lie. I am getting tired of lying. But, hopefully, I am slowly getting out. I have severed my ties with Eddie and am attending night school and slowly setting my life back on track. I am righting my wrongs. So I leave at that and continue my job.

After work, I walk to the check-cashing place. I carry all these secrets with me, and so I don't want a real bank account, because I figure the less paper trail the better. Afterwards I walk home with a wad of cash in my pocket and, like most other days, when I reach my street, I stop and stare at my building, at the third floor, carefully. See that floor, I own it, I tell myself. It's twilight, and a yellow-orange sun is hitting the window of my room. I see Mami's silhouette pass by the window in my parents' bedroom, and I smile, thinking they must have been fighting and she moved herself to the living room. On the first floor, I see a brother from Maritza's crazy church fighting with the entrance gate that is stuck. Tonight they have service, and though Maritza keeps inviting me, I never go. I also see Helen walking into the building, coming back from work? I think. Her petite figure is elegant and curvy. Her hair is in a ponytail that bounces with each step. I forget about her making me ring the other night, because she looks so vulnerable, so small and fragile.

Next door, at the botanica, Papelito comes out to empty yesterday's glass of water. He delicately tosses the old water onto the street, getting rid of the impurities in his botanica.

"Julio, *mi amor*," he spots me and shouts from across the street, "watchoo doing there, *hijo de* Chango, uh?"

"I got this month's," I yell back. Papelito waits for the cars to go by so he can join me across the street and, soon, drivers who know him brake so he can pass.

Black as tar, with no trace of Spaniard blood in his lineage, at sixty-eight, Papelito is a man made up of rumors. It is said he can kill with prayers. Papelito is the only gay man who can walk the streets of Spanish Harlem swaying his hips like a cable-suspended bridge and not be ridiculed. Frail and delicate as if the wind could sweep him away, he has a certain flamboyant arrogance, a confidence, because he is protected by a religion that is as beautiful, as misunderstood and as feared as he is. As a high priest, a *babalawo*, of Regla Lukumi, better known as Santeria, Papelito is feared and loved by many.

"*Mira, lindo*, Trompo Loco is looking for you."

"I heard. What does he want?"

"He didn't say but when I told him I hadn't seen you, he got mad. You know and began twirling himself like a top until he fell to the floor. I said to him, *mijo*, you want some tea?"

"I'll go find him," I say to Papelito and hand him this month's mortgage in cash with an extra hundred for him.

Because it was Papelito who I came to for help when I needed to have someone else's name on the deed of my mortgage. I had saved a lot of money setting fires for Eddie, and I knew the IRS would ask how did I buy that apartment on my demolition job salary and wasn't I a part-time student? I knew I'd be caught. So I had to find someone who could explain the money. But in Spanish Harlem everyone is poor and it was hard to find a front. I knew Papelito owned the largest botanica in the neighborhood and when I asked him for help he looked at me like I was asking him to commit murder. He gave me those *brujo* stares that all the men in this neighborhood are scared of him for. I didn't blame Papelito. What I was asking was risky, and what if I faulted on my mortgage, it would be him who'd be taking the fall, maybe lose his botanica. So he said to me the best he could do was consult the Orishas, the black gods, for advice.

The next time he saw me, he tenderly and excitedly kissed my cheek. "*Mira payah*! How can I refuse a favor to a son of Chango!" A happy Papelito told me that if I get initiated into Santeria, that it would be the Orisha, the god, Chango, a representation of fire and lightning, who would claim me as his son. So that's what he calls me, "*Hijo de* Chango," and because Papelito believes that Chango is always watching over his children, to deny me a favor would be to insult one of his gods.

Don't know whether that's true, I only know that because of his religion's secretive and silent rituals, Papelito is trustworthy and I'd be safe from neighborhood gossip and, more important, the IRS. So I have to keep it all low and under.

"*Mira* Julio, *mi amor*," Papelito takes the money from my hand with the grace of a dolphin, "I had this dream." Papelito elegantly tucks the money inside a pocket of his yellow-white dresslike gown. He will write a check to the bank in his name and keep the extra hundred as a gift to the Orishas.

"Please, Papelito, you always have a dream," I say.

"*No mijo*, I'm serious, I had this dream, that you were getting married—"

"*Coño*, not you too. What is this?"

"I'm serious, *papi*." He brings out two fingers, then they go limp, "Take a consultation *lindo*, ask the Orishas themselves?"

"Some other day. I got to go, Papelito," I say, yawning.

It's as if I said nothing, because all of a sudden Papelito loses interest in telling me about his dream. For some reason he begins staring at a deep and wide oil slick on the side of the curb. A parked car has been dripping all this oil, and the gutter is covered in multi-colored fluid. Greens, purples, blues, and red swirls are coiling around each other all over the gutter before slowly slithering and disappearing down a drain. I think Papelito is caught in the moment. In all that beauty flowing in that filthy water. Papelito can see beauty in anything. When this happens to him he can be as single-minded as Eddie is in setting his fires. If I had time, I'd ask Papelito how an oil slick on a dirty street corner, flowing over cigarette butts, dead leaves, and the torn-off sole of someone's sneaker can consume all his attention? And if I ask, he'll tell me something about the meaning of life being contained in all our throwaways. How leaves die more beautiful and colorful than when they were just born. Something along those lines, count on it. But I don't have time. I have to find out what's bothering my friend Trompo Loco, and later I have class.

Complaint #4

Trompo Loco's place is a squatted walk-up, one of the few pockets left in El Barrio of a time when the neighborhood was cheap, burned, but beautiful, because all you needed was imagination, guts and healthy amount of perseverance, and the place was yours.

When I enter the broken down walk-up, the activist squatters open their doors to see who it is. Some of them have bats, others knives. They don't joke. They play for keeps. These people are going to take what they feel is rightfully theirs. I understand where they are coming from, so I leave them alone and don't ask. I never ask.

"Hey, man, sorry were you asleep?" I say to Trompo when he opens his door. He looks like he just got out of bed, wearing a ripped-up T-shirt and no pants.

"Nah, nah bro'," he says, with the swollen face of an abused son of a mother with past addictions and an entire geography of failed suicides. "It's all right, come in. I been out looking for you."

Inside Trompo Loco's dark apartment there is a mattress on the floor, losing lotto tickets, medicine bottles, and unpaid bills lying on the side. An old table stands in the corner, its third leg held up by stacks of phone books. There are chicken bones, buried halfway, lost inside coffee grounds that somehow got spilled on top of a plate. Coming in through the window is a long electric wire, jerry-rigged to the lamppost outside so as to run electricity to his apartment. Trompo Loco's apartment is really a plea, a cry, an appeal for the survival of a soon-to-be-extinct urban homesteader.

Trompo Loco flicks on the lights. I sit on the mattress.

"Listen man," Trompo Loco says, "you know I'm like a little brother to you, right?"

"Okay, Trompo, yeah, get to the point." Trompo Loco hates it when anyone calls him by his complete nickname. To his face I only call him Trompo. If I'd called him by his complete nickname, he'd get so angry that he'd start spinning. But what would get him even angrier, so he'd spin until he passed out, is being called by his real name, Eduardo.

"Well, Julio. I mean, I wanna work where you work."

"Why would you wanna work when you got disability? I worked hard to get you that. Took you to see doctors, and then all that paperwork. When your mom was sent away, I got that for you, right?"

Trompo Loco's mother was manic-depressive. She was a beautiful woman no one ever guessed needed help. Because of her striking appearance, the neighborhood took her depression as a form of conceitedness or eccentricity, until it worsened and then everyone just called her crazy. In El Barrio few can afford shrinks and fewer designer drugs. Go back three decades to the seventies and you have a *loca* who can't be helped or understood at all.

"I just want a job. Like you have a job. Ask my father, okay? Just ask 'im. He talks to you."

"First of all, okay, Eddie is not your father, and second he won't hire you."

I hate lying to Trompo Loco, especially when he knows the truth. But Eddie wants it that way. Not only did Eddie have an affair with a Puerto Rican woman at a time in America when Puerto Ricans weren't cool, but she happened to have a history of mental illness. It was too much for Eddie, wife or no wife. Eddie would have been the butt of jokes for years to come. His friends would have had an inexhaustible well of fun at his expense. Eddie's mistake would have made its rounds in every bar, coffee shop, and social club in the five boroughs. So Trompo Loco became a nuisance from Eddie's past that he has tried to bury under tons of cement.

"Listen man," I say, "I'm your friend?"

He nods his head.

"So look, I got a big place now. Move in with me and my folks. They know you, helped raise you, bro'. Just come with us."

"Nah, nah, see, Julio. That's what I'm talking about. I want to be help-less."

"Okay, talk to me." I've known Trompo Loco all my life so I know how he talks.

"See, Julio I was on the bus and this guy way older than me, walks in carrying a little Toys R Us bag. And he sits on the bus smiling. And I notice how he carries that bag, like it was his pride you know. And every time the bus made a stop he would bring out a finger. I do that sometimes, so I know he was counting. But see, he was all by himself, no one was helping him and he was proud to be help-less. So, I thought, I'm smarter than him because to me, riding the bus is easy."

"I got a class at eight so I got to go, but I know what you mean. What you want is independence."

"Yeah, yeah, that's it. See this place, I got this place all on my own. I live here all on my own. It's a nice place too, right Julio?"

I sigh, because I have been trying to make Trompo Loco understand that the other squatters in this building are real activists. They don't want Trompo Loco around. Sooner or later, they will turn on him. These activists are intelligent people who need all the help they can get and Trompo Loco is a setback to them. He doesn't understand the work that's involved in legitimizing a squat. The paperwork, the city hall meetings, the protests, and, in time, someone will bleed real blood. Trompo Loco thinks that just because he is here that makes it his. The activist squatters can get nasty, they can be as self-righteous as religious fanatics. I should know, Maritza is like that.

"Yeah, I think it's a good place, you know," he says, looking around his squat.

"*Mira* Trompo, this setup is no good. You're going to have trouble with these people."

"I don't want no trouble, Julio. I always smile at them."

"Yeah, but they're going to throw you out—"

"Don't let them throw me out, Julio—"

"What do you want me to do? Trompo, all I can tell you is if one of these people hit you, you hit them back."

"I hate hitting people, Julio."

"I know you do—"

"I've never hit anyone in my life, Julio—"

"I know that—"

"I've never done anything to them, right Julio?"

"Well, in a way they think you are holding them back. Everyone in this squat has to be on the same page." I sense Trompo Loco doesn't understand the term "same page," he thinks it's a book or something. I shut up.

"All I want is work, Julio. What I need now, I now need to wake up and go to work, like you do. Check this out." Trompo Loco gets up and goes to another room. He keeps talking as he looks for whatever it is he's going to show me. I stay where I am, I don't want to see how the rest of the house looks. All I know is I have to get Trompo Loco out of here.

"I found this on the street and thought that I can work. Where you work, Julio." He reemerges with a hard hat. It's got a huge dent on the side. Whoever it belonged to must have had some serious accident.

"*Mira*, Trompo you can't work where I work."

"Why not? I got a hat now."

"Because you can't, okay?"

"But why not? I can fix the hat and it'll be like new, and then I'll work."

"You can't work where I work, okay?" I notice he's getting mad. "Don't fucking start spinning now. I'm serious." I look in his eyes. His hands are fists and he's doing his best not to spin. "Okay I'll tell you what I can do, I'll try to get you a job on the condition you move in with me and my folks." Trompo's eyes light up.

"You serious, Julio?"

"Yeah, now I got to go." I get up from the floor.

"So you gonna talk to my father, then."

"No! I didn't say that, right?" I say, a bit upset, "and I told you, he ain't your father. But I'll try and find you a job."

"All right, all right, all right," Trompo Loco backs away, he doesn't want to upset me. "Hey Julio, thanks man. I really will make it up to you."

"Like the last time?"

"No I mean it this time, I will make it up to you."

"You can start by not going around that coffee shop." Trompo gets nervous and clears his nose. "You know what I mean? Right? I heard you've been going around that coffee shop. Now, that guy is not your father. If he was he'd be here, right?"

Trompo just clears his nose again.

"Good, now are you reading your Bible?"

"Yeah, and Maritza is taking me to her church."

I am glad for Trompo Loco, because Maritza is the pastor of this really wacky church. Maritza gave Trompo Loco this illustrated Bible with big letters. Trompo Loco still has problems reading it, but the pictures help. Maritza's church is one of the few churches where Trompo Loco would be welcomed without being looked at as a freak. Maritza's church is really a socialist racket. She doesn't even believe in God, but she wanted to mobilize the poor in Spanish Harlem and so she brought God into the mix. It worked, and her church is so progressive that other churches shun her. I was never surprised at people's acceptance and sweet trust they had for Maritza. Nothing is too doubtful or unimaginable if God is deftly placed into it. I also wasn't surprised at other churches for shunning her. Church buildings are never built out of glass, that way they can throw stones at will.

"Good Trompo, go to church and read your Bible." I hug him and get ready to leave.

"Julio, why did God send a bear to kill those kids, just for making fun of that prophet's bald spot?"

"Wha'?"

"Yeah, God killed these kids who made fun of his prophet. I wouldn't have sent a bear to kill the kids. I would have sent them home with no play."

"You serious? God did that?" I had forgotten that story but I now do remember reading it in the Old Testament, where God is a warlike, jealous God, right before He does a turnaround and becomes love personified in the New Testament.

"Well I don't know, Trompo. Ask Maritza, okay? I got to go to school," I say and hug him again on my way out the door.

M any times people from the neighborhood have asked me why I take so much interest in Trompo Loco. They tell me, if he wasn't around, the time and energy I'd save, maybe even find myself a woman. But I can only think that he reminds me of this terrible feeling I had when I was a kid. A feeling that I can't stomach. It began when I was ten, and my mother, after I had been kicking and screaming, finally let me try out for the Little League team from Yorkville that met in Central Park's baseball fields. We had missed the deadline to sign up to play with the league that was from Spanish Harlem, and it cost fifty dollars to join that other league from Yorkville.

But I won and my mother went with me.

When I approached the coach, a white man with a beer belly and hair on the sides, he only let me try out because my mother was there, plus I had the fifty bucks.

"You'll still need to pay for your uniform," he said to me, and I didn't say anything, because I knew I could cry and kick some more so my mother would somehow come up with the money.

"Take right field, you're batting ninth." I was happy, because I was playing. But I knew right field was for scrubs who the coach didn't trust. No one hits it to right field. And batting ninth was an insult. But I took it, because I wanted to play. I wanted to play baseball, I wanted to play that great American game that I loved.

That day I went three for four. I hit a single and two doubles, plus when the only kid from the other team hit the ball to right, I caught it. During innings, I'd take a sneak peek at my mother, who was reading her religious books, bored out of her mind, sitting among other bored mothers. But she loved me, so she sat there through seven innings.

We won that game and I knocked in four runs.

"Here's your money back," the coach said. "I don't have a place for you."

"But I went three for four?" I said, and the coach shook his head and started putting away the bats and gloves. The kids and their parents were all getting ready to go out for pizza or Burger King.

"Aren't there any Puerto Rican Little Leagues?"

"Yeah, but they're full," I said, and I knew these white kids could use me.

"See, you should have joined sooner, that right there tells me you have no discipline." And he walked away.

When I went over to my mother, I knew she would not understand. So I just handed her the money. She was kind of happy she had her money again. She told me, next year, I would make it on time to play with the Spanish kids. I knew that, I knew there was always a next year. But I had been cut. And that my mother would never understand. She'd never understand that no matter how much you try, how much effort you put in, and even if you do good, you are still considered not good enough. She wouldn't understand that I also wanted that wonderful feeling of acceptance, the sweetness of being part of something. Even if I had to pay for it.

Instead I had been cut.

That's why I loved Trompo Loco, because all he wanted was to join the team, to be everyday people. Trompo Loco was always trying. He was giving his best, as little as it may be to some people. He gave it all, but it was never good enough. Yet he was out there, swinging, like when we were kids and he was downstairs watching us play, absorbing all those insults so that maybe one day he could be like us. Instead Trompo Loco had been cut, he always got waived.

Complaint #5

After night school I enter my building, walk up one flight and find Helen sitting alone on the steps. Helen is wearing a black skirt, black top, black stockings, and her shoes are these ugly, black earth shoes that look like clunky boxes. Her hands are hiding her face, and her shoulders jerk up and down as she wails and whispers little things to herself. I notice a half-empty bottle of vodka standing upright and proud near her shoes.

"You all right?" I ask her, placing my hand lightly on her shoulder.

She shakes her head and her blond hair falls over her hands, which cover her face.

"Something happened to you?" She stays quiet, doesn't even look up.

"You can just knock if you need anything," I say, stepping over her, and walk up the stairs. I turn around to make sure she's still there, watching her shoulders resume their motion, rise and fall, rise and fall.

*M*ira, *Julio, se fue Kaiser,*" my mother tells me when I enter.

"Wha'?" I get upset, the image of Helen on the steps still clear in my mind. "Ma', how could the cat escape?"

"Your stupid father left the window to the fire escape open."

"How could that happen, ma'? That was a nice cat."

"I know, I loved him, *'tava mas lindo.*" Mom is a little sad. "I looked all over for him, *en el rufo, la escalera,* by the hallway, in the bodegas, I even went inside Papelito's botanica next door, and you know I hate going in there." She whispers, *"Si entras allí, se te puede pegar algo."* Meaning something dark would cling to you. This dark thing was bound to come into your house, curl up in a corner and wait until you were sleeping, then uncoil itself and roam—maybe open the refrigerator, take the phone off the hook, leave the faucet dripping. This evil thing that all Pentecostals were warned about would hover over your dreaming body, hissing and murmuring unintelligible sounds. It'd lurk in your tiny apartment, and you'd feel its cold presence increase each day, until it became part of your dark family.

"Allí no vive Dios. But I went inside that botanica only to look for my cat, so *que el Señor me perdone.*"

I shake my head, not just because the cat is gone, but because my mother believes botanicas are houses of fallen angels. The angels Genesis speaks about, the ones that had left God's heaven and materialized their bodies to have sex with the daughters of man. We were taught that, during the great flood, these angels left behind their bodies of flesh and returned to their celestial forms. But they were not let back inside the fraternity of God. Instead they were cast down to Earth where they played havoc on mankind. To Pentecostals like my mother, these demons are as real as invisible companions that lonely children play with in their made-up worlds. It was this fear, the fear of wicked angels, that prevented anyone from our Pentecostal church from visiting botanicas. These beliefs are so nailed into my mother's head that the older she grows the deeper those nails are driven; by now, it's hard to find their points.

"I even asked that horrible man if he'd seen a cat, and no one has seen him."

"Well, maybe he'll turn up," I say, looking around as if the cat is going to walk from under the couch any minute. I liked having that cat around. I especially liked it when he would run around all over the apartment. My apartment has a huge hallway, and having Kaiser run around reminded me how big this place is. Made me love my house even more.

"Is Pops up?"

"No, sleeping. That's all that man does."

"Is there food?" I ask her. I just want a quick bite.

"Only *pegao* left," Mom says.

"*Pegao?*" I say, "why not?"

I get a good, strong spoon and start scraping the burned rice left over at the bottom of the pot. The doorbell rings and Mom goes to answer it.

"Hi, I know it's late—"

"No, it's not that late," Mom says to Helen. "Come in. Want some food?" Mom offers, though I wonder if Helen would like *pegao*.

"No, I'll . . ." she hesitates for a moment, "have coffee. If you have any?" I think she really didn't want coffee, but judging from the expression on her face, something made her knock. Helen shyly walks in. When she walks inside, her shoes clank on the new wooden floor we placed in the living room. It was an expensive renovation, and I'm wondering, as her shoes sound like two-by-fours hit against each other, if she'll ruin the floor. Because of Helen's presence, my mother's face becomes a lamp. She could care less about the floors. My mother pulls me back inside the kitchen and I let her.

"*Mira*," she whispers to me, "*quiero nietos con pelo bello.*"

I introduce my mother to Helen, but they had seen each other before. Mom smiles like a ditz, because she is happy we have a white person in the house. So Mom leaves us alone in the kitchen right after she has set the coffee pot on the stove. She repeats her whispers to me that she wants grandkids with blond hair, as she leaves us alone.

"I'm sorry about the stairs." Helen's blinking a lot. There's a rim of smudged mascara under each eye.

"It's cool," I say.

"Can I ask you a question?"

"Yeah." I start eating as we sit at the table.

"Why are some people in this neighborhood so mean?"

"Like what, you got robbed, is that it? Hey, I'm sorry." I shrug. "It happens."

"No," she says, "I was at the fruit stand and this woman looks up and down at me, and when I smile and ask politely, 'Yes?' she says to me for no reason, 'White bitch get out of Spanish Harlem.' " Helen hides her face in her hands, and her blond hair falls over them.

"Hey, it's all right. Don't cry, it's all right." I touch her hair to comfort her.

When she uncovers her face, she isn't crying. Not at all. I get a peek at her bra when I look down her blouse.

"I'm angry," she says. "I'm angry at myself, at that woman. At what I'm doing here." She clears her dry throat. "Angry at what I'm doing to this place. What is it with me?"

"Where you from originally, Helen?" I ask her, just to talk about something else, because I understand what that woman meant. I know the origin of her distrust. It's been hard for us in Spanish Harlem to negotiate a whole new series of relationships across lines of race and class even. We had lived among ourselves for decades, here in El Barrio, and not too many of us had to live with white people next door to us. And now, in the new millennium, the melting pot did melt, and it wasn't just us who were clueless, Helen and her people were in the same boat.

"I was born in Howard City, Wisconsin," she says, "it boasts the world's largest ball of twine."

The pot whispers, and I go to pour us some coffee.

"Where I'm from," Helen says, "they don't burn crosses, but if you're not from around those parts, they don't look at you with the same eyes. You can be as white as the Grand Dragon, mister, it doesn't matter, a stranger in my town is a stranger. So yes, I understand but—"

"So if you understand that woman," I cut her off, "why are you angry?"

"Because," she nods repeatedly, "still, does it make it right Julio, does it?"

"I'm not saying it's right," I backpedal a bit, "Helen, all I'm saying is you got to understand."

"Yes, I understand. I'm not that stupid. My business partner bought a brownstone in Harlem and he got death threats in his mailbox. Is that terrible or what?" She looks around, I think she wants a drink.

"Yeah but," I say, "it's still better than what would happen to a black man buying a building in a white neighborhood."

She blinks rapidly again.

"I didn't mean to bother you Julio," she says to me.

"It's all right." I know she wants to talk, so I let her. And truth is, I want to hear what she has to say.

"Can I ask you something?"

"Sure," I stare at a roach on the wall. It's the first one I've seen since I bought this place. The building was in need of work but it was clean.

"I'm opening up an art gallery on 118th and Second Avenue. What do you think about that?"

"I think it's good. I hope you sell a lot of paintings." I look at the roach again. Should I go kill it? Then it might not get a chance to multiply.

Helen lifts her hands up and shakes her head.

"No it's not. It's not that good of a thing."

"It's an art gallery," I say, "not another Starbucks."

"Yes, but don't you see, Julio, I'm bringing art to a neighborhood that has art. Its own art. My business partner says, 'White people don't need a gallery, they have SoHo. This neighborhood, on the other hand, needs galleries. The exposure itself is priceless.' But I know that's bullshit and I still go along with it. Did my business partner ever think that," she says, as if she was talking to her business partner, "that this neighborhood has art. Tons of art. De la Vega's gallery, the Mixta Gallery, Taller Boricua, el Museo del Barrio. That's a lot of art. Now if you ask me, the real reason we are opening a gallery here is because it's a hell of a lot cheaper than opening one in SoHo."

"Wow." I am surprised. "You know those places? Taller Boricua,

Mixta. Some people have lived their entire lives in this neighborhood and don't know about those places, wow."

"Well I did my research on this neighborhood before I put up some money. Didn't you?"

"No. I always lived here."

"Oh my," she says.

"Listen, Helen all I can tell you is that you are here, and there are these unspoken rules, a way of life here. You have to claim your territory. If you are going to make this neighborhood your home, you claim it. You don't just pay your rent or put money in, the people in this neighborhood could care less, they will bug you until they see some guts in you—"

"But what about the Dalai Lama and compassion?"

Where did that come from?

"What?" I say, totally caught off-guard. "What does he have to do with this?"

"What about understanding?" she says.

"Look, when we arrived in Spanish Harlem the Italians beat the shit out of us. But we hit back, we claimed it. If you are going to now live here you will have to bleed sometimes. I mean not bleed but be hurt, just like today, don't let those women fuck with you is what I'm saying. You make allies and you hit back. That's what you have to learn. You learn when to hit verbally; humor is good. Making someone feel stupid. But you make friends as well. You also claim it by not going to Starbucks or Old Navy but the Latino stores too—" I stop, because she stares at me like I had said things that shouldn't be said. Like I have just shot her dog. Right then I realize I have too much going on in my life to evaluate who is right or wrong. I have labored hard and even took shortcuts to get what I have. I feel that Helen hasn't yet put her time in Spanish Harlem to talk to me about right or wrong. She didn't have to sell a piece of her soul to buy anything, then again, I don't know her. I didn't want to talk about what white people bring to us or what we bring to them. Maybe in class, not here. Not now.

"You are so small," she says in almost a faint whisper. The corners of her eyes shudder, as if her worst suspicions had been confirmed. "You believe two wrongs make a right."

I have some idea why she gets defensive, but what does she want me to say?

She puts her cup down. She waits a second for me to escort her out of the apartment. I stay sitting, and so she leaves.

I finish eating and then put my books away.

I fix a window that needs adjusting. Just some screws that were always loosening. I'm done in a few minutes, and afterwards, I open and close it to test the window, then I step outside onto the fire escape.

I gaze up at the empty, blue-black sky. It looks like an ocean with clouds. The moon is full, and the glittering outline of an airplane collides with its round whiteness.

Looking downward, I make cat sounds, hoping Kaiser will answer me. I look around in the darkness but never see him.

Nothing.

I stare across the street and see no one sitting in front of the buildings. It wasn't always like that. Before people like Helen arrived, those buildings didn't have spikes on the side of the stoops. People would sit on the stoops and talk all night as they watched their children play. The spikes are offensive; it's saying "We don't want you sitting here. We don't care that you sat here for decades, bringing those tropical customs from your old countries, this is a new neighborhood now."

I know, all neighborhoods must change, but if you are Puerto Rican and need to learn where you came from and who you are, you need to start in Spanish Harlem. The spiritual landmarks are still here, in El Barrio. Helen's people don't seem to have mystical places like ours. They don't have a sacred Harlem, an East L.A., a South Central. They don't have poor, holy places that speak to your soul, vibrant streets that tell you about those who came before you. All they have are small towns that either die or stay the same. Small towns they don't care to romanticize. Small towns they try to kill inside themselves when they leave for New York City or wherever and not look back. There's no place like home, Dorothy had said about Wisconsin, or was it Kansas? I never cared for the movie or the book. All I know is many want out. What Dorothy really wants is to come to Oz. And Oz is running out of room.

Complaint #6

At work the boss is complaining about thieves coming at night and stealing all the expensive pipes from the buildings we are stripping. He lines us up like we're in the fourth grade.

"It's got to be one of yous," he says with no apology. "You people have a bone in your bodies that makes you take things."

For years the windows and entrances to these buildings were cinder-blocked. Not so much so junkies wouldn't use these hollow walls for shooting galleries, more so that thieves wouldn't steal the brass pipes and expensive wires that lay hidden behind the walls. The landlords knew that in time the neighborhood would bounce back and they would someday rebuild. But if the pipes are stolen it makes the renovation more expensive.

As the boss rattles his accusations, I have this idea.

I will ask Maritza to get Trompo Loco a job at her church, collecting coats for the homeless or something. I'll pay her, and she will

pay Trompo Loco as if it was a real job. Trompo Loco will never
know. If Maritza can't do it, maybe Papelito will do it, but I don't
want to ask him, because he is already helping me so much by
fronting my mortgage for me.

"Which of you came in during the night and stole some brass
pipes?"

The workers are all quiet, looking at the ground. Mario is smirk-
ing, nodding like he knows who did it. But no one pays him any
mind.

The boss paces.

"All right, I just want those brass pipes back. I don't care who
took 'em."

"I'll give them back," Antonio says in Spanish. "I'll give them
back when you give us Texas back." All the workers except Mario
laugh.

The boss is furious. He looks at me.

"What he say, Julio? What he say?" the boss asks me, and I realize that all this time he never bothered to learn any of his workers'
real names, except for mine and Mario's.

"The truth, maybe?" I say.

"You too, Julio?" he's surprised at my answer, as if he and I had
been friends.

"Look, I think we all just want to go back to work," I say.

The boss spits on the floor.

"I know who did it," Mario says.

"Yeah, who?" the boss walks over to Mario, "tell me."

"Just pick any one of them," Mario says, "you can't be wrong."

Mario laughs like an idiot. The boss doesn't bother to answer
him. Instead his eyes stare at Antonio. Antonio stares right back at
him, like he is daring the boss to either fire or fight him.

"I know you understand me," he says to Antonio. "And I understand you. So don't think I didn't get your joke. I don't have to understand Spanish to know what it's about."

A half-smirk rises from the corner of his mouth.

"You have a beat-up pickup," the boss accuses Antonio. "I've seen it, you must have come here during the night and loaded that pickup. Is that right?"

"No boss," Antonio says in a heavily accented English, "at night, I am a drunk Mexican. I can not steal nothing."

I laugh.

Boss doesn't.

Antonio stands there, defiant.

"Is that so," the boss says, "maybe I should report your drinking problem to the INS. How about that?"

Antonio's eyes finally fall to the ground.

"I want those pipes by the end of the week. Otherwise, there's plenty of other Mexicans who'd kill for your jobs." He walks away as all of us go back to work.

I tap Antonio on the back.

"Good job," I tell him in Spanish, "don't worry, he's a son of a bitch but he knows if INS raids this place, it's his ass too. There are rules about hiring undocumented workers."

"I know that, Julio," he says, "but I know who stole those pipes." Antonio gets back to work without telling me more. I leave it alone. I don't ask.

Just then I look ahead and see Trompo Loco come into focus. He sees me and smiles as he points at his hard hat. I get angry at him. I don't want to be embarrassed, which is exactly what Trompo Loco is going to do. I hope that the boss doesn't see me talking to Trompo and tell Eddie that Trompo Loco was around.

"Hey Julio, you know, I got this great idea that I can just help you. I can just work next to you," he says with the sunniest of smiles.

"Trompo," I sigh, "you got to go home, come on."

"But I can help you, look," he takes a wrapped sandwich out of his overalls, "I even brought us lunch, see. Half of this is yours, but I want the bigger half."

"Trompo go home," I raise my voice and he closes his lips real tight. I look behind me to see if the boss has noticed me not working. I see Antonio making fun of Trompo. I look back at Trompo Loco and can't tell if he is about to cry or spin.

"You can't work here, because I already got you a job," I lie, because I know he is about to spin. If he does, there's no stopping him, at least not without knocking him down to the ground and maybe hurting him.

"Really," he gets closer to me, "a real job?"

"Yes, I'll tell you later."

"What do I do?"

"You go home."

"That's not a job, Julio."

"I mean you go home now, I'll tell you later. And then you have to move in with my family, right? Right?"

Trompo Loco is beaming. He licks his lips, like he's been starving and a plate of food has just been placed in front of him.

"Okay, okay, you can have all of it," he hands me the sandwich. "I'll go home and make a new one. I have some Wonder Bread left over, the jelly and all." Trompo Loco turns and walks away. I'm glad he is leaving, but then he turns around. "Hey Julio why do fat chance and slim chance mean the same thing? I heard a guy say it. Then another guy, and it means the same—"

"Go home!" I yell at him, and he covers his mouth real fast, like he had said something wrong. He turns around and begins to walk away whistling, happy he is going to have a job soon. And I go back to work.

The boss taps my shoulder.

"Hey, wasn't that kid Eddie's retard?" He winks at me, and I ignore him and get to work. Boss trails me, grabs my shoulder, because he feels he can command any of his workers' attention at any moment. "Let me tell you something Julio, being that we are both friends of Eddie's." I stop to listen, maybe it'll be short and then he'll leave me in peace.

"I knew that retard's mother. We all did. Know what I mean?" He gives me a wink.

Like I don't have enough problems.

Waiting for me downstairs at home is Maritza. I haven't seen her in a while. I only hear echoes of her voice at night, when the services in her church would start. Bits and pieces of her sermons enter through my window and sometimes, when her church is really high on the Lord, my entire floor shakes.

Maritza is holding on tightly to this very scared girl. She clings to Maritza, like she has cat claws. The girl's eyes never leave the ground, and she's silently crying. Her heavy tears roll off her cheeks and splatter on her blouse. The girl is short, and I can tell by her beautiful, long, black hair and her silence that she is a new immigrant from Maritza's church.

"You have to drive us, Julio." Just like that, no please or thank-you.

"Wait, aren't you supposed to be at church right about now?"

"We snuck out. We have little time, Julio. You have to drive us—"

"Where?" I say.

"To Queens. And I don't drive, let's go," she says. "This is important, Julio. And we only have two hours." I stare at her for a second, because Maritza is like that sonic boom that you hear seconds after the electric storm hits the city and all the car alarms go crazy. That's what she does to me when I see her, and it takes me a while to shut them off. I used to be in love with her for so long, but later it wore off. Like that number that you keep playing that never comes up, yet you still play it, but now it's more out of habit than love or want or need. Basically, I've known her all my life.

"Look Mari, I'm not in the God business, that's you. I got my own things to worry about."

Maritza sighs heavily. She has taken off her usual pastor gown and put on a dress that outlines the shape of her breasts. As she impatiently sighs, her breasts slowly rise and fall in unison.

Maritza's attention shifts to the scared girl. She whispers something quick and loving, with something about God at the end, and then pulls me aside.

"Where you going that's so important?" I ask Maritza, whose hair is always kept short and kinda of moppish and raggedy. If she were a petite girl, she'd be considered perky and cute. But because she's tall, taller than me at five-eleven, what her hair tells you is that Maritza is too preoccupied with matters she deems more urgent to care what her hair looks like. So she just keeps it short and out of the way.

"Just drop us off at the clinic, just drop us off. We got two hours before the service is over, come on."

I think I know what's happened.

"Is that all, cuz you always have something else in mind."

"That's all, let's go. Come on, this poor girl is getting married next week."

She gives me a desperate look. Maritza knows that I can never refuse her anything; though I've tried, I could never do it. For years I've tried to shake her loose, and like a pit bull's jaw I can't let go. She commands me to do this or that, and I always complain, but in the end I always give in and do what she's asked of me.

Like now.

I drive her and this scared girl to a clinic in Queens, where during the entire trip no one says anything. Complete silence, except for the girl's sobs and sniffles. I take the FDR Drive along the Upper East Side.

In the silent car, I think about how the Upper East Side always reminds me of when I was a teenager and I started to realize I was being lied to. I believed in "The Truth" back then, and these people walking around the Upper East Side were people who were destined to be destroyed by God. These rich people were sinners and didn't love their children, because they were not walking in the ways of Jehovah God and their thoughts were not His thoughts. They didn't know the Bible and they didn't read it to their children every day and they didn't preach the good news of the Kingdom. They were part of the physical world. The governor of their world was Satan, and all those shop windows with Rolex watches and silk dresses, and all those penthouses, and all those cars and good furniture were material things that were there to entice us into the world. Our reward was Heaven.

Yet I walked around the Upper East Side and saw how these people, too, had churches and they, too, believed in God, and they, too, took their children to church. They called their God the same name as we called ours, and He, too, had a son, his name was Jesus, and he, too, died for all sinners. The churches and synagogues on the Upper East Side were big and wealthy. They had real wooden pews, not folding chairs, like ours, and their rugs were clean, not gum-stained. Their worshipers didn't wear the same two or three good dresses

they rotated every other Sunday. They bought their children pres-
ents, real expensive ones, like trains and cars that ran on batteries.
These people were Christians like me, believed in the same Christian God as I did. The Upper East Side and Spanish Harlem were two
neighborhoods that existed back to back and were like the prince and
the pauper. But our Christian God was the same. And our God was
supposed to love us the same. Our God was supposed to bless us the
same. We were supposed to live by His word and take part in the
same blessings. But that's not what I saw. I remember how, when we
were teens, Maritza made fun of me one day by saying, "The Upper
East Side God can beat up the Spanish Harlem God."

My mother kept saying that it's only a matter of time, and that
the more years go by the closer to "The End" we get. Mom would
hear in the news about some earthquake in India or some mud flood
in Colombia and she'd see them as signs of "The End." That still
hasn't changed. But not me, I got fed up. I wanted to do something
with my life other than just wait for the world to end. Maritza went
to school and graduated college. She studied civil rights, and when
no one in Spanish Harlem was buying her socialist agenda, she began
to save the world using the very God she had made fun of me for
once believing in.

"Here's the address, Julio. Hurry."

"All right, all right, God." I say and take the piece of paper she's
handed me. I cross the 59th Street bridge, not feeling groovy at all.
So I'm thinking that this is a Planned Parenthood branch or some
back-alley shanty Maritza knows about. Instead this clinic is located
on Northern Boulevard, the aorta of Queens. The clinic is right
smack in the center, where all types of businesses hit you at once—
dentist offices, real estate brokers, jewelry stores, restaurants,
banks—they waren't hiding anything.

"You have to come inside with us," Maritza demands. The girl is still shaking.

El Centro de Cirugía Plástica is not a name used in disguises, it's not called that to divert attention, it's called that because that's what it is. Surgery. The plastic kind.

I park the car.

I walk in and, except for Maritza and the frightened girl, the waiting area is empty. The room is a soft pink and there are tastefully framed posters of beautiful women on the walls. A television is playing MTV *en Español*, with the volume down. Shakira is shaking her Arab roots like she has been thrown in a body of water right in the dead of winter.

The door swings and a woman walks in. Her hair is beautiful, her legs long and slender, her breasts the size of baseballs, with a perfect rise you only get from implants.

"So," the woman says coldly, writing on her clipboard, "she needs to be a *señorita* again?"

"Yes," Maritza answers for the girl, who all of a sudden starts crying like her mother had died in her arms.

"It's all right sweetie," the woman says, laying her hand on the girl's knee, "*es muy simple, no tengas miedo*. We'll sew it back up like it was before, like nothing has happened."

"Will she need anesthesia?" Maritza strokes the girl's hair as the girl cries on her shoulder.

"Not much, just local. *Mira* sweetie," the woman tells the girl whose head is buried in Maritza arms, "*no te apures, todo se cose. Serás virgen de nuevo.*"

"*No sé lo que me hará,*" the frightened girl sobs, "*él cree que soy virgin . . .*"

The girl can't finish her words before breaking down. I think she can't say that her father might kill her if her husband brought her back as damaged goods.

The woman with the clipboard isn't moved, like she's heard all this before. She even whispers a little curse when she writes something down incorrectly. She begins to erase it, candidly speaking to Maritza.

"Don't worry, the doctor is licensed and knows what he's doing," she tells Maritza. "Your cousin will be fine. We do this all the time. We leave a small opening unsewn for the, you know, her period. But everything else is put right. Her hymen will be intact like before. He won't know a thing. On her wedding night, the walls will be tight and there will be blood on the sheets. Sign here." Maritza signs. "I need the credit card," and that's when Maritza points at me.

I back away slowly, like a gun has been pointed at me. I see Maritza telling the woman to take "her cousin" inside for the doctor to start the operation.

I exit the clinic and walk to my car. Maritza catches up with me.

"Wait Julio, wait," she pleads. Of course I stop.

"I knew it, I knew it," I say, "you needed something else, I knew it. I'm not going to pay to have that girl's thing done."

"So you'd rather have her beaten up by her husband or killed by her father? Look, this girl came to me for help. I'm trying to help her."

"Did you ever think Maritza that you can't always help people? That sometimes it's better to just let things happen."

"No it's not."

"I can't believe you, I've known you all my life, and you still surprise me. I can't believe you."

"I have a scared girl in there who made a mistake! I need your credit card!" She is already losing her patience with me, as if I am the one who is responsible for all of this.

"Maritza, I'm not the guy who did this to her, and I'm sure that the guy she is marrying is also a new immigrant, cuz Nuyoricans aren't into this virgin bullshit. We like our women whether they are pushing strollers or not. Look at Zulma, she has like four kids, but she still looks good and all these men want to marry her. So it's not only my problem it's not even my people's problem."

"Well, for your information, the guy she is marrying is Puerto Rican."

"Yeah, from the island, right? That's different, they buy into this marrying-a-virgin shit. They think their wives should be pure like sugar or something, like their mother, or some—"

"I'll pay you back!" She yells in annoyance at my rattling. For a split second only the sounds of sirens and cars passing us by can be heard.

"I'll pay you back," she says calmly. "If I could put it on my card, I would." And she stares at me like she has hypnotic powers.

"Aren't you against all of this?" I say, calming down a bit and shaking my head slowly. "Isn't this something that you speak out against in your church?"

"Yes, of course it is, stupid. God you're so stupid, Julio," she says, "of course it is, this is female genital mutilation. Of course I'm against it. It's really about control over women. But right now, I have a scared girl who if she doesn't bleed on her wedding night is going to get the shit beaten out of her."

"At times I don't get you, Mari," I say defeated, "I don't, but all right, all right how much?"

"Two . . ."

"Yeah, two? Two what? Two hundred?"

"Two . . . Two thousand."

"Two thousand! You bugging, girl!" I can't max out my card, two thousand, I have a mortgage to keep, tuition, books, my parents.

"Wait, wait, wait," she holds my arm, "I have three hundred and she has six, so you will only be paying eleven. I'll pay you back."

I stare at her. Her face is lit by a lamppost on the corner. I once dreamed of wanting to know how Maritza's face looks in the dark. When you turn off the lights and your eyes have begun to adjust and all things take on new shades and different hues. I used to think maybe one night I'd wake up for no reason and she'd be next to me and I'd get to see that image in real life. But then I got kicked around by her so much that I realized that she was more like a big sister slapping her little brother around.

"You'll pay me back?" I say knowing she will not, she can't, like many do-gooders, Maritza is always broke.

"Yes, I'll pay you back now let's go."

"How about giving Trompo Loco a job at your church," I say. Maritza looks at me like I'm insane.

"Fine, but I can't pay him—"

"No, you pay him what you owe me. You just let him do stuff—"

"Whatever, okay. Trompo can clean up and shit, let's just go back inside."

We walk back in the clinic.

I pay the woman.

Maritza and I don't talk. Maritza is watching the clock. She knows she has to get the girl back in time before the service is over. I can tell the girl's mother is in on it along with Maritza. The girl's father must be a nonbeliever and so he is not at church, and they can use the time to sneak out and get the girl revirginized.

We sit and do nothing but wait. In the waiting room the beautiful woman with fake tits, fake ass, fake nose is talking to a future customer.

"*Hay una problemita.* You're getting married next week," she says in Spanish, "you can't get married next week. You need at least a month or two for the stitches to dissolve."

"Stitches?" the customer frowns.

"*Sí* sweetie, stitches. If you have sex on your wedding night with the stitches intact, *ay dios mío*, the infection rate is so high that I can't begin to tell you."

"But we are getting married next week. Is there another way?" the customer says.

"No sweetie, you have to find a way to postpone your wedding, otherwise, if you have sex with stitches, well, you'll fool your husband but you could die."

Maritza had been listening to the conversation as well. She shakes her head in sadness, disgust or disbelief. Her eyes focus on the young woman whose head is hanging and who is about to cry. Maritza wants to get up and do something, but the woman hugs and coos her.

"*No te apures,*" she says. "It's no big deal. I had mine done, too. I had my whole body done. The only thing real are my teeth," she says and the young woman forces a smile. "Good," she tells her, "smile, we women, we have our little secrets." Then she looks my way, "We trick you men all the time."

COMPLAINT #7

Dear Julio,

When I moved to Spanish Harlem I was so concerned about
being politically correct and nonracist that I inadvertently did
stupid things that demonstrated my fear and ignorance. I was
hyperaware when I was the only white person walking on the
street. So many men have said "hey baby" to me and "God bless
your eyes" that I started to avoid looking at people's faces. But
that didn't work, because then I neglected to see one of my
neighbors saying "Hello" to me three or four times. That neighbor
was your mother. I find that I still can't say "gracias" instead of
"thank you," because I'm afraid I will mispronounce it and sound
stupid—despite the fact that I'm proficient in French, Italian and
Portuguese.

Let me explain that I have a weird blend of haughtiness and

guilt. The haughtiness comes from abiding by the manners of the environment I am used to, an environment where it is rude to catcall and where people handling food wear plastic gloves, and no one shouts in the street or anywhere else outside. But my guilt becomes frustration in the fact that I don't know how to reconcile the fact that I didn't cause these discrepancies, *other white people who aren't even related to me did.* Still I am being held responsible in this neighborhood by *some* individuals who react to me like the embodiment of the Evil White Empire. Similarly, I react to some individuals as if they are the typical stereotypes I have encountered on TV.

Of course, I could take Spanish lessons and it would be so, so easy for me to learn the language. But to hear Spanish without understanding it is like being in front of a great work of abstract art. I feel slightly overwhelmed but I find new things every time I hear it, like I find new things when I look at Pollock. Part of me likes being surrounded by my own personal un-understanding because it feels more real and more interesting than my world where everyone assumes authority, expertise, and therefore control.

My parents moved to that Wisconsin town I was born in after they met in Ithaca, NY. After they got married, my father's company sent him there. My parents weren't native to small-town customs. As soon as they arrived driving foreign cars and not American-made ones, the town suspected them of being communist. During the Cold War, my mother was labeled a lesbian when she protested the Arms Race. What did that have to do with her sexual preference? My father laughed at it. My mother worked as a librarian and fought tooth and nail for books that the library had banned. Yet through all of this they won the

town over and in the end, decades later, they now consider
themselves from Wisconsin. But not me, I longed for their past
at Cornell and so I counted the days till my departure.

I don't plan on changing anything in Spanish Harlem, but like
my parents I will be myself. Yes, New York City can be so
materialistic and superficial. Breast implants and bleached hair
have become armor women wear to prevent themselves from
actually feeling anything. I don't want that NYC. I want to live
in a place where people actually eat real food they made for
themselves, stuff that doesn't come out of a box or get delivered
in Styrofoam.

The longer I live here, Julio, the more I begin to understand
the depth of complexity of what I have previously romanticized.

But I'm beginning to make sense of it. My sense, Julio, not
yours. It is my way of dealing with it all. I used to see an old
woman selling homemade soup from a shopping cart in the
street and thought she knew the meaning of life. I'd buy soup
from her, thinking it was special soup, made by wise, age-old
hands. Magical soup, like something out of a Gabriel Garcia
Marquez novel. How stupid of me. It's really simple, she's poor.
I've been told I'm better at expressing myself on paper than I am
in speech, and so I just wanted to let you know these things.

Helen

As soon as I finish reading Helen's letter, I think of her hands.
The letter is handwritten in black, bold lettering that was as graceful
as Papelito's movements. I can picture her hands skating over a white
sheet of paper, doing all sorts of circles and swirls. Helen's letter is
beautiful. I have never received a letter like this one, ever. I don't

want to fold it. I think of taking the letter with me everywhere and rereading it at every possible chance, in subways and at bus stops. During coffee breaks at work and during class, especially when the subject is dull and mechanic. I think I will discover new things about her. New things in me, too. But if I take the letter with me, it might get ruined and I don't want that to happen.

So I iron it by placing it flat inside a book. It's all I can think of doing to protect it. I'm an amateur in these things. After putting her letter away, I feel bad I said those things to her the other night. And I wish I could express myself the way she does. I feel both terror and joy that she explained herself with a letter and feel I should do something. I don't know what. So, I feel even dumber but I will do what many do when they are in situations like this one. I'll go see Papelito. Since I have to pay my mortgage anyway, he'll never know my true reasons for being there.

Papelito's botanica, San Lazaro y las Siete Vueltas, sparkles with glorious light. Even the life-sized tortured plaster saints look alive, like plants that instinctively sway toward the sun. It is a botanica so clean and saintly, you feel you have to whisper once inside.

And it is always full of women. The place weeps femininity. Women walk in and out of Papelito's botanica as if it was a beauty parlor. They adore Papelito, because he'd let women in on Yoruba secrets. He makes them love potions for their men, or spells for women they hate.

Papelito is wearing a blue-and-white dress, the colors of the Orisha, the black god that had chosen him, and Yemaya, the goddess of the sea. I enter with this month's mortgage payment, as I always do. Papelito is whispering something to a woman and I try not to disturb him.

"*Mira mi amor*, wrap a single strand of your hair around his mail box," the woman listens intently, "melt red wax over the photographs of her. Place them in a black shoebox and hide it in a closet." The woman nods her head. "Say the prayer to Ochosi, the hunter, and your man will come back to you."

She believes it. So I guess it'll work.

The woman tries to kiss Papelito's hand.

"No, no *mija*. Kiss the Orisha's hand," he says, pulling his delicate fingers back, "thank them, *mi linda*. Make the offerings and pray to them. They will show the way, girl."

"But what if he doesn't come back to me?" she whines.

"Have faith in the Orishas," he says and she almost weeps. Papelito holds her close to him.

"Don't worry, trust them," he repeats. As the woman pulls away from him, Papelito holds a strand of her hair in his hand.

"Such beautiful hair," Papelito says to her. "*Pero* Irma, you got split ends. So young and with split ends, I got something for that."

I wait for him to finish with Irma, so I look around. Papelito's botanica also doubles as a pawn shop. It has so much junk that Papelito sells milk crates full of bric-a-brac for three dollars. Rumors had spread that a woman had bought one of Papelito's crates and had supposedly found a gold ring at the bottom. Others said they bought a crate and found a diamond inside a half-empty bottle of baby oil. Some had found less enviable things but useful things nonetheless, like spoons, detergent boxes, small radios, toothpaste, charged batteries, pens, canned goods, books, and toys (some broken, some not). These objects came courtesy of thieves, addicts, winos, and other down-and-outs who regularly arrive at San Lazaro y las Siete Vueltas to hock their loot. They'd walk in and ask if Papelito would take this or that off their hands for loose change. Papelito accepts everything gracefully, then he'll throw the items in one of the milk crates.

I wait patiently for Papelito to take care of his customers. I walk over to an elegant corner of the botanica. There is an altar erected to the Orisha Chango. Papelito loves Chango, because Chango is the god Papelito always wanted to be chosen by. Many years ago, when Papelito was being initiated, during the *asiento*, when an Orisha is placed on the initiate's head, Papelito didn't lose faith hoping Chango would claim him. He kept reminding anyone who'd listen to the story a part of Chango's legend, "*Ese* Chango, he once dressed as a woman to escape, and he dwells inside a woman, Santa Barbara. *So mira*. He will choose me and accept me how I am."

But during the sacred ceremony, it was the Goddess Yemaya who claimed Papelito. His *padrino*—his teacher/godfather—let him know this, and Papelito embraced Yemaya with all his soul. Blue and white, the Orisha's colors, is all he wears, and he does things in seven, because seven is her number. But Papelito still keeps a lit candle in his heart for Chango.

The altar to Chango is erected on a sturdy table covered by a red-and-white mantle, the colors attributed to the Chango. A tall statue of the regal Catholic saint Santa Barbara, who shares a duality with Chango, stands in the middle. There are symbolic representations attributed to the Orisha: a double-headed ax, various volcanic rocks, an image of a horse, bowls of hard candy, nuts, seeds, and, on the floor, a full-size bata drum with a gold cufflink on the side. On the wall, above Papelito's altar to Chango, hanging straight and upright from a carefully hammered nail, is a framed autographed picture of Robert F. Kennedy. I pick up the portrait and stare at it, like at captions from an old magazine or a sixties song playing on a far-away radio. The picture makes me think of the "might have beens" of the world. Maritza would be proud of me for thinking these thoughts.

Papelito walks behind me and lovingly takes the portrait from my hand.

"I got to touch him, Julio. He showed up in El Barrio and we mobbed him," he says, placing the picture carefully back where it belongs. "I grabbed his arm and *fua*, his cufflink came off." Papelito's face saddens. "I was so young in '68. Didn't even wear dresses yet."

The bells chime again. A woman walks in and whispers something in Papelito's ear. Papelito nods. They talk briefly.

"I took up a collection, Papelito. This is *el derecho* for the Orishas," she hands him a wad of money, "can you do the *trabajo*?"

"*Pero contra mami*," lightly placing his fingertips on his chest, near his heart, "of course I'll perform the *trabajo*." When Papelito talks, his whole body moves with fluidity, gracefully as oil slowly pouring out of a bottle.

The woman looks my way and gives me a distrustful stare. She says something to Papelito behind her upheld hand, to be sure I can't hear.

Papelito nods again, gently kisses her cheek, and escorts the woman out. He shuts the door behind her, turning over the CLOSED sign.

"*Mira mi amor*, your mother was here a few days ago asking about a cat," he says in a low voice as though a scandal may erupt simply because my mother spoke to him.

"Yeah, I know. Don't worry about it. I'll get her another one. Here," I say, handing Papelito the money so he can deposit it and write a check to pay the bank as if it is his mortgage. After I hand the money over to him, I stand there like I'm waiting for a train. I want to tell Papelito that a woman wrote me a letter, and ask what the Orishas might have in store for me. I want a consultation, but I feel stupid asking for one. Especially after I have rejected Papelito's offer to try one out, time and time again. I stand there, all nervous, and no words come out. Instead I think about psychic networks and horoscopes and stuff like that, stuff I have no faith in. I have always believed that you can fit any situation of your life into a horoscope and those readings. That's why they hold no water for me. But Papelito's religion is a religion of survival. One that took certain steps in order to keep itself alive. A religion of cunning. Santeria is something else. Something real. But, above all, I have faith in Papelito.

"I have to talk to you," he whispers after he takes my money. He stares at my eyes as if he has seen something that he knows I'm afraid to tell him. Like he is making it easier for me, like throwing me a lifesaver. "Come, come." He takes my hand.

"I gotta go Papelito," I say, because I feel like chickening out. "I have night school, then help Mom put in those new tiles in the kitchen. That apartment needs work—"

"No mijo, mira," blinking his eyes and pausing to make sure he has my attention, "que this is important, mi amor," he says, and I have to laugh inside, because it's not what he says but how he says it. The way he choreographs his hands with his speech is like watching a ballet. But I'm happy, because it's really what I wanted all along and couldn't push my pride, fear, doubts or all three, far enough to do it.

We go to the basement.

It's where Papelito has set up the Ile, the house of the Orishas. It's a magnificent room, full of fresh flowers and plants. At the feet of every saint are fruit offerings, bowls of sweets, and symbols attributed to each Orisha. Nailed to the wall are bows and arrows, spears, and entire sugar canes along with flags of different colors. An elaborate altar for Ochun is assembled on a knee-high table. Next to it, upright and loving, stands a life-size statue of La Caridad de Cobre, the Lady of Charity, the Catholic saint with whom Ochun shares a duality. There are five baskets filled with fruits—five because that is her number—and feathers of a peacock, the bird associated with her. Yellow silk scarves and other similar fabrics decorate the altar, celebrating the colors of the Orisha.

Papelito asks me to sit down on the floor, where two pillows face each other, and then he asks me for the *derecho*, the fee for the Orishas. I want to tell him I didn't ask him for a consultation, that it was he who wanted me to come down here. Instead I dig in my pocket and bring out three twenties. He instructs me to fold them and cross myself with them by touching my shoulders, then forehead, and then stomach, kissing the money at the end. I do as told, because I don't want to offend Papelito or his religion.

I hand the money over, and Papelito takes the *derecho* and puts it in a colorful jar next to a statue of El Niño de Atocha, the saint the Orisha Elegua shares a duality with. Papelito catches me staring at Elegua.

"Elegua is both messenger and gatekeeper, he has the keys so we can speak to the black gods. It always starts and ends with Elegua."

Papelito then joins me on the floor.

"Let's see what your *letra* is today, *mi negrito*," he tells me. Papelito takes a necklace made up of tortoise shells and starts casting it down between us. After each cast, he writes different combinations down, numbers I can see or words he only understands. Papelito mumbles to himself quietly. He instructs me to hold on tightly to some objects he hands over to me. A stone. A bone. A shell.

He writes down more combinations.

"No one has asked the Orishas to harm you, *mijo*," he tells me.

"So that's good, right?" I say, trying to be cool about the letter. I really want to ask him if love is in the cards for me? Or something along those lines.

"*Pero perate*, two women are coming your way, Julio."

"Get out," I'm excited.

"One is white, she will have money, the other is dark but she will love you and give you children."

It's a religion of poet priests yanked out of their beloved Africa and forced to embrace not just slavery in the new world but also Catholicism. And so these poet priests preserved their religion by hiding their gods inside Catholic saints. The Spaniards bought the hustle, and, in time, the two religions merged, forming the way of the saints, Santeria. A religion born out of a need for survival, of diversity, of color and magic. The Dark Continent was in our blood and Africa's religions were part of our cultural heritage. Like the blood of our people, Santeria became one with so many other things in order to survive. It adapted and transformed itself into something new. It is this instinct of survival that lives to this day in botanicas all over the country.

"Wow, two women," I whisper to myself, "what do I have to do?"

"You have to make a decision, *papi*."

"I can't keep both?" Man, I'm thinking, when it rains it pours.

"No, greed is not the Orishas' way, *mi amor*."

"You sure?"

"*Sí mijo*, I'm sure. They love to eat, but they are not greedy. Now, *mijo*, you have to erect an altar for Ochun, goddess of love and marriage. Five yellow candles, five sweet cakes, a peacock feather, that's Ochun's bird. After five days, throw the cakes in the East River as an offering. *Me entiende?*"

"Okay."

"Julio, the East River, not the Hudson, the women are coming from the east."

"Sounds good."

"You know what saint shares her duality with Ochun, right?"

"La Caridad de Cobre, right?"

"Good, learning, *mijo*, learning." Papelito then checks his numbers again. "*Sí pero*, there is still harm in your *letra*. Some harm is coming."

"Like what?" My eyes narrow and I fear the flames of those fires I set are reaching their arms to grab me. Engulf me maybe.

"*No sé,*" Papelito shakes his head, deeply looking into his calculations. "But the harm is coming from a powerful force, Julio," he stares at his numbers as if double checking.

"Hey, Papelito," I pause, because I've been wanting to ask him this for a long time and want to say it right, "why do you believe in the Orishas so much?"

Papelito laughs a little, his head drops back. He starts to put away his numbers and with his finger he taps a glass of water that is sitting on a table. The glass makes a pretty, crystal-like ring that drones for a few seconds. Papelito gets up and goes over to light a blue candle to his Orisha, Yemaya. Then he bows to Elegua, because all things start and end with Elegua.

"This is a holy room, *ven mijo*," he says, and I follow him back upstairs, where a couple of women are waiting for him outside the door. The women's Latin American faces let me know they are from Maritza's church. They have been waiting patiently and silently for Papelito to reopen his botanica.

"*Momentito, momentito!*" Papelito kindly lets them inside. He hands them each a small statue of the saint San Lazaro, who shares his duality with the Orisha Babaluaye, saint for the sick and diseased. The women take the statues and hold them close to their chests, as if they were some miracle vaccine, something as vital as water in a desert. Papelito tells them to thank Maritza, and the women silently leave. They don't go through the front but take the back exit. Maybe they fear that their friends, who don't understand the religion and might see them coming out of a botanica, might judge them.

Papelito's attention returns to me. He puts his hand on top of mine, which he does when he has some revelation to tell you.

"Your question is easy, *mi lindo*," he says. "Regla Lukumi is really the *patakis*, the stories I have chosen to live my life by."

"Stories?"

"Yes, powerful stories that teach me how to experience life, my life. How to live my life within nature and my community."

"Why do these stories hold so much power?"

"Because they are beyond stories, Julio. They hold power for all of us, *mijo*. Listen. These stories are really our search for truth, for meaning, for significance. These stories are us in disguise. *Mira mi amor*, some people choose to live their lives by Christian stories, Hindu stories, Muslim stories, Buddhist stories, or, like me, Yoruba stories, but if you take all the stories, you will see similar patterns, similar characters."

"Like who?"

"Like Elegua earlier," and he points at another statue of El Niño de Atocha. "Elegua is not just the gatekeeper but the trickster, a joker. Many religions have a joker, Julio. In your Christian beliefs, just when God had given man a job, a woman, and eternal life, the serpent had to stick its nose in. The joker is there to tell you, just when you think you have it all under control, *Sape! Te jode la vida.* Depending on the stories you have chosen to live your life by, Ganesha, Hanuman, Lucifer or Elegua will throw things at you. They are really the same character in different stories."

"Stories, huh? Any love stories in there?"

Papelito smiles the brightest smile I have ever seen decorate his face.

"All the good ones are love stories, *papi*," he delicately swats at my shoulder. "It's really what it's all about. The real hero in all stories is love."

I get nervous and feel embarrassed to be asking him about this. It makes me feel like the women that visit him. Truth is, I want to hear more but I switch gears.

"Stories? I see," I say, lifting my head a bit, like I understand it.

"Yes, stories that if you listen closely will tell you things about yourself that deep down you know are true."

"But I like the Christian stories. What I don't like is the church," I shrug.

"Then *mijo*, what you don't really like is their *rituals*. These stories come with rituals. It's the only way these stories become real to us."

"So Regla followers make their stories real by possessions and potions and stuff?"

"No different than the pope telling you to eat the body of Christ, *verdad*? Or a pastor speaking in tongues, that's possessions? No? *Mira*, they're all rituals, all relative. Maybe it's time that you exchanged your stories. Maybe you'd like to live your life by another culture's myths and rituals. Pray, Julio."

He takes his hand off mine and winks and goes to attend a customer who had walked in while we were talking. He sways his hips towards her, hugs her like he's known her for decades. Maybe he has, the woman is as old as Papelito. They start to gossip.

"When? No? That husband of yours!" Papelito exclaims as he and the woman both laugh and continue to whisper like meddling witches.

T hat night, I buy the items I need for my offering. I go home thinking about rereading Helen's letter and about exchanging my stories. Why not? It might do me good. At school I'm getting a BA in management, because I know I can get a good job; problem is that management is really boring, like playing bilingual Scrabble with my parents. In night college I'm not learning stories to guide me, I'm just getting a bunch of information. A series of technologies for a new and supposedly improved job market. But stories interest me. I know some of the Yoruba stories and many of them are beautiful, colorful and lovely. The black gods speak from the wind and thunder. The spirit of God flows in every mountain stream and glade of grass. It's an earthly religion with poetry. There was no poetry in growing up Pentecostal.

As for Papelito asking me to pray, I never doubted the power of prayer. Both good and bad. I had witnessed it myself when I was a little kid and our pastor had asked the entire church to pray on behalf of this brother who was unemployed. This brother had to feed his wife and five kids but had no work. Jobs were hard to come by during the recession. Unemployment was at an all-time high. New York City was near bankruptcy. If things broke, they stayed broken. So, the pastor pleaded week in and week out for the congregation to hold this brother in our prayers. I remember praying something silly, like, "Lord Jehovah, you have a job. Please help this brother have a job, too." Something along those lines, something that would only make sense to a seven-year-old. When the brother landed a job driving a milk truck, our entire church rejoiced. He even donated milk to those in the congregation who needed it. But on the third month on the job, a fire engine crashed into the brother's milk truck, killing him. I felt betrayed. Did my prayers kill him? Did God? The pastor got up in front of the platform and said, "He was probably singing a hymn when God took him. He was a sweet brother, like honey. His death was a reconciliation of milk and honey." And the congregation laughed at his little pun. But I was sad. I nervously confronted our pastor after the service, and he brushed aside my question of "why" by telling me to listen to my mother. I was a kid, so I didn't bother him anymore after that. But even at that age I began questioning our beliefs. There were other forces at work here. My religion wasn't the center of the world, like I had been taught to believe. There were other sets of truths that my religion feared, and didn't want to challenge, or didn't know how to address when brought up. By anyone of any age.

That's why I believe in Papelito. To him all religions are streams, rivers, bodies of water that lead to the same ocean. It matters little to Papelito if his religion is considered a great lake, a pond, or a puddle; as long as he keeps his water clean, he believes his life is enriched by his faith. No matter how foreign that faith might sound to others. So, maybe I should take Papelito's advice to heart. Maybe I should trade in my Christian Jesus for another culture's Christ.

Complaint #8

The last thing I expect to see when I get home is Helen sitting so close to my mother on the couch it looks as if she's perched on Mom's lap. The two are looking at family albums. My father is sitting across the room in his favorite chair. Piled on his lap are his old salsa albums. No doubt he was showing them off.

"Julio loved school," Mom says, which isn't true. I hated school.

"And this," Helen points at a picture I know too well.

"That was his clubhouse, he loved it," Mom says. Helen shoots me a sly smile, like one does when something is cheesy.

"Julio loved church," Mom says, pointing at another picture, and that, too, is untrue. I liked church, but it was far from love.

"Julio loved cats," Mom says. "Brought me a cat once."

"Julio loves a lot of things, Mrs. Santana," Helen says, laughing.

"Oh, yeah, and he's so smart." My mother wants to sell me, like she needs to let Helen know I'm good. "This is Julio graduating."

Because Helen is white, my mother assumes she has to speak clear, good English, like it will indicate that she is civilized. Though Mom has a slight accent, there's no trace of Spanglish in her speech.

"Show a picture of when I had a salsa band," my father says, but Mom ignores him.

"He loved to play, Julio was always playing," she says, and Helen is enjoying this. But I really don't want her to see those pictures. I know those pictures well. I see them in my mind's eye all the time. It isn't my childhood that makes them so memorable, it is the time they represent. The burned buildings, the vacant lots, the graffitied trains, the broken elevators, the heaps of garbage, the many buildings and places that no longer exist in a fading neighborhood. And I know Helen will only see me laughing or playing and ignore what's behind me. She'd ignore the glares of truths in those backgrounds. It was my neighborhood, with all its wrinkles and warts, before the surgery.

"There's a picture of me with Hector Lavoe," Pop says, and Mom knows that if you leave Pops alone, he'll dream off on his own. Which is what she wants.

"Who are those two, Mrs. Santana?"

"That's Julio's friends, they grew up together. Eduardo and Maritza." Of course Mom doesn't mention that Trompo Loco is slow and that Maritza runs a commie church.

"She's beautiful. Short hair doesn't go well with her though."

Mom had gone too far. I am about to take the album. I reach for it, and when Mom shifts her weight the album falls on the floor. Many of the pictures spill on the rug. Helen excuses herself as if it was her fault. They begin to pick the pictures up. Helen looks at me.

"I just dropped by to apologize for the other night."

"It's okay," I say.

"Julio, Helen is having dinner with us," Mom says proudly.

"Only if it's no trouble, Mrs. Santana. I mean I'll invite you over and reciprocate as soon as I can fix my kitchen. It's such a mess. But the gallery opens in two weeks."

"It's too bad I can't stay," I say.

"Re . . . ci . . . pro . . . cate?" Mom whispers slowly to herself, because she doesn't know the word.

"*Mira*, that's wrong," Pops says. "We have a guest and you have to go. *Que modales son esos?*"

All of a sudden my father cares about manners, like we are at church or somewhere public.

Helen and Mom are through picking up the pictures and are back on their feet.

"I know it's wrong but I'm sorry. I just came to change and pick up a book for class," I say. Truth is, anything would be better than where I'm going. And I want to talk to her, at least apologize for that night. I don't want her to think that I'm jumping the gun in thinking that just because she wrote this nice letter she's crazy about me.

Mom cuts me her evilest look.

"He is embarrassed of us," she whispers to Helen, "because we are not as American as he is."

"I don't think so, Mrs. Santana. That's not true," Helen says. I, on the other hand, let Mom say whatever she wants. I do my best not to fight with her.

"I have to go. Sorry I can't stay, Helen." I go to my room and change. I open the book where Helen's letter is and reread it quickly. I tell myself there is nothing in there that should make you think anything. She is only stating her side, and she does it beautifully and nicely, and you should be just as gracious. I place the letter back inside the book and close it.

When I come out of my room, all three are in the dining room. I make believe I'm getting things ready, but I look at them and see that Helen seems comfortable. She smiles when my mother serves her some food.

I do want to stay. I do. But I have to go.

"Julio, wait," she calls out and gets up from the dining table and runs over, before I step out, "I apologize for the other night."

"Oh, that, don't worry about it," I say, not looking at her.

"Was Julio rude to you?" Mom joins us by the door.

"No, not at all," Helen says to her.

"I have to go," I say, about to turn around.

"Did you get my letter?" she calls out.

"Oh, that, yes," I say and I notice that my father smiles the shiest of smiles. That man has read it. Jesus! I'm wondering if Mom has, too? That's what you get for living with your parents this long. You idiot. "Yes, I should apologize as well," I say.

"No, no," Helen's small mouth stays open for a second, like she's heard a rude remark, "no, no. No need to. I'm just trying to make friends here, okay? That's all. I didn't come to fight. I just want peace," Helen says. "Thanks for reading it."

"What letter?" Mom says.

"Nothing, Ma'," I say, to calm her suspicions down. "Nothing."

Miraculously, Mom lets it drop. But Pops still has that sly look on his face.

"Poor thing," Mom says, petting Helen's hair, "getting called *la rubia* all the time in the street." But I know Mom would kill for that title.

"I just need peace," Helen repeats, "what you told me about claiming my presence here is just so brutal. Like pioneers, this isn't the Wild West." She smiles, and I notice how pretty her nose is. How she has tiny freckles that join together when she smiles. "Allies and all that stuff, I just want peace. Okay?" she says again as if that word had power. Maybe it does; I like the word as well. I sometimes believe it can save us all. I want to talk to Helen about this, but I can't right now.

I park my car outside the coffee shop on 118th and First. I enter to collect for my very last job. Eddie is sitting at his favorite table. He's on his cell phone and glancing through a limp *New York Post*. With only a third-grade education, he's a wizard at numbers and trivia. Eddie has a calculator in his head, and every morning he reads all four city papers, the *Times*, the *Daily News*, the *Post*, and *Newsday*. If he knew Spanish, I bet he'd read *El Diario*. His Sundays are practically devoted to reading his papers. But I know he isn't making bets.

Still on the phone, he motions for me to come in and sit.

"Why not take my car, honey," he doesn't lower his voice or anything. "No, I'll be here awhile." He pauses and then looks at a picture on a wall. "I don't know when I'll be back, all right? But when I do get back, I'll fix the car," he says and I pretend not to be listening. His coffee shop's walls are bare, except for the wall behind the cash register where it's crowded with dusty bowling trophies and pictures of his wife and children. The entire history of his family, from when they were kids to adults. There's no picture of Trompo Loco on that wall. "Yeah, yeah, I love you too," he says and I cringe, because Eddie has no problem with those three words. At least not to his wife. Eddie can be the coldest of people, yet he can say those words and say them while someone else is in the room.

"Bye, I love you too," he repeats, hangs up, and then looks my way as if he has said nothing embarrassing, which I guess he hasn't.

"Hey, it's good to see you," he says in the nicest of tones as he folds up the *Post*. The other three city papers are neatly piled on the floor, waiting their turn. He then gets up, gets me a cup of coffee and hands me an envelope with my pay. I take it; no need to count it.

I tell him that was my last job.

"Are you sure? It was just yesterday that you started, time flies." He stands up, steps on his papers and hugs me.

"So why you quitting?" he says like I haven't told him already.

I tell him I can't do jobs for him anymore. I need a lot of time. I tell him I'm going to go to school full-time. But I'd still like to keep the demolition job he got me at the construction site. I never heard any names, I don't know anything about the insurance, never saw any faces, I always worked alone, and now I want out.

"Out? Out where? What you mean out?" Eddie is getting old, but he still has the same young voice he had when, as a kid playing stickball, he yelled, "Safe!"

"But Julio, what I'm 'spose to do, call the union? 'Hey, send me another arsonist, the last one quit to go to school?' "

He smiles at me, and I smile back and think how beautiful this old man could be. How he still loves his wife, believes in God, and how his clothes smell of newspapers and sweet coffee. He would make a great old man if he only knew how to be one.

"You can't just quit, Julio. You're the best. What I'm 'spose to do?"

I plead with him. Because I also know he is fair.

"How you going to keep that mortgage, Julio? No way, you gonna give away money to the banks."

I tell Eddie that's my business. I look into the old man's eyes for no reason other than so he can see I'm not hiding anything. The mortgage is my thing, he has nothing riding on it, it's mine and mine alone to lose.

"Come here, come here, give me a hug. Give me a hug."

I hug him again. Still, as good as he's been to me, we're in business and business is the hardest thing, harder than diamonds and harder than raising babies.

"Listen, I always liked you."

I know the reason this old man likes me is because I look after his son. It's Eddie's way of justifying his guilt trips, a chain he has created with my help. He takes care of me, I take care of his son. In his own way Eddie believes he is performing his fatherly duties. Not only that, but he can take communion and be at peace with his God.

Eddie learned the fear of Jesus when he was a kid, baptized at Our Lady of Carmel on 112th and Lexington. He loves that church. Later his mother groomed him to be the priest in the family, but he lost his way or found it, I'm not sure. He likes to tell the story of when Spanish Harlem was called Little Italy, how on every Friday, when it was fish and no meat or you'll go to hell, his mother would give him a quarter to get fresh fish at the market. It was also the place where men played craps and took bets. He'd watch those games but, more important, the faces of the players. He soon recognized who was working with who and would place his bet only after the dealer's accomplice had placed his. Soon Fridays were more than fish, Fridays were young Eddie's days to make money. That was until those craps players caught on to him, and then it was on to something else.

That something else turned out to be an old gun Eddie won playing poker. His mother hated the gun, and the story goes that Eddie himself didn't know what to do with it. Then came the knock at the door.

A woman wanted to know if Eddie would put her dog out of its misery. It was cheaper if Eddie shot the dog than if she took the dog to an animal hospital, to ask for a humane injection. She was pooped. The dog was suffering. Eddie agreed and soon the neighborhood knew him as the man who will shoot dogs. Soon, many knocked on his door asking for his services. Eddie obliged for a price. He saw it as a good business. A single bullet costs three cents, and Eddie would do the job for five dollars. Bury your dog in Central Park for an extra ten. His only condition being, the dog had to be old and suffering. They say that Eddie hated the job. He confessed to his priest that he hated the job because the owners would knock at his door in tears, telling Eddie stories about their dogs when they were puppies. The shoes they mangled. The way they used to run and stumble. But Eddie needed the money, so he did what he had to. He went to church every Sunday to wash his sins clean. Eddie did so many jobs that word spread fast among all the Italian neighborhoods in New York City. By then Eddie was nineteen and was putting down three dogs a month.

Until he broke the gun. One day the old gun fell on the floor and broke to pieces. The handle, trigger and barrel lay sprawled out on the floor.

Then it was on to something else.

For a few years Eddie worked in a supermarket as East Harlem continued to change in color. People like my parents arrived by the load. East Harlem became known as El Barrio or Spanish Harlem. Then, during the late sixties the property value of the neighborhood fell. And that something else that Eddie had been waiting for arrived in name of Slum Clearance. This was no longer small-time hustling, there was a fortune to be made. And he set out to make it.

"You Porto Ricans, I never lost money on any of you. I once bet five Gs on the Benitez–Sugar Ray fight." Eddie does have a weakness, he loves to gamble. If Eddie sees two roaches side by side he'd freeze, to bet you on which roach will get to the wall first.

I tell him, Benitez lost that fight.

"Exactly, and he didn't let me down. Imagine if he'd won. I'd be out five Gs. But you people never do that to me."

But this old man doesn't believe in a lucky gambler, only winners and losers. And the winners are the ones who control the game. So if he bets on the roach that's to the left, it's because he has seen something, a missing leg, a lost antenna or something that the roach on the right is lacking. It's the reason why he reads all the city papers. He feels bits of trivia on various subjects gives him a gambling edge. Once he told me that, since I don't read papers, never to gamble, because I would always lose.

"All right, good luck."

I thank him and just when I'm about to go, his cell rings again, and Eddie motions with his hand for me to wait.

I stare at the photographs by the cashier. I see the story of his family. There's a picture of a younger Eddie taking his kids to church. Trompo Loco, of course, is missing. Trompo Loco is a sin that Eddie denies ever committing, a sin he never confessed to his priest or anybody. And, just like saying "I love you" to his wife, without an ounce of embarrassment or discomfort, he tries to ignore Trompo Loco's existence, just as naturally. But somewhere in Eddie's being there is Catholic guilt that gnaws at him, that eats his liver every night and grows a new one in the morning. I know, because he always manages to ask me about "my friend." I know that's why he wants me to wait, to ask me about Trompo Loco. There are times when I just want to snap at him and say, "How should I know. He's your son, you go ask him yourself."

"That's great, dear," he says, "I'm happy you got it started." Eddie talks to his wife like a newlywed, he says "I love you" often. I mean, he has said "I love you" already, now hang up! But no, he is still on the line.

"No, I like Father Hernandez, I like him, sure I'll throw some money his way."

Eddie talks and performs at different speeds, as if he has created two new languages, feelings, and faces. One for his wife and the other for the coldness of his profession.

Finally Eddie says to his wife in the sweetest of tones, like many times before, "Yes, okay, bye, I love you too."

"Can I go now?" I ask him.

"I heard your friend was at the demolition site?"

"Yeah," I say, "he was there, I told him to go away, but he doesn't listen," I say.

So, I know that the boss squealed on me. Which should be the clincher for Eddie, letting him know for sure that the entire world knows the truth. The only one who still thinks people don't know Trompo Loco is Eddie's son is Eddie.

"You keep your friend away from anything that has to do with me."

"I try, he just doesn't listen," I say to Eddie. Then—I don't know where I get the guts to say this, but I do—"He thinks you're his father."

Eddie's face collapses like he was smacked in the face.

"You don't believe that do you?" he gets really defensive.

"No," I say, "of course not, but I just wonder why he thinks that?"

Eddie grumbles. He lies back against his chair.

"Listen, I appreciate you looking out for him. So, I'll tell you that, yeah I had a thing with his mother. That don't mean he's my kid. A lot of men jammed that broad. She was a mental case, you know. I confessed that, I did my retribution, long ago. But now, no way I'm going to be the sucker who takes responsibility for that kid. That's why I don't lift a finger for that kid. I would if the kid was mine."

I want to tell Eddie that Trompo Loco is no longer a kid. He's man. A bit slow, but a man.

"Damn right I would. But I never lifted a finger for that kid. And you know I'm not like that at all. I help people too. I helped you out when you needed a job, right?"

"Yes, and thank you," I tell him. "Don't worry, I'll keep my friend away from here."

"Good," Eddie says, "but take him to church. It's the only way he's going to find some direction. Some people are saved by it. His mother could have used it. So take him. Okay?"

"Yeah, I got him a job at a church." Though I don't tell him which church, because Maritza's church has got a crazy reputation.

"Good, that's good," Eddie's eyebrows lift up. I think he is glad. "Good, Julio, now, here, take these."

He hands me car keys.

"What is this?" I say.

"A favor, just a favor. Pick up at 82nd and Park and drop at Hunts Point, you know where."

I had just told him I wasn't doing jobs for him. Any type of jobs, not anymore.

"The father buys his kid a Lexus for his birthday. Kid wants the money. Kids these days, you were not like that. That's why I always liked you."

I shake my head, extending my hand with the keys toward him. I can't. Don't want to do it. Can he get another guy?

"Julio, one last favor," he stands up again and holds my face with his hands, they are wrinkled and hard but he holds my face as if he was holding eggs.

I'll do it but I repeat that this is my last. I say, this is only a favor. I make sure to repeat it.

I turn to leave.

"Good scout, don't be a stranger and let me know when you graduate. And remember, don't take nothing. Don't even open the glove compartment. And keep that kid away from here."

I walk out of the coffee shop to find Trompo Loco across the street, staring at me. I work up a slow anger at seeing him. I fight it, but get furious at the complex mess I have to manage while I had nothing to do with creating it.

"Didn't I say not to come around here." I push Trompo Loco to keep walking. I want him as far away from here as quickly as possible.

"Did you talk to him? Did you talk to my father?"

"How many fucking times I'm gonna tell you he ain't your father." We turn the corner and I hope Eddie hadn't seen Trompo.

"Did Maritza talk to you," I ask him and his head drops. "You going to work for her church, right?" I say, demanding more than asking. Trompo Loco nods.

"You gonna move in too, because those people where you live hate you, Trompo. Those people are playing for keeps. You just holding them back, okay?"

"But I want to be help-less, I just want a little help and then I want no help at all. Less help," he says and I look at Trompo Loco and see a man who just wants what we all want. There is nothing outrageous in his wanting, no fancy cars, women, or fame. Trompo Loco just wants a real life. A job. A house. A father. I can't keep discouraging him. It is his right to have these things. And he is working towards obtaining them, too. He is plugging away, he is trying to make the team, and I keep cutting him. So I hug him and tell him to go home and I would talk to him about it. Really talk to him about it the next day and help him on his way to being help-less. But the father thing? There is nothing I can do about that.

My favor for Eddie has to do with a Lexus. This kid wants his car stolen so he can get the insurance. The kid gets in touch with people that know Eddie. The kid gives Eddie the keys, tells Eddie where the car's parked, and my job is to go steal it. I drive it to wherever it is that Eddie tells me to, park it, screw off the license plates, and let the vultures pick it apart. The insurance company investigates, and when they find it, it's a skeleton. This has nothing to do with chop shops, it's plain insurance fraud. The kid gets investigated but he didn't steal it, I did, and they have no idea who we are. Even I have no idea who "we" are, I only deal with Eddie. These jobs are almost gimmes. I've done tons of these. The only danger is if the police stop you for some violation. Then you're busted. You got grand theft auto on your hands and Eddie don't know you. So you drive carefully. No running through yellows, and you use signals.

The car I am going to steal is supposed to be parked on 82nd and Park Avenue. A black Lexus. I have the number. I have the keys.

I spot it and approach it. I get the key out of my pocket, open the door and get in as if I own it. I put the key in the ignition and fire up the engine. I check out the glove compartment. Only Gloria Estefan CDs in there. What kinda music is that? This guy's car deserves to be stolen . . . without an insurance kickback.

I drive past the Willis Avenue Bridge. I throw Gloria out the window and into the East River, cross over to the Bronx and dump the Lexus at Hunts Point. I ride the 6 train back to El Barrio, pick up my car, drive to my night class happy with money in my pocket.

Complaint #9

"**Qué** *es eso!*" Mom screeches.

"That is an altar, Ma'," I say.

"An altar? *Dios mío.*" Mom's mouth drops. Not only does her Protestant religion forbid Catholic saints, it also forbids lighting candles and offering fruits, cakes and feathers to them.

"What are you doing opening and checking inside my room?"

"Something smelled real bad and I had to see what it was," she says, knowing she did something wrong so she'll make up an excuse, because these candles are odorless.

"Ma', it's my business if I erect an altar in my room. It's my house too."

"Not if you are bringing demons into the house and I live here with your father too," she says, and my father enters my room.

"*Ave maria, una ofrenda* Julio?" My father knows what's up.

"An offering for what? *Porque yo voy a tirar eso a la basura,*" Mom yells.

"You better not throw anything away, Ma'," I yell back to her.

"Oh man, Julio, that's Ochun," he says. I want him to shut up. "You want love to enter your life."

"Pa', stop it, you're talking crazy," I say, because I don't want Mom to know this. I'll feel so stupid.

"Love? You want love?" Mom says.

"Well, maybe. Yeah, I want love," I say.

"You find love by going back to the meetings and finding a good sister in church."

"Can I find love my way, please," I say to her. "Ma', you always say that 'the same recipe for *pasteles* always comes out different in other hands.' So let me find it my way, okay?"

"Not with *Satanas* helping you like this—" she says.

"Hector Lavoe was the biggest *santero*," Pops interrupts, "and he was always erecting altars to Ochun. So, I know. One day, we were together—"

Mom returns the favor and cuts him off like always, before he finishes his story.

"Santeria, *en mí casa!*" Mom begins to plead with God to forgive me, "*Dios mío, no sabe lo que hace.*"

"I know what I'm doing Ma', okay? I'm doing it for my own peace of mind, okay? It's about stories—"

"Stories—*que tu 'ta hablando?*" Pops says.

"It's about stories telling me how to live . . ." then I stop, because I can't say it like Papelito can.

"Nothing," I say, also knowing they won't understand. I gently push them both out of my room, because I have only a few minutes to work on my love ritual to Ochun before school. I just dropped by to change and to pick up the sweet cakes. The five days that Papelito had told me to keep them by the altar are up, and now I need to throw them in the East River so Ochun could help me.

But Mom is really disturbed. Like I really did bring demons inside the house. Which, in her religion, I have. When she sees me pick up the cakes she snorts like a sow. I laugh at her, because she sounds silly.

"I hope I don't have to lock my own room now Ma'?" I say, because I know she is capable of getting rid of my altar as soon as I've gone to work. Pops, though, thinks it's funny when he sees Mom go to the kitchen, grab a mop and start mopping the house, as if that would keep spirits away. I go over to kiss her, and she brings her cheek toward me, but I know she's unhappy.

"Bendición," I ask.

"Que dios te bendiga," she says in a tone like it'll do me no good, but she'll do her motherly duty and bless me anyway.

Outside the air is crisp and clean. Not a trace of smog in it. I decide to walk to the East River pier. I have time to kill, because my class doesn't start till later. Around dusk El Barrio fills with hardworking people coming back from work and picking up their kids from school. The neighborhood buzzes with a huffle and shuffle, just like Midtown during rush hour. I'm about to cross the street when I spot Trompo Loco looking down at a homeless person passed out on the street. The homeless man has plastic bags tied to his wrist, to make sure no one steals his possessions while he sleeps. Though inside the bags are only old newspapers and cans. His sneakers are laceless and bulging, like his feet don't fit in them, and he has on layers of clothes. Trompo Loco is looking down on him, and I wonder if they know each other. I cross the street. Trompo Loco sees me, smiles at me, and then goes back to staring at the homeless man.

"I like to watch him, Julio," Trompo Loco says to me. I stare at the hard hat he is still wearing. "You know, keeps me alive. I could be there one day, right?"

"Never, you're too bright," I say, lightly tapping his hard hat. Trompo Loco's face lights up like a candle.

"Has Maritza paid you anything yet?" I ask him, because she owes me from that day. That was our deal.

"Pay me what?"

"Pay you what? Money, what else."

"Why? You helped me fill out those papers years ago."

"What papers?" I say.

"To get money." He shrugs. "Those stamps and WIC—"

"Yeah, yeah, okay," I now know what's he talking about. "Yes but Trompo," I say to make it clear, "this is different, when you work you get paid."

"Why?"

"Because work sucks. No one would do it otherwise."

"But I like to work—"

"Has Maritza paid you, Trompo?"

"What?"

"Money!"

"I don't want money," he says, "I want work."

"Never mind," I say, "I'll talk to Maritza." A van honks at us.

"Julio, I got to go to work," he says, all excited, adjusting his hard hat.

"Who's that?" I look at the driver, a middle-aged woman with rollers on her head, peeking out from under a bandanna.

"That's Sister Centeno. Maritza wants us to collect can food and coats." He says proudly, tapping his hard hat, "Can't stay and talk to you. I got to go to work."

Walking by the new Starbucks that just opened, I look to see if

Helen is inside. I look and see all these white people that have moved into the neighborhood. A few Latinos are there, feeling hip and looking stupid. The old residents of Spanish Harlem still prefer the coffee brewed in bakeries. I don't see Helen, and start heading for the East River.

On my way I see a huge tour bus full of white people stop in front of the Salsa Museum on 116th and Lexington. The tour guide, a white guy, erroneously says, "There are many salsa museums all over Spanish Harlem." I want to ask him, where? Because there's only one. And I watch how these white people enter the museum, as if they are entering a pyramid in Egypt. Full of wonder and discovery. I continue to walk, asking myself who in their right mind would visit Spanish Harlem in the 70s, when it was burning? When did it become cool to visit this neighborhood? Is it cool? Then I think of Helen.

Helen, Helen, why am I looking for Helen? Get that broad out of your head, I tell myself as I turn east, toward the river. As luck would have it, I see Helen walking about half a block in front of me. I notice, when she walks she moves like she's dancing in her room, thinking she's all by herself. Her feet and shoulders bounce and her head moves slightly. If she saw herself walking she'd probably feel embarrassed, like when someone is caught dancing alone and they quickly stop and shut the door.

When Helen stops for a red light, I catch up with her.

"Hey, what's up?" she says, smiling.

"Hi," I say, looking across the street where two old men are playing chess.

"I'm sorry about the other night."

"Hey, it's all right," I say, continuing to look at the old chess players. I've always wanted to go over and introduce myself and play. But I never have.

"Where you headed?"

"By the East River," I say, but I don't tell her I'm going there to throw sweet cakes in the river.

"No way, my gallery is by there, on 116th and First. I just bought all this booze for the opening night. Come, check out my art gallery. Check it out," she says, lightly slapping me on the arm.

I should just go take care of my things, but a good drink always sounds better when you don't want to go to school. Especially night school.

"Okay, yeah."

"Great," she says, "let's have a drink?" We walk past men playing dice. When they see Helen, they pick their dice up. As she passes by them, they hiss and catcall her.

She smirks and shakes her head as if to say, how childish.

"You're not going to fight for my honor?" she says, half joking, knowing it's not worth it.

"As long as they don't touch you," I say, "hey whatever."

"Guess not," she says, visibly uncomfortable. "What's with the *mami* shit. Yeah, I can't stand that. Guys blow kisses going, *mami*, *mami*. Do you guys see your mother in my ass?"

I got to give her that.

"I'm sorry Julio, am I being offensive?"

"No," I say, "I think that's stupid. Besides, I've never seen one guy ever pick up a girl by doing that. If it really worked I'd be the first one on the corner."

"Latino men are so Oedipal. Calling girls *mami*, like do you guys want to fuck your mothers? Do you?"

"Hey my Mom was hot," I say, trying to inject some humor here, "okay? See, that's what I meant when I told you to claim your place here. Making someone look stupid is big here."

"Why?"

"I don't know, it was once called snapping, or dissing. It gets you respect. Claim your space." From the look in her face, she doesn't buy it.

I had seen Helen's gallery space, it's a block away from Eddie's coffee shop. I have never entered, because there was always a sign saying OPENING SOON. The sign had been up for months. Until Helen must have taken it down when she moved into the neighborhood. But the space was still closed, and I would see Helen and some people always trying to get it in shape. I had no time to stop by, because the only reason I was around that part of El Barrio, the old Little Italy, was to see Eddie.

"The stairs in our building," Helen says, "are so old they creak, but the floors in this gallery space creak so loud they make everyone sound like Hamlet's father."

"I read that last semester," I say.

"Oh? What are you studying?"

"Management, but I had to take a lit course. Which I like."

The gallery is small but neat. It's very well lit, with a large window facing a lamppost. The paintings are leaning against the walls, ready to be hung. Objects from other parts of the world, masks, rugs, jugs, small statues, are on the floor, waiting to be placed in their proper spots.

"So, what's up?" she says, like we haven't been talking.

She leads me into her office. A tiny window faces 116th and Lexington, the aorta of Spanish Harlem. We sit down, both of us barely fitting in a small but neat room filled with office supplies.

I point to a picture of a man standing on a wheat field. "Who's that?"

"Oh, that's my dad," she pours us a vodka and adds some tonic water, "yeah, corporate farmer, you know, thousands of acres. Other people's farms. I hate the place. No imagination. At fourteen I couldn't wait to drive so I could escape everyday to Concourse, the nearest big town to where I was. A post office, a book store, a restau-rant-slash-Laundrymat, whoopie. When Concourse got old—real quick it got old—I couldn't wait to go away to college. Cheers."

"Thanks. Where did you finally escape to?" I ask.

"Cornell, that's where my parents are really from. Where they met," she tilts her head, "didn't I tell you this before?"

"Yes," I say, "in a letter."

Helen snaps her fingers. "That's right."

"It was a beautiful letter," I say, "I still have it." I stop when I see her blush.

"Anyway, my dad got this big job for a bank." She returns to the same corner, so I let her. "Not the nicest of jobs. People hated him."

"Why?"

"The bank sent him to take care of farms that people had lost to the bank by defaulting. My dad made sure all was working well."

"I see. So, why you choose to come to New York?"

"You're kidding me, right? Capital of the art world, Julio. Be-sides, when your town tells you all your life never to be with a certain kind of people, when you leave that town, naturally that's the first thing you do." She stops her glass right before she takes a drink, "I'm sorry, am I being offensive?"

"No. And screw that, just talk."

"Good. So after grad school—"

"You got your master's?"

"Is there something wrong?"

"No," I say, wondering if I'd ever reach that far in my goal to-ward higher education.

"You okay? What's wrong?"

"Nothing, keep going."

"All right, so I meet this gorgeous guy, Russell Running Water Means. Little by little he gives me bits and pieces of his life. He had told me he was Native American, turns out he was Mexican American, real name Julio. Like yours. Actually you two kinda look alike. I'm sorry, am I being offensive again?"

"Are you going to keep this up? Just talk." I down my drink and think that I'm supposed to be offering my sweet cakes to Ochun at the East River at this very moment. I don't want the Orisha angry at me.

"Okay I'll stop. You want another one?"

"Sure." I hand her my glass.

"So Russell Running Water Means, or Julio Silver, born Julio Plata from California, shares the same passion for art that I do, and then—poof! He's not from California but Utah, and three wives later, I find out, the Mormon Chicano boy—" and when she walks over to hand me my drink she catches me not listening to her, so she cuts her story short. "But at least we got to open this gallery. Are you all right, wanna tell me what's wrong?"

"Okay," I say, taking my drink and downing half of it. "Promise you won't laugh."

"Maybe a little."

"Okay, I have these sweet cakes in my bag that I'm supposed to offer to a goddess, Ochun—"

"Wait, that nice old man next door to us put you up to this, right? The botanicah," she pronounces the last word like she was from Boston. "He's really nice."

"Yeah, it's about stories. Powerful sto—"

"Hey," she doesn't let me finish what I was going to tell her and gets up from her chair and goes over to a desk. "Come to our opening next week. De la Vega said he's coming, others too."

She hands me an invite postcard, SPA HA GALLERY.

"There will be lots of free drinks."

"I'll try to make it. I got to go."

"You gonna let me drink alone?" Her eyes drop, like a child left at the doorstep of a church.

"I'm sorry, I have to go," I say but don't go anywhere.

She drinks up.

"Try to make the opening, okay?" she says as her shoulders slump.

I've heard the strangest things happen to you when you're drunk. I never believed it. I never get drunk, just tipsy. I think weird things happen because we let them. They don't always happen at unfortunate moments, only that it is at these times when we will purposely forget about what we're really supposed to be doing.

I walk toward her.

Helen stands up and faces me. I wait for her to touch me, and when she does, I kiss her. Helen pulls her sweater off above her shoulders. She pauses and then, with her hands behind her back, reaches for the clasp of her bra, like she was going to surprise me with flowers or bring out a gift. When Helen's breasts spring loose, she looks down at them. And after she takes off the rest of her clothes, I think she apologizes for her body.

"This is it," she whispers with a small shrug, "this is all I have."

Then there are all these silences around us. No one is doing anything but just standing here. We just hover, loitering like muggers, until the silence becomes too cold, so chilly it seems not even blankets could warm us up. And it is only when Helen realizes how silly all this is, how absurd, that she begins to giggle. And only then do we decide to inject some sense into this odd situation by kissing each other's body.

The few times in my life I'd had sex, it had always been on the run. During improvised events, with girls I barely knew, or girls I knew too well from the neighborhood but didn't care for. I've had sex in borrowed, inconvenient places, sandwiched between a new building I had to burn and a mortgage check I had to hand over to Papelito. This time, it was different. Sex with Helen was like a process of continual adjustments. Like living in a foreign country. You learn the language, the currency, the method of transportation, the good stores and restaurants. You try to feel like a native, like you belong, careful not to embarrass yourself. Still you never succeed in feeling at home. You remain a tourist in her body.

The gallery phone has been ringing nonstop throughout. And as soon as we have stopped and it is over, Helen goes to answer it. She talks naked, and I stare at her white legs and thin waist. How her pallor offsets the dark wooden floors. She is tiny and her hair is not as short as I thought it was. It reaches all the way past her shoulders, and her back is covered with freckles.

I get up to dress and sense that something has changed in the room. There is this uneasy thinness in the air, enhanced by the medical smell of used condoms on the floor. As I get dressed, the feeling only intensifies. I feel like I just took part in some large event, and a tiny residue of shame hovers above me. Now that it's time to go home I just hope that I said and did the right things. That I didn't fail anyone.

I say I have to go, and grab my bag. Helen nods, covering the phone's mouthpiece and says something to me, but I don't catch it.

I'll soon have to confront that half smile, that shy embarrassment that always arises when you've slept with someone for the first time. But not now, not yet.

Outside.

The walk toward the river does me good. I arrive to find the moonlight has cooled the river, turning it a heavy, clear gray. Above, it's all white clouds and blue-black sky. I sit on a red bench, facing the traffic of tugs and freighters that float by the river's breeze. I sit there and watch the currents go by as seagulls bite the water. At my feet, there's scales of dead fish, blood, and used condoms. Someone loved badly but loved here, by this pier.

I get up, unwrap my offering to Ochun. The East River sizzles like seltzer when I drop the sweet cakes in its waters. I see fish underneath come up for a taste of Ochun's offering as the wind plays with my hair, my clothes, my face, like telling me change is inevitable. I beg the goddess to make me better. To help me find out things about myself, because some change has occurred in me. Papelito said so, and he is an expert in these things.

So, before I head off for school, I ask the goddess, what should I do? As I drop my last sweet cake in the river, I ask her. Helen is supposed to be a spy in my country. What should I do? Because it's not only Spanish Harlem that's being gentrified.

Complaint #10

Passing by Modesto Gardens, on 104th Street and Lexington, I see Papelito inside. He is beside a rose bush, looking down at the ground like he lost a contact lens. I'm hoping he doesn't see me, because I don't want to be late for work.

"Hey Julio, *mi amor.*" He spots me.

The garden is beautiful, with imported trees, sand, dirt, flowers, benches, and a little man-made waterfall and fountain.

"*Qué pasa*, Padrino," I say looking around the garden. Many years ago this place was vacant lot, filled with carcasses of dead dogs, cats and rats. An ex-junkie named Modesto, along with Hope Community, a church-based organization, had turned this desert of rubble into a little oasis in El Barrio. They couldn't afford top soil, plants, flowers and rocks, it was just too expensive. So they *borrowed* some from Central Park.

"*Mira hijo de Chango*, help me find these rocks," Papelito shows me the rocks he has already collected.

"Rocks? Why?"

"If you look right," he says, delicately bending down and looking at the ground, "you will find what's left of the Orishas."

"In the rocks?"

"Some rocks, not all rocks. More like stones *mijo*. *Mira* Julio, centuries ago the Orishas left their homes and bodies and descended to the earth, to show us their way. Now, all that remains of their presence is in these rocks." He spotted another one.

"Like this one," he says. He picks it up, blows on it, and polishes it with his sleeve, *'ta ma'*, cute."

I look at the rock Papelito shows me. It's a simple and ordinary rock, but it's the story Papelito just told me that makes me get on my knees and join him in looking for stones on the ground. Growing up Pentecostal, God lived in the temple. I never understood why God needed to live in a house with walls, windows and locks. When I asked the pastor why, he told me that God really lives in heaven. So I always thought we should worship outside, at night, when we could gaze up and see His reflection in the moon and the stars. Instead we praised Him in a building. We kept God locked up in a house, like an old man in a wheelchair. Papelito's gods, on the other hand, lived outside, in living things. The black gods hadn't kicked mankind out of the garden. Nature is good, and so, even in this concrete jungle, Papelito can still find traces of his gods, in stones.

I pick up a stone that looks just like the one Papelito held in his hand.

"Like this one, too?" I show it to him.

"No, baby," he says, "if you learn to listen you'll hear the *ashe* of the Orishas."

"*Ashe?*"

"*Sí,* the power and life force that the Orishas emit, to help those who seek the help of the Orishas."

"Papelito," I ask, as I continue to look for rocks, "these stories that you have chosen to help you live your life—"

"*Sí mijo.*"

"What are these stories teaching you at this time in your life, I mean, now?"

Papelito straightens himself up. I do, too. Papelito has a handful of rocks, my hands are empty. His eyes hold mine.

"These stories are telling me now to get ready to leave the planet. But to get ready with dignity. The story of Chango's death is very meaningful to me *ahorita.*"

"But you're not dying."

"Not right now, but I'm sixty-eight, it's getting close *mijo*. What the story of Chango teaches me is not to look at my body as the fire, because all fires die. When I was your age, I just thought of the body. Boyfriends galore, *nene*," and Papelito winks. "I mean I still look at men, because you can't shut the body down. But now that my body is failing, I identify myself with the mind. Chango wasn't the fire, he was the heat from the fire that can't be extinguished. So when my time comes, like Chango, I hope to go as dignified as he did. Not afraid. The Orishas tell me this. Now, stick your palms out, *papi*." I do as told. Papelito empties the rocks he had in his hand and fills up my palms. The weight feels good, like holding a pound of hard candy when you're a kid.

"But," he says, lifting a pinkie in the air, "just like with any deities, we must be willing to give something of ourselves in order for them to guide us."

"I built that altar you said I should," I say, holding the rocks out.

"*Que bueno*, did Ochun help you?"

"Yeah, I met this girl."

Papelito elbows me and winks.

"See, because you believed. Who is this princess?"

"You don't know her, just someone," I lie. Papelito then gets a bit serious and stares at my face like he knows I'm hiding something.

"I'm happy for you," he says. "*Pero mi amor,* what you really need to do, Julio, is examine yourself and decide if you want to start your path toward saintliness, toward the way of the saints. Toward letting Yoruba stories guide your life."

"I don't know if I can make that commitment, Papelito," I say to him, because I know that takes a lot of money, time, and what I have less of . . . faith. Without the same faith Papelito has, I know I'll never hear the music he does. The Orishas won't sing to me. Though it seems that Ochun has.

Papelito's lips barely part, and his head rises slightly.

"*'Ta bien.* So, what are your hands holding?" he asks.

"The *ashe,* the life force the Orishas use to help those who need their help," I say proudly.

"Nope," he says.

"What the Orishas left of themselves here on earth?"

"Nope."

"What then?"

"Rocks, Julio. You never give anything of yourself to the Orishas, nothing. So, those are just rocks, Julio. Like stories without rituals are just stories, those are just stones, *mi lindo.*"

At work, it is the same story. Not much has changed.

"That Mario guy is the first white man I ever worked side by side with," Antonio tells me in Spanish.

"*De verdad?*" I say.

We are on lunch break after taking the tar down from the roof via a hoist. We've been working all morning long. We had to make a hole on the roof so we could hoist down large, cut up pieces of roof tar.

"You know, when I first saw him I thought he was going to be a smart, good worker. Now I think he is the laziest of men," Antonio says in nasty, angry Spanish. He points toward Mario, who has fallen asleep by a parked car as his sandwich gets invaded by flies.

"You know, Julio, when he arrived I tried showing him how to work all the tools and he just wanted to know what he could get away with."

"*Mira* Antonio," I say, "that Mario was in jail where someone hooked him up with this job and told him it was easy."

"No?"

"*Sí.*"

"But he is still white, an American. He can find other work, no?"

"Unless he's rich, but then he wouldn't have been locked up in the first place."

"I still do not like him."

"Okay."

"Julio, I am sorry about the other day, calling you a homosexual."

"It's all right. Sometimes I wonder myself why I haven't got married."

"There are so many women, Julio. What is your problem? In Mexico, you would be able to choose them like a soccer star."

"This isn't Mexico, Antonio."

"Yeah, I know. This is America."

"Hey it's got its good and bad," I say in Spanish.

"Yeah, but it is a crazy country. I mean this is the only country I know where you go to jail if you hit your wife. That is crazy."

"Why?"

"Because she is your wife, she belongs to you now. Once you marry her, of course."

"So would you like your daughter's husband to hit her?"

"No, but that is the tradition. I stay out of it. Same as I would not like the father of my wife telling me what to do to his daughter."

"Wow," I say in English, "that's wild."

"What?"

"What you just said," I go back to speaking in Spanish.

"But you know, sometimes I think I don't care about anything. I just came to work so I can have a chance to grow old in Mexico."

"That's a good idea."

"Hey Julio," he gets close to me and then looks back to make sure no one hears him. "I met this *puertorriqueña.*" Antonio tells me about her and how she loves sex. "She tells me to turn her over and hammer her like a woodpecker." Then he howls like a coyote at the moon. I laugh. "She is always stressed out because she runs an organization," he says, and how she does this and that for people, and Antonio again tells me blow by blow what she does to him in bed.

I'm digging it, because he tells it well, and, judging by his enthusiasm, he's been wanting to tell someone about her for a long time. But he couldn't tell any of the other guys, because they probably know someone who knows someone who knows his wife in Mexico. But not me, so he lets it all hang out.

"She likes me," he says. I'm not going to throw stones at the guy for cheating on his wife. He is a long way from Mexico. But, more important, it's none of my business.

"Come to my house and drink beer with me, soon?" Antonio says, and I say, why not?

"We can talk more."

Just then it's time to go back to work. Someone kicks Mario's boots. He wakes up and begins cursing. Spewing out how the boss doesn't give us enough time to eat.

Me and Antonio are still laughing, and I'm happy. I'm finally one of the guys. For once, not locked up in my own little here and there. I'm experiencing people, closely, not just observing. I begin whistling as I work. Antonio has found some sort of happiness, and I think that no matter how miserable you are, how far from home, how rich or poor, everyone is entitled to a quota of happiness. Antonio is living proof. And for some reason I start feeling real smart. I have it all figured out. I have a job and am taking care of my parents. They are living with me and we have our own place and I have quit setting fires for Eddie. I have gotten Trompo Loco a job at Maritza's church, made him feel like he is somebody, which he is and I love to see his face when he smiles rather than when he spins. Maritza is doing what she thinks is right, entangling her feminist, socialist philosophy with God. And I am on the brink of exchanging my stories, my religion for a new one. Things look bright.

Except for Helen. I am thinking, too, about Helen. What happened the other day was great. But Helen, like many New Yorkers that have been injected here, has no clue about my city's past. How, when I was a kid, restaurants and other establishments from the Upper East Side and Greenwich Village would serve us but they'd also let us know, "Why don't you stay uptown, where you belong?" As bad as we got it, black people got it twice as bad. Some Latinos have white skin and could pass, but black people were always being told when to stay in Harlem. I heard it. It rang in my seven-year-old ears like the breaks of a loud and broken subway train. And now that white people are coming into both Harlems, they are whistling a different tune, "Why don't you people get out of Harlem!" So, what's it going to be?

Would Helen understand this?

And what am I doing with her?

I leave it there and think about school. I have a year left, and I have a class that night, and I have done all the assigned reading and even had my papers written up, and so, I feel twice as smart.

"Julio," the boss hollers from afar. "Eddie called, says he needs to see you, now."

At that moment, when I am taking stock, those words awaken me to the fact that it doesn't matter how smart I think I am, it's impossible to see the entire picture. There are glass doors that will take me by surprise and I'll crash against them. The world is too big and I'm just a speck. A dust particle in an evil mess. A mess filled with beautiful people like Helen, like Mom, or Antonio, who might not be doing what's right, only human. And me, who sets fires.

"What he want?" I holler back.

"Just go, he sounded unhappy."

"I'll see him after work," I say.

"No, go now. He sounded unhappy."

"You sure?"

"Yes, I'm sure. Now go, I'll have to dock you though."

Walking toward Eddie's coffee shop, I get this terrible feeling. I remember what Papelito had told me about how all religions have a joker god in them. Loki, Ganesha or Lucifer, they were all the same characters in different stories, Papelito had said. In his beliefs, there was the black god Elegua, who plays with mankind, telling it that no matter what system you got, no matter what you think your life is about, he's going to throw this and that at you. Then he sits back and watches how you get yourself out of trouble. And if you do find a way out, he'll just throw something else.

Papelito said a woman was coming into my life, and Helen arrived. He also said evil things were on the horizon. Evil things, he said, were coming from a powerful source. I was sure that force was sitting, smoking, reading the paper, just waiting for me to walk through his coffee shop's doors.

Complaint #11

HOW nice to see you," the old man says in the nicest of tones, like he was a kindergarten teacher. Eddie is reading the *Daily News* and smoking a cigar. Once again, he has the other three city papers neatly piled on the floor, each waiting its turn. His cell lies silent on top of the table.

Eddie stands up, puts his paper aside and hugs me.

"I have something for you."

I ask again what's happened.

"In D.C., a new policy is going into effect soon. They just informed me."

I understand what he's getting at. Why he wants to see me.

"They're calling it," a sarcastic smile arises, "Urban Centralization. Can you believe it, Urban Centralization? In the country's own capital, can you believe that, Julio?"

Eddie knows they can call it Planned Shrinkage, Benign Neglect,

Model Cities, Urban Renewal, or whatever they want. It means one thing: slum-clearing for industry and expensive housing, the burning of ghettoes.

"I want you in, all the way."

Like tooth decay, it's a slow process, but in time, when all the original teeth have been left to rot and pulled out, brand-new gold crowns can be put in their place. You keep burning a neighborhood down, you keep cutting services. With all the unhappiness, crime will rise. Now you can blame the people who live there for the decay of the neighborhood. The landlords will sit on the burned buildings, vacant lots, waiting it out, because sooner or later the government will have to declare it an empowered zone and throw money their way.

"They'll know you," Eddie looks over his shoulder for someone in the distance and as if what he is about to tell me is top secret, "all of them, adjusters, real estate brokers, fire marshals, landlords, but most of all, the local politicians."

Eddie's eyes are full of light, like he has offered me a chance to go back in time and relive a magical moment I missed by being born too late.

Paris in the '20s.

Berkeley in the '60s.

"I'm getting old," he says. "In a matter of speaking, I want to pass the torch."

The history of all countries is the battle over land. In New York City it's always been a battle over the slums. Real estate is to this city what oil is to Texas. It's precious, because you can't produce more land than already exists. And those who own some want to rent it at as high a price as possible, with as little maintenance as they can get away with. Milking their buildings, providing just enough services so as to keep some tenants paying rent. But soon, the landlord will light a match to it. And when that time comes, they always turn to the back alleys. The buffer zones. A way to distance themselves from the effects of their policies. That's where people like Eddie come in. His coffee shop is where poverty czars and local politicians make decisions that affect the lives of those who reside in the ghettoes.

I tell him, "Listen Eddie, lighting up a private house that the owner wanted burned to collect the insurance that's one thing. The guy knows I'm coming, he won't be there. But if I go burn a building where people actually live, people who are not in on the scam, that's another thing. I don't want to go to D.C. I told you over and over again, I quit."

"Listen to me," he says, "you'll make so much money."

"I like that idea," I say, "but I don't want to set fires anymore."

"Fifteen, twenty years later you'll get to see that part of D.C. all prettied up."

I repeat that I'm out. I never heard any names, I don't know anything about the insurance, never saw any faces, I always worked alone, and he knows that. I take my hands out of my jacket. I tell him I'm going to go to school full-time. But I'd still like to keep the demolition job he got me at the construction site. I like the benefits that I get from the union.

"You sure about this, Julio?"

I tell him firmly, "Yes, Eddie."

"You'll make so, so much money," he repeats.

"I don't want the job, Eddie. Can't you give this job to someone else?"

"It won't be the same, Julio. It was me and you. Always me and you. Once I got too old, it was just me mentoring you, and let me tell you, you never let me down. Doctors get high on the job, pilots get high on the job, lawyers, teachers, cops, senators, they all get high on the job, now you," he says proudly, "I don't know when you get high but you never did it when it was time to work." I nod thanks, like it was a compliment. "And that, kid, is why I like you and won't vouch for anyone else. If those frigging respectable professions have a hard time finding good workers, think how hard it is for people like me?"

"I don't want to keep lighting fires, Eddie."

"I mean, I won't insult you, Julio, this job is what it is. It ain't pretty. But I don't think you see the entire scope here, Julio. What's at stake."

"I do," I say. "I really do."

"You do?"

Yes, I do.

He watches my eyes. He holds them long enough to know that I'm serious.

"Eddie, I just want to work and go to school right now."

The old man drops his eyes to his coffee, he takes a sip.

"All right. What you studying?"

"Management, but right now just electives."

"You never told me. Forget it. Go," the old man says, "go to school."

I thank him. My heart is calm.

"You Porto Ricans. I never lost money on any of you. I once bet five grand on the Trinidad—Mosley fight."

"Don't tell me, you bet on Mosley."

"Exactly, imagine if Trinidad had won?" his raspy laugh returns, "I'd be out five Gs. But you people never do that to me."

I'm ready to leave. I've had it with him.

"But you," his laugh disappears, "you made me lose money."

A quick spasm shoots up the left side of my leg all the way to my face.

I tell him I've no idea what he's talking about but he must see my left side quivering, the tick in my eye.

Eddie barely moves his hand. A waiter, the only waiter in the coffee shop, goes somewhere inside.

I hear a meow.

The waiter places Kaiser on my lap. He curls there like he missed me.

"Never take anything? That beast was suppose to burn in that fire."

"Hey it's not like the adjuster can claim it as valuable property."

"It's a pure breed," he shouts, "you stupid. But that's not the point."

I look down at Kaiser, his eyes are royal-looking, like telling me, I'm a pure breed, stupid, I must cost at least something.

"First you turn me down, second you took, and the dumbest thing you did was to let it get loose."

Like all domestics, Kaiser must have somehow journeyed back to his true home. Someone must have found Kaiser, standing, sitting, or lying by the burned house, weeks after Eddie's adjuster had reported him burned with the rest of the house. So now someone at the insurance company has some explaining to do. About how a cat escaped an electrical fire in a climate-controlled house, unless the fire wasn't electrical to begin with. So now, to shut up mouths, Eddie has to pay for my mistake.

"What you got?" Eddie looks at me half smiling, half angry.

"What you mean?" I reply nervously.

"How are you going to pay me back?"

I ask how much.

He tells me.

I say I don't have anywhere near that amount.

"What you got? Come on."

I don't have anything.

"Every man's got something."

I tell him I have nothing.

"A loyal girl you can turn out?"

He laughs a little, the old man laughs.

"I wish," I say.

"Of course not. You never have a girl."

"Thanks," I say, hoping this is all a joke.

"I'll tell you what you got."

Right there I know he is serious, he has given this some thought, and I'm waiting with my heart pounding, because Eddie is creative. He punishes you like the Greek gods. He'll have you roll a rock up a hill for the rest of your life only to send it rolling back down again and again. Or chain you to a boulder and have some huge bird eat your liver every morning only to grow a new one at night and have that bird visit you again at dawn.

"You got some money coming your way."

I brace for the impact. I brace for his irony.

"I looked into it," the old man takes a sip of his cold coffee.

"Into what?" I say.

"Your building's insured under the company where I have my people."

I know what he wants.

"My parents live there," I tell him. I think of Helen, Maritza's crazy church as well.

"I didn't say burn your parents." He frowns and waves his hand rapidly like there was smoke between us.

"We'll split the insurance. You own it, right, the third floor you told me."

"What about the other people who live there, Eddie?"

"Hey, I'm sorry, you should of thought of that before you took."

"I can't do it." I tell him.

"Well I don't blame you. I never liked it myself. But think it over or take the job," he calmly returns to his paper. When his cell rings, he answers with two words, "Yes, darling."

I leave Eddie's coffee shop carrying a happy cat in my arms. Kaiser is beautiful. His gray coat is soft and sleek, and his purr is steady and low. Someone had fed him well while he was lost. I'm dazed. Without noticing I have kept walking west and have reached Central Park. Somehow, seeing birds and trees makes me calm down some. I enter Central Park and walk around the Harlem Meer. Kaiser digs his claws into my shirt, scared of water. I hold him tighter, reassuring Kaiser that I'm not going to throw him in the pond. Kaiser lets go of my shirt and lets me hold him lightly, like I have before, as though he's still a kitten.

Twilight is falling, and a smoky white mist is rising from the pond. The shadows the leaves throw on the water look like colorless tattoos. Kaiser's head becomes an owl wanting to take in all that nature. I join him in enviously staring at the pigeons and insects that fly freely by the lamppost. Their shadows create giant flying patterns on the grass and pond below. I'd trade places in a second with any of those flying creatures, because this minute I feel like an angry dog tied to a parking meter. A dog that knows he ain't going nowhere unless those that tied him up say so.

"Eddie has no right. No right, fucking with me like that. No fucking right at all!" I say out loud, but I know some of that isn't true. And then I feel embarrassed when a jogger passing by overhears me. He shoots me a look and then quickens his pace.

I turn around and go home. I don't want to think about setting my house or anyone's house on fire. So I let it go for the moment. I don't think about anything except how happy my mother is going to be. How she loved this beautiful cat and how I will please her by bringing him back. At the moment, it's the only happiness I have to look forward to.

Book II

PROJECT FLOORS

Ladies and gentlemen, the Bronx is burning.

—Howard Cosell, 1977. As the Yankees played the Dodgers in the World Series, a camera panned to a nearby fire, showing the grim reality just beyond the comforts of Yankee Stadium.

Ladies and gentlemen, the Bronx is burning,

12A

When I was nine, me and Trompo Loco built a clubhouse on a vacant lot on 109th and Park Avenue. The Brown House, for the president and vice president of Spanish Harlem. Of course everyone on the block wanted to join our administration, because all we did was eat chips and drink soda in there. Word had also spread I had access to *Playboy* magazines that I had copped from the stationery store. That wasn't true, but I let everyone think that, because it explained the sign I had hung outside:

NO GIRLS ALLOWED. ESPECIALLY MARITZA.

Me and Trompo Loco didn't like Maritza, because, growing up Pentecostal, we took a lot of shit from her. Especially me. She took pity on Trompo, because he was slow, but with me she was merciless. She'd say, "You in a white religion, Julio." I'd point out that everyone in my temple was Puerto Rican. "Yeah, but that's a gringo religion, not like Catholics, see. Now that's a religion for Spanish people."

What was she talking about? Maritza wasn't even a Catholic, her parents were big-time socialists. Back in the day, back in the island, they had fought with passion for Puerto Rico's independence. When they reached Nueva Yol, on the heels of the great Albizu Campos, they had Maritza and ingrained in their daughter an almost self-righteous socialist repertoire, one equal to that of a religious fanatic.

Back then, when the neighborhood was burning, me and her were just kids, but she knew that in my church we would always have arts, crafts and bake sales, so she always came for that. On every Sunday during the summer, our temple would close the street off from traffic. The block was then transformed into a paradise of sidewalk chalk, music, dance, jump rope and food. Maritza loved it when my father would teach kids how to play the congas. Me and Trompo Loco would help him bring out all these congas, like twenty of them, and he'd give conga lessons outdoors. Maritza would bang on those skins as if she was possessed by some African river deity. She thumped away, happy and smiling, forgetting for a minute that the class was held in a vacant lot full of charred bricks, dirty diapers and junked furniture.

My mother ran the arts and crafts, and I would help in bringing out those huge communal eating tables. Mom would fill bowls with beads and pins and place them on every table. Kids had to bring their own bar of Ivory soap, and Mom would help them make these soap-bead sculptures. Maritza loved that, too. She'd stick each pin into the soap so violently, it looked like she was doing voodoo on somebody. Throughout the summer, Maritza never missed a single church festival.

But come September, Maritza would see me in school and it was the same shit again: "Your religion is all show and noise." Yeah, I'd

say, what about those free music lessons you got all summer from my
father who was once a top musician? "Yeah, so why ain't your father
playing the Palladium, if he's so good?" I'd tell her because the Lord
spoke to him one night and told him he had to lead others to the
light. Maritza would laugh, "The light? Yo'r pops ain't Con-Ed!"
Other kids would say, man if I were you, I'd kick that little bitch's ass.
I'd say it wasn't the Christian thing to do and that Jesus had said "to
turn the other cheek." Truth was, I was scared to fight girls, because
they scratched, pulled your hair and some spat at you. Besides, I had
seen Maritza fight, and back then, in the fourth grade, Maritza could
take me. I know, because at that time I had gotten my ass kicked by
this nasty, fat girl named Josephine, who beat me up behind the jungle gym. So now the entire school knew I had gotten my ass whipped
by a girl. This gave Maritza new ammunition, "Did you see the
light? Did you see the Lord? She's fat, right?"

So when Maritza heard about my clubhouse, she threatened that
unless I was willing to let girls join, she was going to bulldoze it.
She never got the chance. That same night, her building lit up, taking
the rest of the block with it. Maybe Eddie had been hired to set that
fire, who knows? But back then I only knew him as Trompo Loco's
good-for-nothing father. The man that Trompo Loco would drag me
to 118th Street to take sneak peeks at. Like he idolized him from a
distance. But I don't recall much about Eddie, all I remember was that
the fire that dispossessed Maritza's family was a grandiose fire. Six
houses aflame at once. Unemployed faces staring at a bitter winter,
the only heat arising from the flames that warmed up the entire
square block. Truth was, I was happy Maritza was gone. She now lived
in the South Bronx and I didn't have to deal with her anymore. But it
didn't matter, because my clubhouse didn't last. A week later, these
white men drove into East Harlem. It was not common to see white

people in the neighborhood back then. Me and Trompo Loco were inside our clubhouse eating chips when they burst in: "Get out!" And we scattered like roaches in the kitchen when the lights are suddenly switched on. From across the street we watched the white men burn my clubhouse down and hammer in the ground a FOR SALE sign on the very spot where my clubhouse had stood. The sign would stay there for years and years, and some residents didn't even know what it was that was for sale. I sure didn't, not at nine years old.

When I turned eleven, Maritza was back. Her house in the South Bronx had lit up. Now Maritza and her family had landed in the projects. The projects were dirty, neglected and dangerous, but at least they were fireproof. Maritza again attended the same public school I did, and sure enough, in the sixth grade, we were in the same classroom and Maritza was still picking on me. Walking to school I'd pray to God, "Lord Jehovah, please let Maritza be absent today." But God never listened to me. And Maritza picked on me all year long, especially that year, because that was the year when my father became a little legend in our church.

Unlike my mother, my father joined the church because of the music. He wasn't getting anywhere with his own band, destined to be a studio musician all his life. Plus, in those days, the salsa pioneers were always getting ripped off by promoters. Even the greats were cheated out of tons of money and pressured into playing too many gigs. Many fell into drug addiction. My father was one of them. Depressed and hooked on anything he could cook, after years of playing for peanuts, he was searching for God or anything close to it. What my father really found in the church was not God but a new stage. An opportunity to impose his own style, rhythms, and lyrics. To run his own show. My father began to use the church to create a new gospel and invent the Latino spiritual.

I went down to la bodega.
But the Lord said not to buy anything.
Oh, oh, oh, what can you buy when Jesus is already yours?
Oh, oh, oh, what can you buy when Jesus is already yours?

Not only was my father proud of writing that song, he said that "I Went Down to La Bodega" was just as ingenious as "Come Into the Lord's House It's Gonna Rain."

Don't need to worry if the mailbox is empty
The Lord's work is my welfare check and that's plenty
Oh, oh, oh, what do you need when the Lord is already yours?
Oh, oh, oh, what do you need when the Lord is already yours?

The lyrics were all Pop's and he thought them brilliant. Truth was, they were some of the worst lyrics ever set to gospel music. Still, my father would create Latino gospels that no one had ever heard before, with words that weren't in any songbook issued by any church.

I saw Jesus in the elevator
He asked me to press his floor
    All the way to sky
    All the way to sky
On the elevator of the Lord.
All the way to the sky on the elevator of the Lord.

Sometimes, parishioners would laugh at the lyrics when first presented. But no one laughed at the music. It was what my father was blessed with, and because of his music our temple had the

highest attendance of any Pentecostal temple in Spanish Harlem.
The three head pastors saw this gift that my father had, and they let
him run with it. Soon, our congregation would become a living
songbook. What our temple lacked in preaching, anointing or healing, it made up for with music. The services would start off with
singing, then a prayer, then a brother would give a short speech, then
more singing, then a sister would recount some spiritual experience,
then more singing, a little testifying, then more singing. The new
Latino gospels that escaped from the walls of that building were as
unique as the whispers that a cold winter wind makes as it swirls inside an empty, burned-out building. A sound you can only hear in a
ghetto. People walking by would hear music, this music with strange
lyrics about an urban Jesus who spoke in Spanglish and understood
our wants and needs, for he lived in the projects and suffered the
same injustices. About Jesus who prayed for more heat, hot water,
and no lead paint. A junkie Christ who pleaded with his Father to
help him keep his veins clean.

The super won't fix the tub and my rent just went up,
no heat for the winter, got roaches in my soup,
I want to go to the corner, get me a bag to cook

I'm taking my complaints
Oh, I'm taking my complaints
Oh, I'm taking my complaints

In a few years our temple's attendance was so high, and the funds
just deep enough, that the three pastors rented a bigger space. The
temple moved from this little hole in the wall on 110th Street and
Madison Avenue to a two-story storefront building on 100th Street

between Lexington and Third. My parents and I lived upstairs from the church and so we helped a great deal in fixing the space up. The three pastors bought cans of paint, mom put in the curtains, Pops bought the best used piano he could find, the band came along and the rest of the congregation followed. A sign was placed outside, LA CASA BETEL DE DIOS, and Pops was back in business.

> Oh, I'm taking my complaints
> to the Housing Agency of the Lord
> Oh, I'm taking my complaints
> to the Housing Agency of the Lord

I'm embarrassed to say it, but those were wonderful days growing up, every moment was a Sunday afternoon. Me and Trompo Loco would sing to the Lord and feel as if the angels in heaven were playing the tambourine right next to me. I always sang with terror and joy, hoping and not hoping that the Holy Spirit would strike me. What would I do with all that power? God's power. I had seen many times how brothers who were struck would cry and scream, their faces afire, speaking in tongues, spewing prophecies. How not-so-young bodies danced and jumped, struck by some divine electric juice that reinvigorated their body and soul. How others would give way to those that were struck most often. These holy ones, these saints, were the ones everyone wanted to sit next to, so as to maybe, just maybe, feel what it was like for God to enter you. To live in God's presence. I waited with fear and joy for this to happen. I wondered when Jehovah would gather up some bolts from Heaven and hurl them my way. I got baptized, and years passed by, and it never happened. I mean, I did believe in God. But when I turned sixteen, instead of heavenly blessings, it was our turn to flee.

Mysteriously, like God Himself, at night, the church had somehow caught fire. It burned to the ground. Weeks later, the building next to it was also lit up, and then the one after it. One by one, the buildings on that block were torched, until only a shoe repair shop stood alone. The city placed all the families in welfare hotels, and later we all landed in the projects. The days of singing and glory were over. It was from that day on that, for me, the word of God was never "love" or "light" but "fire."

All these memories invade my thoughts as I take a shower. The silkiness of chlorine-treated tap water that travels through hundreds of thousands of yards of pipes always brings me back to the past. It also reminds me of good memories, of opened fire hydrants on muggy summer afternoons. Of splashing girls and cars with street-made aluminum-can spigots. Squatting in front of a fire hydrant, as if hugging it, and using your hollow can to channel all that water pressure at whom you wish. Everyone's dryness across the street was at your mercy. Cars would roll up their windows in the dead heat of summer so as not to be drenched by you. These boyhood thoughts and the warmth of the shower water make me feel secure, like I'm not just washing away dead skin but my problems as well.

I come out of the shower to a clouded mirror. I take my finger and scribble, "Helen." I step back and look at her name. How much more white can a name be, I say to myself. Then I add to it, "Helen and Maritza, I have to burn the building." And then I quickly erase it, as if I don't have to go through with it. I dry off, remembering the day when Papelito had agreed to place his name on the deed for me. How I told myself that I was starting to live another beginning, a

final one. How much promise my floor was filled with, sunny promise. Like a box I'd open to find gifts. One was Helen.

"*Mira, que* Kaiser wants to come inside," Mom urgently knocks
at my door and I look at the kitty-litter box underneath the sink.
"You've been in there a long time and the cat needs to *caca*." I can
hear the cat scratching the bottom of the door. I hate the cat. I remember once hearing that professional thieves only steal when they
are 99 percent sure they will not be caught. That one percent, well
that's the unknown, the unseen, the off-duty cop who is in the john,
the kid who captures your image on the mini–video camera he got
for Christmas, or the corporate shredder that is out of order. But
sooner or later that one percent will show its ugly face. That one
percent, for me, was a fucking cat.

"So what," I shout.

"You cleaning it then," Mom says.

I grab a towel and open the door. The cat runs inside the bathroom, like he needed to go bad. Mom accompanies him, as if a cat
needs to be paper-trained.

I go to my room, I find my altar dark and fruitless. I feel guilty.
I've let the goddess Ochun down. But I hope she'd understand,
though I know she can punish me, too. So I light my candles, and I
brush the peacock feather. I get dressed and feel clean, a bit more re-
laxed, at peace.

Mom knocks at my door. I tell her to come in.

"*Mira* Julio," she says as I'm putting on my shoes, "I went to the
bank the other day and asked to see if we could get a loan."

"A loan? To fix this place up?"

"*Y pa' que ma?* Of course to fix this place up."

"What you do that for, Ma'?" I say as if it was a bad idea. It was a
great idea. With a bank loan we could fix up the rest of the floor.

Maybe put in a bathroom, splice the wall up and make it into a little studio and rent it.

"The bank," Mom says with eyebrows up, "didn't have you as an owner."

That is exactly why I can't get a loan and fix the place up.

"What do you mean the bank didn't have me as an owner? Well, what bank did you go to, Ma'?" I play it off.

"Banco Popular," she says as if that was obvious, it's the only bank she ever banks with. It is where Papelito has his account, too. Where the deeds of this apartment are filed away in some computer under his name.

"Well, see Ma', I deal with Chase Bank," I say. "I got a better mortgage rate payment with Chase," I say and finish putting on my shoes.

"But I gave Banco Popular this address and they said that someone does pay *un morge* that lives here but it was confidential—"

"So maybe it's the *blanquita*," I say, cutting Mom off. "Maybe it's Helen. Maritza rents that space downstairs for her church, so it has to be Helen." Kaiser enters my room. He starts to sniff at my candles, though the fire repels him.

"Why would a *blanquita* place her money in a Spanish bank?" Kaiser then goes over to Mom and jumps on her back. Mom doesn't flinch. She lets him sit on her shoulder like a parrot.

"A bank is a bank, Ma'." I say as she makes kissy faces at the cat.

" *'Ta bien*," she says, sighing, "then come with me to Chase, to get a loan to fix up this place—"

"Ma', it's not that easy," I say. "Plus I've been thinking that this place isn't that great. Maybe we should sell it and go."

"Crazy, *mira*, unless you get me *Troomp* Towers."

"Trump Towers? Why would you even want to live there, Ma'?"

"*No se*, just to live there. Just to see what it looks like."

"Well, I don't know about this loan, Ma'," I repeat, and now that Mom knows her idea of a loan isn't happening, she stares at my altar with disdain.

"*Eso* Kaiser," she talks to the cat, not me, "is going to bring the devil in this house."

She sees me putting on a tie.

"Where you going?"

"Ask the cat, Ma'."

"Julio, you getting all nice? The *blanquita*, right?"

"No, Ma', I'm going to church," I lie to her, and she knows I'm lying, because it's too good to be true.

"To that church downstairs?"

Why didn't I think of that? I say to myself. That would get her off my back.

"Yeah, and don't touch my candles, okay?" I point at the cat. "And keep him out, too, he might burn his paws or something."

"*Esas velas, pa' demonios?*" she rapidly waves a finger in the air. "I won't go near those candles. My cat knows better than to touch them," she says, walking out of my room.

"Ma'," I call her back, "kiss me good-bye."

"Only if you leave that room."

I close the door behind me and kiss her. The cat jumps down from her shoulder.

"Don't you also have church?" I ask her.

"Yes, I have real church, *me' entiendes*," she says. "I have to wake up your father so he can get ready," and she slows her delivery, "for . . . real . . . church."

"Good," I say, "bring the cat with you."

"Oh you're funny, did you swallow a clown for lunch?"

13B

The lounge is located on 101st Street and First Avenue. It's one of the new, trendy bars that have opened since the face of the neighborhood started to change. I walk in to find all sorts of people, but mostly white professionals. Residents of Spanish Harlem drink outside, paper-bagging their cans of Budweisers, playing dominoes under a street lamp or a tree. During winter, they go to each other's houses and drink in the kitchen. Lounges are alien to Spanish Harlem. Even during El Barrio's glory years of the fifties, when there seemed to be a bar on every street corner, they were always dives, not places with paintings, sofas, cushions and curtains.

I enter, and the music is loud, but not so loud that one can't talk or hear anything else. I see Helen sitting next to this real geeky-looking white guy with glasses. He constantly pushes away a lock of hair that falls below his eyes. I wonder who the guy is. They're playing Monopoly, and I look around some more and realize this place is a haven for people like Helen. It's equal to finding an American bar in Paris, the expat bar that few of the native residents ever patronize. The crowd is young, and as I make my way toward Helen, a young guy in a suit and tie accosts me.

"Hey, *amigo*," he says, "you know where I can find some?"

"Outside," I say, "pick a corner."

"Can you do that for me?" he says and tries to underhand me two twenties. "You know, I'm new here."

"Sorry, man," I say, not taking his money, "I don't do that."

"You know who does? A friend of yours, maybe? I mean I don't mean to be rude or imply anything. Hey I just want to unwind," he says in the friendliest of tones, and I do believe him.

"You need a drink?" he asks me. I say no thank you. So he turns around and walks back to the bar.

A Latin guy, who was sitting by the pool table and probably heard everything, walks over to me. He is wearing a guayabera, a short-sleeved shirt with colorful embroidered patterns running down the sides. A fedora hat sits on his head, and his ears are plugged with headphones from a Walkman he must have at low volume.

"My friend, I tell you," he talks like he just took a deep drag on a joint and he's not trying to exhale. "They see a Latino walk in here and right away he's got to be dealing." I nod in agreement. "Yes my friend, but the worst," he says after he takes a sip of his beer, "is they want it right here, in the bar. Like delivered Chinese food, shit. They don't have the balls to go and cop on the corner like everybody else. Unless they're true addicts, they won't do that. They want takeout. Wass your name?"

"Julio," I say.

Helen hasn't seen me yet. But I can tell she's already a bit lit, because when she rolls the dice, she throws them too hard and they slide off the board and onto the floor.

"I'm Raul. You play pool?"

"Not really," I say as I see both Helen and that guy she's with on their knees, searching for the dice.

"Yeah, well, that's too bad. I'm looking for a partner. I'm next on the table and, you know, that's the only reason I'm here. I'm here to play pool, thass it. I'm getting tired of them always asking me if I'm holding shit." I see them laughing as they fumble through a green carpet looking for a glimpse of white dice.

"This place, is no good. It's like a fucking living room. But they have a brand-new pool table. And you know those tables in social clubs are whack. All lopsided. The balls chipped. The cues are more crooked than a crack whore's teeth." They find the dice under the very sofa they had been sitting on. They plant themselves back on the sofa and continue their game. "This pool table is nice, bro'. Best table in the neighborhood. I like pool, you like pool?"

"Yeah, listen man, it was nice meeting you," I say to him.

"Same here, my brother. If you change your mind, I got next."

I leave Raul and go over to the sofa where Helen and that guy are playing. Helen sees me. Her small face lights up as she leaves the game to come over and hug me. Even in this bar her hair still smells of almonds, like she just got out of the shower. Her black clothes are prim and crisp, like she just bought them.

"You got to help me," she says, "I'm in so much debt."

We join the guy on the sofa who gives me the weakest of handshakes. He is wearing khakis and a white shirt. His red tie is loosened and his blazer neatly folded on the sofa next to him. She introduces him to me as Greg. He talks to me like we are long-lost friends.

"So, Helen tells me you two are good friends—" Helen elbows him, and I get uncomfortable. They must be really close. Like Helen is his fag hag. Not that Greg is gay or anything. Who knows, who cares. But at that instant, when Helen elbowed him out of embarrassment, I could picture me and Papelito doing the same thing.

"Okay," Helen says, tucking her hair behind her ear, "back to the game."

"It's over, Helen," he says, pointing at all his property. I look at what he owns. He has hotels on Mediterranean, Baltic, Connecticut, Vermont, all the cheap avenues. Every time Helen passed Go and collected her two hundred dollars she was bound to land on his slum and fork over the same money she had just collected.

"It's over," Helen says, rolling the dice, "when I'm out of money. I still have fifty dollars." Helen lands on Community Chest. She picks up her card, and it reads, "Bank error. Collect $200 dollars." She sticks her tongue out at Greg, and he gives her the money from the bank.

"Aren't you going to give that back?" I half jokingly ask her.

"No way, it's the bank's fault."

"But it's still wrong. That's not your money," I say to her.

"Why should she give it back, Julio?" he interjects like he is the authority, "that's the rules of the game. If the game says it's fine, then it's fine."

"So you are saying," I say, "that it's okay to steal if the rules let you—"

"Of course it isn't," Greg snaps and Helen gets up.

"Anybody need another one?" she says and Greg and I say yes, please. Helen leaves, walking unsteadily toward the bar. I hear someone yell Raul's name. His turn at the pool table must be up.

"This game," Greg pushes up his glasses, "is wonderful. Growing up, I used to play Monopoly with my family all the time. Didn't you?"

"We're a Scrabble family," I say.

"Yeah, I like that, too. But in Monopoly my father taught me that it's the cheap places that are worth investing in." I notice Greg is a bit lit as well. I was supposed to meet up with Helen here, and she must have been here awhile, drinking with Greg. "They don't cost much and people land on them constantly." He leans toward me and says, "Helen can't play. She's busy trying to land on Boardwalk and Park Place. What a waste of time. It's so goddamned expensive that unless you have an incredible amount of cash you can't build hotels there." He says it with pride, like he is the master at this game.

"Listen, are you a Democrat?"

"I vote," I say, looking around the walls. The place is nice, like a nightclub where no one dances, just drinks and kicks back on the sofas.

"Well, how 'bout contributing to next year's presidential ticket?"

He brushes away the lock of hair that has fallen over his eyes, covering his glasses.

"Hey, I'm broke," I say. "Greg, right? How'd you and Helen meet?"

"We went to college together," Greg tells me. "I just bought an old townhouse in Harlem. See, we're neighbors now, see?" he says to me.

"Oh, yeah," I say, remembering that Helen had spoken to me about this guy before. "You're the one that got those bomb threats in your mailbox."

"Hey," Greg says, "I understand their anger."

When Helen returns with our drinks, she also gives up playing.

"I don't get those threats anymore. I think the people of Harlem have accepted us now. Don't you think so, Helen?"

"What?" Helen says. She begins to put the game away by placing all pieces and the board inside the coffee table drawer.

"The people of these neighborhoods, you know, they have accepted us." He pushes up his glasses, which have slipped again, and a lock of hair falls down over his eyes. He brushes it away again, freeing his vision.

"Yeah," Helen says, looking my way. "I know one has." And she winks at me.

We talk.

Mostly about junk. *Seinfeld* episodes that I never saw. Helen and Greg talk about college. About friends they knew at Cornell when they were students there.

"I hear she works for Schumer," Greg says.

"No way," Helen says.

"Yes, she's his assistant. Though her title is fancy—"

"That airhead?" Helen says incredulously, "at Cornell she was always stoned. Stoned Joan, we'd call her."

"Well, Stoned Joan is now 'Special Liaison Stoned Joan.' "

I'm getting a buzz and I'm thinking about telling Helen everything. About me and what trouble I got myself in. But then I look at her smile as she talks, and all of a sudden I get overwhelmed with happiness. Like I am going to be saved at the last minute. Dostoyevsky at the firing squad. Somewhere, somehow, something would intervene and I would not go through with what I had to do. There was no way I could pay Eddie back all that money and I wasn't about to go to D.C. Seeing her laugh and get all silly with her friend gives me hope that I can find a solution to all this. So I laugh along with them as they continue talking. Helen tells me, someday she'll take me to her favorite student bar at Cornell. "The Chapter House, Julio," she says, taking a deep sigh.

Outside.

Greg just sticks his skinny white arm out and cabs flock to him. He kisses Helen good-bye and shakes my hand, saying something I can't make out but I know it's friendly. When the cab speeds away, Helen embraces me and says she needs to go inside a bodega to buy water. As we enter the store, Helen trips a little, and I hold her up. The corner boys who had been eyeing us start laughing.

"Yo, you can't control your woman?" they shout and laugh at us from just a few feet away from the entrance to the bodega.

Helen hears that and faces them.

"Excuse me?" she says to them, "control . . . your . . . woman . . . ?"

The four corner boys don't move from their spots but do turn their faces away from her.

"I'm no one's woman," she says, moving her body so that they can see her. The corner boys want nothing to do with her or anybody. They are working and don't want anyone calling attention toward them. So, they look at me.

"Can you take your woman home, okay?"

This irritates Helen, who seems to get brave when she's lit. Reminds me of the first time she talked to me.

"Listen, you—" I don't let her finish. From behind her, I pick her up by the waist and take her away.

"Hey what are you doing?"

"You're drunk, Helen," I say. "Just leave them alone."

A few feet away I put her down and let her break free of my loose hold. She's not having any of it.

"Don't you ever grab me like that," she warns me and starts walking back toward the corner boys who curse in Spanish when they see she's back, "*Coño, esta blanca no aprende,*" one of them says. "Go home, lady," they say to her but their eyes focus on me. "Go home."

"Hey, look at me when you say that," she says, but they don't listen to her and start getting angry.

"You don't take this midget away we're going to have to hurt you," they say to me, pointing out how small Helen is.

"Midget!" Helen shouts. For a second I thought she was going to kick that guy in the shin.

"Hey, man," I say, trying to see if I recognize any one of them. Knowing just one of them could put an end to this scene. But I don't recognize anyone. "She's drunk, okay? What you want?"

"I'ma fuck you ups, is what I'm going to do if you don't take that bitch home."

"Threaten me!" Helen's so angry she's almost yelling. "I'm not invisible, your problem is with me!"

The corner boys no longer think it's funny, they consider me pathetic. Like I have no authority. They give up on a peaceful solution.

"That's it, I don't care." One of them moves toward me, making fists. I get ready to take him but I know I can't win.

"I know that guy." Raul appears. He must have just walked out of the bar and witnessed all this. "He's all right."

"You know him?" The guy lets his fists become palms again. "Raul you know him?"

"Yeah, I got this," Raul reassures them. "I got this."

Helen directs her hurt and anger toward me. "What, you think I'm your woman now?" she yells at me. "All of a sudden I belong to you?"

"You sure you got this, Raul?" they say, knowing that Helen and I are still there, causing a scene. Raul nods.

They shake their heads. They aren't going anywhere. It's their corner, and I'm sure they are paying whoever owns that corner to peddle there. It's an underground economy that Helen is disturbing. But because she is lit, she thinks she is back at Cornell, back in the classroom, and can confront sexist remarks at will.

"*Mira*, you got to go home," Raul says to us. Helen is huffing and puffing like the day she stormed out of my house, but this time she storms into the bodega.

"Okay, thanks man," I tell Raul, "let her just get her water."

"You know you were lucky this time. I can't be Mighty Mouse and save the day again. You got to tell that girl of yours to stay on her side. You know."

"Yeah," I'm glad Helen isn't around, because then the fight would start all over again. "I know."

"She can't just go up to my boys and say shit like that. And you know, bro'," he says, pointing at me, "that's your mistake, bro'. You got to train that white girl."

"I'll look into it," I say, knowing it's too late. Too late to debate anything right now, especially on the street. We both make a fist. We give each other a pound by clashing our knuckles together.

Helen walks out of the bodega, screws open her bottle of water. She drinks half of it down. Her lips are moist and cool when she kisses me shortly afterwards, and I realize she is more drunk than I thought, because she has forgotten all that's happened.

On the way home she talks about Greg and what a good friend he is. How he'd stay over at her dorm and sleep on the floor after they had been drinking all night. Once we reached our building, I can tell Helen is fading, and I open the door and help her up the stairs. I reach in her purse for her keys and open her door and take her shoes off and put her to bed. Helen passes out, and her small frame reminds me of fairies, like Tinkerbell sleeping. I kiss her good night and she only moves slightly. Like a cat yawning. That overwhelming feeling of hopefulness returns. I feel like I can do anything. What was I so worried about? I'll just work twenty jobs to pay Eddie back. I'll work twenty jobs for twenty years if I have to. But I can do this. I'm the master of my own destiny. The Orishas have smiled upon me. Maybe I'm just drunk. But at that moment, all things seem possible. I kiss Helen's cheek one last time and walk out as the door locks itself behind me.

14C

The boss is in no mood to abuse anybody. The copper and brass pipes and wires that had been stolen a few weeks ago have not been returned. Usually the boss hands out the checks by lunch time, giving the system of exchange enough time to work. When the owners of the social security numbers collect their checks and hand the workers some cash, this exchange takes time, it always cuts the lunch hour in half. But this payday the boss is holding on to every check. Many of the workers are nervous, rightfully thinking they might not get paid at all.

"What you think he's waiting for?" Mario asks me.

"I don't know," I say, taking my hard hat off, "don't look good though."

"You smoke?" he offers me a cigarette.

"Nah, thanks."

"No come on," he says, "have one, no Bloomberg bullshit law here."

"I know, I just don't smoke," I say and look at the trailer where the boss is talking to the rightful owners of everyone's names, except for me and Mario. "I got nothing to do with this shit. I need my check."

"You and me both, pal," he says, lighting up.

Pal, I say to myself, who uses that word these days? How long was Mario locked up?

"Say, you know Eddie, right?" he says, smoking away.

"No," I say, still looking at the trailer, "I just want my check."

"Whatever you say pal," Mario knows I'm lying, "but word is you owe Eddie a lot of money."

I almost sprain my neck as I quickly face him.

"Hey, you got something to say?"

Mario pats the air as if calming me.

"Nah, nah pal," he says, still patting invisible air, "I know one thing. I stay out of people's business."

"Good," I say, looking back at the trailer.

"But I also know when two people can help each other."

Mario moves his entire body in front of me. He wants to make sure I listen to him. He can tell I'm not.

"Listen, Julio," his face is in front of me, "you ever heard of N-50s?"

I sigh like I'm bored, and then shake my head no, because I don't have a clue what N-50s are.

"Listen, N-50s are American citizenship certificates. Know what I mean? It's what a naturalized citizen is awarded after he passes that citizenship test, making them Americans. N-50s are worth more than gold. Now imagine if there was a load of blank N-50s around. Blank N-50s? Blank American citizen certificates and all you had to do was write your name and place your picture and just like that, you're an American? You know the price they go for!"

The boss comes out, the owners of the names stay inside the trailer.

"You listening to me, pal?"

"No," I say, "I just want my check."

The other workers all fear what I fear. That we're all getting docked or worse, not getting paid. "Listen up," the boss hollers, "Julio tell them, until those pipes are recovered, I'm forced to dock all of yous."

"Hey man that's not right," I protest.

"Damn right it's not. I'm docking you too."

"Me, you docking me?"

"And you too," he looks at Mario, who shrugs like he could take the hit, but I know he can't. He is just playing it cool, though he plays it badly. "When the office comes to ask for those pipes they better be here or there's going to be hell to pay."

"What are they doing?" I say, pointing at the owners of the names who are in the trailer.

"They," the boss says, "are adjusting these tacos' money."

"They can't do that. They don't lift a finger—"

"If they don't like it, they can go," he says, "and when are you going to break the good news to them?"

I know the workers already know. They don't speak English well but they understand it and they can sense bad vibes in any language. The boss leaves and the workers surround me. Asking me in Spanish if they are going to receive the same amount of money as they always do. I tell them that none of us are. They begin to curse, and conspire. I hear all sorts of ideas, like beating him up and taking the money.

They quiet down some, but they're still angry. When the owners of the names come out of the trailer, the workers all settle down and their eyes focus on the ground. White men scare them. They'd rather not talk or look them straight in the eyes. To them, white men are nasty and abusive. And when white men are polite and friendly, they get suspicious wondering what it is that they want.

The white men, owners of the names, aren't happy either. They talk among themselves about "getting rid of all of them and breaking in a new crop." A new crop that won't steal from them. Another white man disagrees. "They all steal," he says, "these tacos have no honor." Another says they shouldn't be paid at all. But in the end the white men give in and pay the workers some money for their work. I can only think that the inconvenience of "breaking in a new crop" exceeds what they lost.

The workers aren't happy but they take what is given to them. Many don't bother to count their bills. They curse, spit, curse and spit. But they take the money and place it in their pockets.

I join the boss at the trailer. I knock and enter. He is making changes to the books.

"Hey," I say, interrupting him, "how long you gonna keep docking us?"

"Till it's all paid. Every single pipe," he says, "tell Mario to come get his money."

"Where's my check?" I say. Dock or no dock, I need the money.

"Eddie has it. Says you owe him money."

"Wha'," I protest.

"Take it up with Eddie. I only know those pipes got to get paid for."

"That's not right."

"Look, go talk to him if you like. Just go. I'll have to dock you an extra hour for no work though."

I walk out of the trailer. Antonio is staring at Mario like a dog does when he hates another dog. They can't look at each other for a second without a growl. Mario arrogantly blows smoke like he is royalty. Antonio's thoughts must be about killing and strangling Mario.

"Mario, boss wants you," I say.

Mario grins, breathing in smoke through his teeth.

He kills his cigarette and brushes by Antonio, daring him to push him aside. Antonio puts his hard hat back on and drinks some water out of a plastic bottle. The owners of the names have all cleared out, their SUVs nowhere in sight.

Antonio and the rest of the workers have gathered in a tight circle. I don't join them. I hear them speak about some woman. Antonio says that he doesn't know her name, but they say she can make you an American. Supposedly she has that much power and she can do it for free. They get excited and Antonio tells them about a friend of a friend who can now travel back and forth to Mexico, or his country of origin, because of this woman. The workers become more animated when Antonio tells them he will find her, somehow he will find her, talk to her, and maybe they will be citizens, Americans soon. I think Antonio is just making them feel better. Talking tall tales, like Christ's second coming, he is giving them hope.

A t the coffee shop, a waiter tells me Eddie takes late afternoon mass at around this time at Our Lady of Mount Carmel. I walk toward the church a few blocks away and think if Eddie keeps my pay I'm done. If I can't pay Papelito, Papelito loses his botanica and I lose my apartment. If I fault, he faults. If it was just my house, I'd burn it. As much as it'd kill me, I'd do it. Being dispossessed by fire never scared me. As a child in Spanish Harlem, I'd go to sleep with the lullabies of fire engines. It was a sound I had adjusted to. It was as natural as my father's snoring. At school, firemen would visit to give demonstrations of what to do if your house was on fire. "It's not the fire," they'd tell us, "it's the smoke that will get you. So drop to your knees." Still, you knew when someone had burned to death by the smell of burned hair. It was a powerful odor that could engulf a whole city block.

I remember a fire, nasty and vicious, that had taken the lives of seven lonely women. The mother of the brood was a beautiful lady who had been blessed with a long and lush mane that draped all the way down to her waist. This feature was inherited by her six daughters, who were only one year apart from each other. But that's where it ended. The daughters were not so easy on the eyes. By the time the girls were in their teens, four of them were extremely overweight and the other two had bad cases of acne, so bad their faces always seemed wet and slimy. The father had deserted the family by then, and people would cruelly joke that his daughters had scared him away. The girls were not popular, they stuck to themselves. At church I remember seeing all six of them sitting together, four of them stealthily eating chocolate as the sermon was in progress. I never spoke to them, because they were older than me at the time, except for the youngest, Aracelis. But I did like to sit one row behind them, because all you saw in front of you was this amazing jungle of hair. The image was perfect, beautiful and subtle. It was only when the congregation had to stand and praise the Lord in song that the cruel reality would hit you. The mother had hoped that one of her daughters would find a man and marry. She had spoken with the pastor, asking for answers.

Why had God played a joke on her daughters? How could He tease her girls like He had? Who would take them? Who would marry them? The pastor suggested she exhaust all her savings on a used car and give it to the eldest. A man was sure to be lured, if not by the girl then at least by the car. The mother did as told. But the car was stolen, and soon the fire arrived, and none of them would ever marry. After the fire occurred, the five-floor walk-up they had lived in was cinder-blocked. The windows and doors were boarded. And it stayed that way, shut like a trunk, like a box hiding dirty secrets. But it is said that years later, when the neighborhood bounced back and the building was set to be renovated, when the first board was removed from the entrance, a thick and misty black cloud escaped, screaming. Those who were there said it smelled terrible. Those who were there said it smelled like burned hair.

Our Lady of Mount Carmel on 112th and Lexington is beautiful. Made of lime and stone, it's always cool inside, even in the summer. Eddie likes this church better than Saint Cecilia's on 106th Street, because it's closer to his side of the neighborhood. The side that was Italian. And now, like the rest of the neighborhood, you can only find pockets of its past.

I'm not dressed to be in church, and I'm holding my hard hat at my breast, as least to show some respect. I see Eddie by the altar, kneeling down, praying and waiting for the wafer to dissolve in his mouth. Next to him are four old ladies. Probably the same four who have been coming here every day, year in and year out, for this service that no one attends or deems important.

The mass has just ended, and I sit on a pew and wait for Eddie to see me.

A young priest walks by Eddie and hugs him. Eddie spots me and comes over.

He sits next to me, rosary beads still in hand.

"I grew up with his father," Eddie points at the priest with his chin, "now his son puts things in my mouth."

"Why you doing this to me?" I ask him.

"I always got lost in altar pieces. Crucifixes, stained glass, triptychs, murals. Christ dying alongside robbers." I let Eddie ramble. This isn't a good place to complain about money, especially when I do owe him. Or maybe being in church is the best time?

"See over there," he points with his chin again at a stained-glass mural of the three Marys. "As a kid I always wondered who had been Mary Magdalene's last client? It drove me crazy. Was it Christ? Drove me nuts. Just like this place drives me nuts. Look at it, Julio. People like me and you, those three." I gaze at the three old women praying. They are dressed in gray and look like mice. "Then you have saints, prophets, angels, devils, demons all under one roof. How can you have all these opposites under one roof?" he says and I notice his voice is scratchy, like he has a cold.

"I can't do it," I say. "I know I owe you money, but I can't burn my building."

Eddie stops rambling.

"Then take the job," he says as he examines the stained-glass windows.

"I can't do that."

Eddie stops looking at pictures in the stained glass and turns his face toward me. "You think it's easy. You think it's all so easy."

"No," he cuts me off. "I never enjoyed one bit of it. I never enjoyed it at all. Seeing all that destruction, all those lives ruined, those children burned. Some landlords would send flowers to the families. But I knew their condolences were lies. Every building that they burned was money. Others hired guys like me, didn't care. The city didn't care and I'd put it out of my head for as long as I could but then, when I had my own children, well, I did what I could. I sent out feelers. I'd pay a snitch to spread the word of the exact date of when the fire was coming. You should have seen the faces of the firemen, Julio, when they saw entire families outside, packed up with suitcases as if they were going on vacation." Eddie lowers his head. Is it shame, guilt, that I see in him?

Once again I think about how, when I was a kid, fires were so common. A way of life even. Sometimes the date of when the landlord would set his building on fire did leak. The date of the fire had been thoughtfully sent around, so people could escape. Just like Eddie says. Kids would come up to the teacher and say, "I can't be here for the test on Tuesday because that's when the fire is." And the teacher was as lost as Oscar Lewis. But us kids knew that kid would not be back to the same school. I lost so many friends from relocation. Until it was my turn. Until me and my family were burned out.

"But you people, you people fought back beautifully." Eddie raises his head again. "Families doggedly resisted. When landlords cut your heat, you people survived entire winters bundling up, gas stoves on all night. When the gas bills were too high, you people didn't pay them but sent the bill to the landlord." Eddie smiles, like he is proud. "Con-Ed was in on it too, though, and they just turned your people's utilities off. So you jerry-rigged wires to tap hall currents or street lamps. When junkies stole the expensive pipes and the plumbing was out of order, you fetched your water from fire hydrants. Filling empty milk gallon after empty milk gallon with water." Eddie's voice has become a proud whisper. "For showers and bathroom duties you visited relatives or a friend whose building had not reached that state yet." Eddie looks at me and I want to tell him his son is like that. That Trompo is remarkable. But I sense Eddie wants to tell me something. "When the Sanitation Department wouldn't pick up your garbage, the rats arrived. You people bought cats. Those with asthmatic kids got rat traps. The ghettoes got crazier and crazier and crazier. You people held out as long as you could. But the city fought back with what they knew you people couldn't fight against—fire."

Eddie stands up.

"When I met her," his eyes are distant, like he sees something out there from a past he can't kill, "she was living in such a wretched building. It was only a matter of time before they'd ask me to do that building in."

I lowered my head.

I had had my suspicions, but I had nothing, nothing at all to back my belief that Eddie had torched his own lover's house. Trompo Loco had been burned out, but so had the rest of us. That held no weight. The stories that Trompo's mother was mentally unstable were true and some had said she lit the house herself. But I never believed it. I had seen that woman, and as scary as she was she was all talk, there was still some good in her, a part of her could still be saved. What I know now is that those stories neglected to add that Eddie drove her past help. He drove her into a character so sad that she became a neighborhood joke that wasn't funny. She became a myth, the crazy lady that children are spooked by. The lady on whose door your friends dare you to knock on Halloween.

"Whose house, Eddie?" I ask. "Who was she?"

Eddie swallows hard, then clears his palate, like he has a bad taste in his mouth. He turns his head toward me and then back toward the altar.

"I'll tell you who the real villain in all of this is."

I know then he isn't going to fess up anything. At least anything that has to do with him.

"The real villain in all of this was the man behind the men who hired me. Moses. Robert Moses. He relocated people like cattle."

Eddie's done talking—or was he reminiscing?

"But I'm not like that. I did what I had to, but I did what I could to reduce it. I'll let you in on a secret, Julio. The hardest thing in this world, Julio," he says, pointing a finger at me, "is being a good bad-guy."

"You don't want that job in D.C. any more than I do, Eddie." I just figured that out. "They've asked you to look for someone. Someone you can vouch for. Someone you trust who won't cost you more money."

"Unless you do your own home in, it's your only way, Julio."

For seconds, neither of us says a thing, and Eddie just stays there like a kid playing red light, green light, one, two, three. He just stands there silent, towering above the pews. I drop my head and realize that silent churches make noises. They hum, like Buddhist motors. Our Lady of Mount Carmel is silent, but somewhere there is this white noise. This hum.

"I don't think I need to take confession." Eddie breaks his trance and starts to walk away, then looks back at me, "take care of your friend. Make sure you do that."

"My check?" I say.

"I'm holding on to it. I'll see if you get that back. I'll see."

And Eddie goes back to the altar. He slowly kneels. His old knees bother him somewhat, because I hear them crack all the way from where I'm still sitting. His knees make a sound like bones being stretched and broken apart. The sound echoes until it dies and blends itself into the holy sounds that surround us both.

15D

Trompo Loco is sitting on the sofa with a bag of ice on his head. My mother, father and Maritza are tending his bruises and bloodied nose. I'm outside by the door, talking with three of the activists who dragged him here. They are very apologetic and have even brought with them most of his possessions.

"We didn't mean any harm to him, *tu sabe*?" says a lean man with a mustache, "but this is serious stuff. We tried to just carry him out but he began to spin like crazy and hurt himself."

"My wife and kids live there and you know, I'm fighting to keep it," another activist tells me as he pushes at me a box filled with clothes. "If he wants to come by and pick up the rest of his stuff, he can."

"Yeah, we're not going to throw any of it away," the fraud activist, a woman, reassures me. "Can I tell him we're sorry?" She tries to peek inside my house.

"Let me ask him," I tell them.

"No hard feelings," she says.

I pick up the box of clothes and go back inside. Trompo Loco is taking deep, angry breaths. I'm not worried that if I let the activist in to say sorry Trompo would punch them, I just don't want him spinning around and hurting himself some more.

"Trompo, you feel better?" Mom says to him, and he doesn't say anything but puckers his lips real tight and turns his head toward the wall.

"Julio," Maritza tells me, "those people did to him what they hope the person who owns that building doesn't do to them."

"No, I told him that was going to happen to him," I look Trompo's way, "didn't I tell you this was going happen? There, you happy now? See?"

Trompo shrinks, he shrugs his shoulders high and in. He slouches on the couch like a puppy, a puppy with a bag of ice on his head.

"Julio, *bendito*, the poor guy—"

I cut Pops off.

"Poor guy nothing, he doesn't listen to me." I look at Trompo again, "You don't listen to me."

"*Basta ya*," Mom says, "no yelling."

No one listens.

"That was wrong, Julio," Maritza says, "that was not right. We got to do something—"

"Like what, Maritza, like what? Those people are just doing what they know is right. They aren't hurting anybody, they just want a home, like everybody else."

"Like Trompo wants a home too—"

"Trompo needs to listen to me!" I say to Trompo again.

"Still doesn't make it right, Julio," Maritza says, "what are we going to do about it?"

"No one is going to do nothing," Mom says, "*gracia' a dio'* that he's okay. Now Trompo will live with us—"

"No he can't," I jump at that, "we need help too. I don't think we can stay here Mom, didn't I tell you this?"

"This is Trompo, of course he can live with—"

I cut Pops off again.

"No he can't, we might all have to go—"

Trompo cuts me off.

"But you said to move in. You told me to come. I want to come. I want to come."

"Now you wanna come motherfucker, now right—"

"*Mira*," Mom snaps, "*esa boca*. No cursing in my house."

"My house too," I say and feel this rage like I have all this stuff to worry about and it keeps piling up. "He can't move in."

"Talk to my father," Trompo whimpers like a puppy who's lost his mother, almost crying. "Talk to him, Julio."

My parents wait for my response. Like everyone, they know who Trompo's father is. I look back at them and yell in disgust.

"I'm not going to talk to your father, all right?"

"I thought you said he's not my father?" Trompo shoots up.

"He ain't your father—"

"Nah, nah, you just said he is my father—"

"Listen, he ain't your father! And even if he was he ain't never going to do a thing for you! So stop crying, stop that shit, 'talk to my father, talk to my father' baby whining, and deal with it that he ain't your father, and start listening to me when I tell you to do something!"

The doorbell rings. I go get it. I tell the activist to go home,

Trompo isn't talking. I close the door. Maritza has her arms crossed like she is waiting for me to give her something.

"What, Julio," she says, "are you going to do about this?"

"What do you want me to do?"

"Something."

"Well, why don't you," I sneer at her, "why don't you start. Why don't you start by paying Trompo for the work he does. Huh? What about that, huh? And leave me alone."

Kaiser appears out of nowhere, like he was sleeping and we woke him.

"Fine!" she shouts, "still look what happened to him and you just want to blame someone else instead of doing something—"

"Like what Mari, like what? You want me to go there at night when everyone's asleep and burn the building down?"

Everyone looks at me in disbelief. Except for Trompo they all have this intense expression as if they are trying to solve a puzzle.

"You want me to do that, Mari? Cuz I can. I can make all of them homeless and then you'd be happy, everything would be just great!"

"What are you talking about?" my father asks, "burn what down?"

With all this yelling and screaming, all this anger, I let that slip.

I point at the cat.

"This is your fault!" Cat licks his whiskers like he could care less. "I should have let you burn!" I yell.

No one knows what the hell I'm talking about.

The doorbell rings again.

"Fuck!" I yell, "I told those fucking people to go the fuck home." By now I've lost Mom, Pops and Maritza. They can't stand me and I know it.

I don't answer the door, I yell at it.

"Go the fuck home!"

The doorbell rings again.

"You need a fucking map?" I shout, and a disgusted Maritza goes over to answer it.

It's Helen.

"Hi," she says a bit embarrassed, because she must have heard the shouts, "there's a group of women downstairs, by your church, asking for you."

"For me?" Maritza frowns.

"Yes," Helen says. I think she senses something is wrong, not in my living room but outside. "They said to get a . . . broom?" Helen says. "I don't know why, but they said to go get you and a broom?"

Maritza looks back at us. Her face turns pale in total horror. Something about that broom makes the entire household shake with fear as if it wasn't a broom she has been asked to find but a gun.

"Señora Santana, I need your broom." Mom leaves Trompo's side as Pops takes over tending him.

"I'll go with you," I say to Maritza.

"No, you can't, Julio," she says nervously and looks at Helen. "It has to be handled by us."

Helen nods repeatedly and fast, like she's already made up her mind to go, though she is as lost as I am.

My mother brings Maritza a broom. She grabs it.

"Be careful, *dios lo cuide, santo Señor.*" Mom says, knowing something urgent is happening, something more urgent than what has happened to Trompo Loco, and only Maritza knows about it. The immediacy of the situation shifts Helen's attention as well. From the look in her eyes, she has seen something really ugly outside, like a lynch mob. We haven't talked since that night we went drinking. She hasn't written me a letter but, looking back, she didn't really need to.

That night wasn't that bad at all. Right now, there is something that needs direct attention, it can't wait and, knowing Maritza, I know it's ugly.

Maritza dashes out of the house and Helen follows her. Though Maritza said not to come, I don't listen and trail behind Helen.

Outside, Papelito is surrounded by angry women. Many are from Maritza's church, newly arrived immigrants. Helen joins them, sticking out like a goldfish.

"Mari, Mari." The wrinkles on his face make perfect channels for the sweat to pour down, like water in an aqueduct.

"Papelito, *qué pasó?*"

"Oh God, Mari." Papelito can't find the words.

"*Cálmate, cálmate*, what happened?" Maritza says.

"He touched her again, Mari. He did it again."

Maritza's face turns pale. Her eyes grow wide. She grips the broom's handle tight, like she is about to twist off a chicken's neck.

"He's on the corner of 103rd," Papelito says, and about a dozen women with brooms follow Maritza. Helen has no broom, but she is taken by the moment and follows the crowd. I trail behind. We reach 103rd, and all the women surround this man that is just standing in front of a bodega. The short, barrel-chested man looks up from his beer and stares at the women. He asks in Spanish, what do they want? They don't answer him. I think he recognizes someone in the crowd and starts to walk away from them, but the women follow. Led by Maritza and Papelito, the women begin to swat him with their brooms. Instead of fighting back, the man drops his beer and runs. The women chase him, swatting him with their brooms and mops. He stumbles down and gets back up, tries to run again, but stops and finally faces the women. He is panting and could kill the women by hate alone. His eyes are huge, and both parties stare each other down as if it is a game of chicken. Maritza starts chanting, *"Pa'que nunca ma'la toque'."* The other women join in the chant, *"Pa'que nunca ma'la toque'."* The man's hands are fists and his teeth are clenched, but he stays standing there, panting and hating. The reason the man does not charge at the women is not because he is outnumbered or too tired, but because several men who have witnessed this public display of humiliation have started to ridicule him as well. Other corner men keep laughing and saying *"Toma!"* and *"Pa'que aprenda!"* Making fun of the man who somehow knows that if he hits any of these women, the men would no longer ridicule him but join in the beating, and the men don't have brooms or mops but fists.

The other corner men keep laughing at the man who had been chased by women with brooms. The men say, "Hit him harder," or *"dale un mapaso!"* The men's laughing becomes greater when the man's wife comes out from the crowd of women and starts yelling at him. *"Y nunca mas vengas a casa,"* for the man to never come home. The wife continues to yell at her husband, telling everybody about his drinking habits and transgressions, which brings more laughter to the corner men. But then the wife breaks down and falls to the ground, wailing, *"Porque?"*—Why? I spot the girl Maritza and I helped to re-virginized. She is crying again, and this time it is Papelito who holds her tightly.

"El doctor le dijo que tiene el monstruo." The corner men become silent. The sick wife's words fill the street and hang in the air like hateful silent bugs swirling around. In that awful moment, everyone stands still, staring at one another in silence, not knowing what to make of anything. The wailing wife's eyes are full of questions, full of whys, and the man's are still full of hate. The street is crowded by women with brooms and men whose ridicule has been silenced by what has been revealed.

The murmuring slowly begins. Then it quickens—"SIDA"—and the men who had joined in begin to slowly walk away, whispering to each other, "That's out. Got his whole family sick." The women with brooms help up the wife who continues to wail and crumples to the floor like dry clay. *"Después que operaron a mi hija."* The wife cries, *"Tu tienes que tocarla otra vez."* I know then what's happened. I understand Maritza's horrified expression of earlier. The girl that Maritza and I had taken to get her hymen restored was going to marry, but her family was afraid the husband would send her back once he found her to be spoiled goods. The operation would take care of that, except that it was her father all along who had been touching her, and worse, he was sick with the monster. The big disease with a little name.

Helen and another woman coach the wife to take deep breaths, for the wife had begun to hyperventilate. "Breathe, honey," Helen coaches her. "Breathe," Helen says, and the wife is swallowing her dry, sobbing hiccups. *"Respira mija,"* Maritza joins in, because the woman is in danger of silently hyperventilating and passing out. Maritza pats her back, *"Respira."* "Get some water," Helen says to one of the women, who runs inside a barbershop. Papelito is holding on tightly to the daughter, who has her face buried in Papelito's chest. "Breathe, honey," Helen coos to the wife. *"Respira, Carmen, respira,"* Maritza says, and as soon as Carmen's dry sobbing takes sufficient air into her lungs, she begins wailing again, emptying her body of sound.

The husband is still standing, his hands clenched into fists. He digs his nails deep into his palms. His face is red, and he stares at his wife with an anger that dries your throat. For a second, he tries to speak but his mouth just nervously shakes.

The women with brooms shelter Carmen. The daughter leaves

Papelito's comforting side and hugs her mother. The daughter is still crying; Carmen has stopped. Papelito digs into a pocket of his gown. He brings out a cigar and lights it. He expertly blows out enough smoke that it quickly surrounds us all. Papelito then begins to blow smoke and speak in a dialect none in the crowd understands. Papelito digs in his pockets again. He hurls some white powder at the husband's face. It rains down on the husband's head, sprinkling his head with a touch of white chalk. The husband doesn't move. He breathes so hard I can hear every angry breath. He is so enraged that silent, defeated tears roll down his face.

Everyone slowly begins to walk away from him. He stands still, like his soles were stuck in cement.

"Maybe you think you was made of iron, the monster would never catch you," a woman spits at the husband's feet as she walks away.

Carmen takes her daughter's hand and follows Papelito, who leads all the women back to the church. Out of the corner of my eye I catch Antonio crossing the street. When he meets up with Maritza, he holds her like he had been with her throughout all the ordeal. Maritza holds on to him like she's been waiting for him. He brushes her hair away from her face, and they, too, walk in the direction of the church.

Helen doesn't follow the crowd. She's a bit shaken. Helen stands still, her eyes looking at nothing in particular. Her nose begins to run, and she fights back tears. I walk up behind her. She turns around and looks at me with both sadness and disbelief. For a wonderful second I'm sure Helen would fall into my arms. Sob on my shoulder. I will hold her tight, brush her hair away and kiss her. Tell her it's okay, that the other night was okay. That today is okay. Instead Helen wipes her tears with the back of her hand. I stretch my arms out to hold her, but she pushes them away, like she needs to be alone.

I leave Helen alone and she walks in the direction of her gallery.

I look back at the husband. He hasn't moved an inch. He has fallen to his knees and is praying in front of the barbershop. He holds a tiny, gold cross necklace out in front of him. He kisses the tiny figure nailed to it as he whispers little prayers.

The three barbers who run the shop have witnessed all of what's happened and come out. One of them holds a pitcher of water.

"*Pa' fuera! Fuera de aqui!*" he says as he drenches the husband with the water. The husband shoots up, as if the water was scalding hot or ice cold.

"If the *santero*'s evil doesn't kill you first, I'll kill you," another barber says.

"*Cabrón*, get out. You're fucked." The third barber kicks the humiliated husband as he starts to walk away. With no complaints the husband walks as if he had been broken, as if he didn't care anymore for his life or dignity.

"Don't ever show up here again!" The one holding the pitcher throws the empty pitcher at the husband. The plastic container hits the husband on the head, bouncing off his scalp and into the sidewalk, where it lands on top of a garbage heap.

"Praying to God?" one barber sneers as all three begin to go back inside the shop. "Where was God," the barber says, "when he was doing that to his daughter? *Pa'l carajo.* You don't whip out that cross, not in front of my barbershop you don't. *Pa'l carajo, qué se cree.*"

16E

I go to the bodega and buy five mangos, five Snickers bars, five Hostess Sunny Doodles, and five yellow candles, big ones, too. I stop by the Chinos and buy a nice, silky blue scarf and some colorful beads. I return home, go upstairs and arrange the offering. I place the scarf on the corner of my bedroom floor, like I'm about to have a picnic, and I place all the sweets neatly into bowls. I light each candle with a prayer that Papelito taught me. I get mad at myself for not getting a new peacock feather, since the old one is fading and dull. I apologize to the goddess Ochun, and hope that she helps me.

I am now ready to go downstairs and see Helen.

I climb down the stairs and knock on Helen's door.

When Helen opens her door, I don't know what to say except, "I got your letter," I say, "it was beautiful." I smile and say, "My father thought so too."

"Well, I wish I hadn't sent it," she says, unfazed, "because you're so full of it."

"Sorry," I say, "I'm sorry." I only know that after that incident of the other day, I don't want to fight or argue with anyone.

"You know Julio," she says, not inviting me in. "You made me feel so bad. So bad."

"When?" I say, though I'm sure I must have. I do it all the time and don't even know it.

"That night you said all this stuff about this being your neighborhood." She switches her weight, so she can hold the door with one hand and her glass in the other. "So I felt like, okay. Maybe he's right. I have to make it mine, too. I have to claim it. I wanted to talk to you about it so badly but I couldn't find you, and so I wrote you that letter—"

"It was a beautiful letter—"

"No, wait," she interrupts me and takes a sip. "Because of what you said, I went to a community board meeting. I was thinking, okay, if this is my home now, I should be in touch with my community. I was also sure you'd be there from all that stuff that comes out of your mouth. I thought you'd be there. Well there were about twelve people there. Just twelve, Julio. I'm saying to myself, they talk all this stuff about gentrification and they don't really give a hoot. Look at these empty seats. Not only that but the board meeting wasn't about white people like me moving in, they were discussing the next block party!"

Helen opens the door wider. Her house is very neat, clean and in order. I had heard the white girls were slobs, at least that's what Mom had told me and I was stupid enough to believe it. "Come in," she finally says.

"I'm sorry, let me tell you about those meetings," I say, walking inside.

"No, let me tell you. I was the one that went. So, I raise my hand like a nice stupid white girl and say, What about gentrification? And a nasty woman, nasty Latina woman says, 'That's not today's agenda.' Like I'm an idiot—you want a drink?"

"Uh? Sure," I say as Helen gets one for me and another for herself. She's wearing a skintight, long, black skirt that reaches all the way down to her ankles, and a skintight black top. She looks like a goth Laura Ingalls. The clothes trace an outline of her curves. Her small frame looks even smaller.

" 'But what could be more important than that?' I say at that board meeting, and that nasty woman, she says, 'You go get your nails done, sweetie, go get your nails done.' And everyone in that auditorium laughed at me, Julio. They all laughed—here." She pushes a drink at me.

"I'm sorry," I take it, "those meeting are useless—"

"Well at least they meet, you just talk," and she makes a hand puppet, "talk, talk, talk."

"You sound nothing like the way you write," I say, taking a long sip.

"Who does, Julio? Who does? But I meant what I said to you in that letter. I was feeling really guilty. But after that meeting and after what I saw the other day with those women? I'm thinking this place is screwed up. This place is like an abstract, you can describe it any way you want and you can't be wrong." Helen places a hand to her chest, "I'm not wrong. This whole place is wrong." She sits next to me and cuddles her drink with both hands.

Helen stares at her ice.

I can hear the ice cracking in our drinks.

"You know, Julio," she turns her face my way, lost in another thought. "I was dating this guy who took me to see *Rent*. The theater was full of all these upper-middle-class residents of Westchester or Long Island, all excited that for one night they were about to live through an urban struggle. We were going to see poor New Yorkers deal with addiction, homelessness, squatting, evictions, real estate gouging, AIDS."

And fires, Helen. Always fires, I say to myself.

"I thought that was reality," Helen blinks a lot. "How could I, or anyone, be that stupid? In Bloomingdale's there's a *Rent* boutique, so you can 'look poor,' " she says, letting out a quick laugh, "like it's cool to be poor?"

"You mentioned something like that in your note," I say. "Helen, you okay? Something else happen to you?"

"Yes," she says, "then the other day happened to me. I just can't get the other day out of my head. If those people would have seen what happened the other day, they'd know it's not hip to be poor."

"What people?"

"Those people," she says, pointing outside, her words a bit slurred. "You were there. You saw all that."

"Yeah," I say, "so?"

"All that time, not a single cop car came by. What's wrong with this place, Julio?"

"That's why those women took it into their own hands," I say, "Helen, this place is a place where you count on your friends more than the cops—"

"Oh shut up. You talk like you're the authority around here. You didn't know what was happening the other day. Maritza did."

"Oh that's twice you said her name," I say, upset that she cut me so coldly. "You guys are chummy-chummy now?"

"I like what she's doing, Julio. I like that she's actually doing things. I thought her church was a joke, but after the other day, I think I want to go and see her in the pulpit—"

"Let me tell you a little bit about your new idol. She doesn't believe in God, her church is all about her politics. She's so single-minded that she'll take advantage of you, me, anything, I mean that—"

"So what. I don't see it. And what about you?" Helen gets up and goes to get another drink. She stumbles a bit. Her walk is slightly unsteady. "Why don't you tell me about you. Since you seem to know everything."

"All right, all right. I'm a criminal, Helen. I'm a criminal," I say. Helen puts her glass down. "I'm into insurance fraud."

"What do you mean?" Her eyes narrow in bewilderment, forming two parallel wrinkles just above her nose. "Like you sell insurance under a bogus company and if something happens you can't pay it, like that?"

"No, Helen, I set fires." It comes out so natural, as if I am a bus driver, locksmith or doorman.

"Fires!" She pushes her drink aside, like she doesn't want to pick it up because she wants to hear it all without any alcohol in between. "What do you mean, fires?"

"I've done things," I say, putting my drink down as well, "I set fires not just for money but out of some sort of vengeance, an anger I have. When I was a kid, the property you are standing on top of was worthless. Many landlords burned their own buildings for the insurance." Helen is listening intently, her face is expressionless and she's stopped blinking so much. "One day this photographer came to Spanish Harlem. She was a white woman, very friendly and nice. She began taking pictures of all the burned-out buildings and vacant lots. Blocks and blocks of burned buildings. I was with my father, who led me by the hand, and when we saw her taking pictures, my father said to her, 'Take pictures of this place so the city can know what's happening here.' You know what she said," Helen shakes her head, "she said, 'The city knows, they even have a name for it, Planned

Shrinkage.' And then she took a picture of me and my father and asked us for our address so she could mail the picture to us. Know what happened?"

"What," she whispers.

"My mother was very religious, she still is, but back then we lived sandwiched between a Pentecostal church and a Jehovah's Witnesses Kingdom Hall. My mother believed that fire would never touch us, because we lived next to people who loved God and He would protect us. My mother believes that Spanish Harlem is a spiritual place, because it has more churches than hospitals or schools put together. So, before that nice woman could get her pictures developed, our building caught fire, and then the next building we moved into caught fire, and then the next. So she lost track of us."

"Julio," Helen places her hand on my thigh, so naturally, like she has known me for years.

"But wait, Helen. Years later, my friend Trompo, his father placed an ad in the paper."

"For?"

"For someone to work in his coffee shop. It was legal work at first, but I knew what went on in that coffee shop. But I thought if the city can let those things happen and get away with it, then I can too. And soon I was offered a real job. I was lighting fires. You wanna hear a funny story?" I say, because I start feeling sad.

"Yes, tell me," she tightens her grip, like she wants to switch conversational gears as well.

"When I was a little kid, Ronald Reagan came to Spanish Harlem." Helen laughs. "No, I'm serious. Reagan was running for office and he stood on a mound of rubble surrounded by burned buildings and gave a small speech about how he was going to save El Barrio from all that arson and neglect."

Helen laughs hysterically.

"What happened?" Helen is all teeth.

"People across the street started shouting, 'We want Kennedy, we want Kennedy!' "

"Teddy? Are we that old now?" she says to herself and to me.

"I'm almost thirty," I say.

"Same here," she says and takes my hand and pulls me up from the couch.

"Let me show you my house."

Her place is like her gallery. Paintings and artifacts from all over the world. There is a statue of Pavrati and another of Ganesha. She has paintings on her walls and African masks, along with rugs, from Latin America, I think. There are vases, and framed photographs, bookshelves, ivory elephants and carved plates. Helen's house is all artifacts and, except for a little boom box by the kitchen, no audio or visual appliances.

At times Helen picks up one of her artifacts, explaining them to me, telling when and in what part of the world she bought it.

"It's my planet," she says, "and I'm going to see every inch of it before I die."

There is a scent of Murphy Oil Soap in her living room, and it intensifies as she walks around her house. She has a little studio where, she says, she paints, badly but paints. I think she has more space than she needs or realizes, not being from New York City. But I need to stop making these assumptions about Helen.

So I ask.

"Space?" she says and then nothing else after that.

She shows me a framed poster in her hallway that has a little kid being potty-trained. Its caption reads, "Are you raising Bolsheviks?" She says she loves the poster, it can be taken either way, she says. It was a gift. I spot a bucket and mop standing by the corner, full of Murphy Oil Soap. Helen catches my eye. "If it's good enough for the church, it's good enough for your floors." She recites that jingle we had heard sung many times in daytime commercials, when we stayed home from school and tried to avoid talk shows that crowded the channels.

Helen leads me to her bedroom, where she lights some candles. She excuses herself and leaves me alone there. Her bedroom window faces the Jefferson Projects and a few renovated tenements. There's a signed photo of the Dalai Lama hanging above her bed, where one would place a cross, if Catholic. She returns with the radio that was in the kitchen. She plays some music and lights another candle.

"You don't really," she says as she strikes her next match to light another candle, "you don't really light fires, right?"

I don't say anything. But I did tell her facts about my life. Maybe she needs to hear less, because facts are tricky. I myself have never believed in facts completely. Like people, facts need other facts or they can't hold their centers. Facts need people to come together in a room and agree on something. That's the way they are born. Helen and I are gathered in this one room and now she wants us to come to an agreement on certain things. But I stay quiet. I'm not telling her the whole story. Which is what facts are supposed to show, the entire picture. I'm withholding from Helen the most crucial of all facts:

I'm burning your house.

"I believe you." Her eyes have this glint, like it isn't the candles reflected in her eyes but her belief that by staying quiet I'm telling the truth. "I believe you, Julio."

Afterwards, I'm sure that Helen has become another fact in my life. Like my parents, like Trompo Loco, like Maritza, like Papelito, Helen is now so real. Is she an intruder in Spanish Harlem, is she not, it's all in the interpretation. Like who's on top? Or who's coming or going? It matters very little. The fact is, she's here. Right now. And I want her here, with me. Each time I'm with her, I feel like less of a stranger in her body, as if my mind and body stop rebelling. I enjoy discovering the constellations her moles form, the tiny wrinkles around her eyes, and what sounds escape from her lungs.

This time with Helen is like visiting a city that you love. Knowing you will never get lost. Feeling that you know exactly where you're going, the streets, the corners, the buildings, and the places where you're welcome. A city that you always want to come back to. From certain places, from certain angles, Helen feels familiar, her body is no longer so alien to me. Helen's body begins to naturally contain every architectural form I have ever seen in this city. I picture spiral tunnels constructed underground, as if the earth was Helen's ear. Subways I've listened to and taken all my life. Noisy inner tunnels, like circulatory systems that mimic both mine and Helen's respiration and exchange of breaths. Kissing her body, I picture double-helixed bridges, as if magnifying Helen's DNA. And aqueducts, where her sweat can channel through, rushing quickly, like her pulse. All these organic structures are replicated on the streets I have walked on all my life.

Realizations like this make me want to tell Helen everything. But telling Helen all could be an overdose of data, and then anything can happen. I might lose perspective and get lost. Become unbalanced. Forget that I have something to carry out, something I've been putting off. So I hold back and orient myself.

elen's laughing. She's happy and doesn't ask me anything. I let things stay quiet and let them happen as they may. Let the candles die, get up and get a drink, or begin all over again. I don't know or care what's going to happen.

I just like being here. In her bed. Doing nothing.

Helen then says that was great, and I leave it at that. But for some reason now, I want to know about her parents. I want to hear about her origins, her past, her town. She asks why? And I say, I just want to. In your letter they sounded interesting. She smiles and adjusts her weight, she leans her elbow on the bed as it holds her head up, like a buttress holding up the roof of a cathedral, and then Helen begins to tell me many things.

17F

As soon as I see him outside my classroom, pacing, waiting for the class to end, I know what he really is. He has fooled everyone, though he isn't dressed any different. His clothes are still wrinkled and old-looking. He has come to get me at school. He knows where it is and what time to be here. Cops don't do that unless you're in some serious trouble.

"Mr. Santana?" He calls out to me as the class ends.

"It's you," I say with a confidence that is pure smoke and mirrors. I'm thinking, I'm done.

"Is there a place we can talk?" he asks, as other night school students rush by us, getting ready to head on to their next class.

"There's an empty classroom, right over there," I say and lead Mario toward it. We enter and he closes the door, but he doesn't sit down. He remains standing.

"I won't take too much of your time. Sorry for not introducing myself."

Mario's voice is unfamiliar, like he is two people. He extends his hand toward me. I shake it. He doesn't show me any identification, he doesn't have to, he would if I asked but there is no need to. He doesn't talk like a cop, but he is one.

"You work for Eddie Naglioni. He's being investigated for insurance fraud, sound familiar to you?"

I don't say anything.

"Well it should, because it was you who set those fires for Eddie, while he cleaned up. Made a killing. You bought a floor in a building on 103rd Street and Lexington. You paid a certain Felix Camillo, an owner of a religious store, to sign his name on the deeds, but it's your mortgage under someone else's name and you paid off some notary to backtrack the dates. All this to escape the IRS who would ask you how could you buy an apartment on your meager salary." Mario doesn't need notes, he has me down right, and he recaps my life like he is reciting performance poetry.

"Mario," I say, "if that's your name. I have a class. Just tell me what you want?"

"I'm sorry to disturb you." I think he means it, too. "Let me get to the point."

Outside, I can hear students waiting for this very room. So they can sleep till their next class.

"Listen, I don't really care about you. That's not what I'm after. I'm after your friend."

The students knock on the door. Mario pays no mind to them.

"Eddie?" I say innocently. "I haven't seen that guy in a long time. You say I worked for him? Lots of people work for him, he owns the coffee shop."

The students give up knocking.

"I don't know anything about Eddie," I say.

He stares into my eyes again, he doesn't say anything. He knows I'm lying.

"Mr. Santana, you do no good to anyone in prison." His eyes never leave mine. "I am willing to," he pauses and clears his throat, "to look the other way on your errors."

I hear a student outside recite her graduation speech.

We've placed in your hands our dreams and hopes because we trust your generosity.

We know we still have work to complete in defining ourselves and our mission in life.

"You will be on parole for a few years, but you will not serve any time if you become a source of information," Mario says politely. Like asking me for a quarter.

"Listen I don't know anything about Eddie," I repeat.

"Eddie? I'm after your friend." Mario makes it clear, "You saw her earlier, I want your friend. Maritza Lisa Sanabria."

"Wait, wait, wait, you want Maritza?" Mario doesn't want Eddie. He wants Maritza?

"Are you involved with this woman?" he asks me.

"Involved? You mean romantically."

"Yeah, that's right."

"Ah, ah, no," I say.

"If you are, tell me now. Maybe you can persuade her to, cooperate as well. I don't know, you tell me?"

"Well what do you want from her? What's she done?"

Mario stays quiet and doesn't say a word for a second.

"About a year ago, the INS was clearing their offices out for relocation. Someone made the mistake of throwing away a cabinet full of blank N-50 certificates. Are you familiar with these certificates?"

"You mentioned them once, at the site. They certify you as a naturalized American," I say and can't believe the difference in him. If I wasn't in so much trouble I'd tell him to switch careers, because his talents are going to waste.

"That's correct," he says as he takes a document out from his coat. Mario hands the paper to me. It's very regal-looking, thick like a diploma, its edges green like money, only there is a box for a head shot and a line for a signature right next to the eagle of the United States of America. It's a document that many Americans have never seen, because they have no need for it. Therefore, these papers could be anywhere. Even an undocumented person could have his hands on them, and because they are written in English, he himself might not know what they are. I sure didn't know what they looked like. I knew they existed, but I didn't know what they looked like.

"I've tracked them down." Mario takes the document out of my hands. "Supposedly the filing cabinet full of N-50s was last seen by the side of the FDR Drive. Left to rot, somewhere in the old Washburn factory in Spanish Harlem. I have reasons to believe your friend knows where those certificates are."

I really want to laugh, but I know Maritza well. Mario could be right. Maritza might have those certificates. Give them away. She could very well be making Americans. Just like that. No permanent residency. No test. No learning of English. No pledge of allegiance to Old Glory. Nothing. Her church was always full of undocumented people. Maybe Maritza knows the true reasons for their attendance but is too proud to admit it to herself. It's possible that her followers care little for her causes, they just want those certificates. They want to be Americans.

"Illegal immigrants are not my concern. It's others who might get their hands on these certificates and obtain an American passport,"

Mario twirls his finger in the air like a propeller, "and go 'jack a plane and do flying tricks. You know what I'm getting at?"

"Look, man," I say, dropping all my education and social graces, and turning street. "Mario, I know you got me by the balls here. But you're asking me to inform against my own kind. All right, let's leave that out," I say when he squints his eyes a bit, "but you're just giving me hearsay. You know, in the street, there's a lot of rumors. That don't mean they're true."

Mario smiles a half smirk, half smile, as if he now is certain who I am. As if he is proud that he has finally brought out the real me.

"Just know that my job is to get those certificates by any means. I'm not going to do anybody's work for them. I don't like that site," Mario explains, not really answering my question. He doesn't have to answer anything to me. "I don't like what's happening there but that's not my job. So I'm not going to share any information on anything, for what? So some other agent can take the credit? No way." Now he sounds more like the Mario I know. "I only do my job. I was assigned to find those certificates and that's what I'm going to do. I'm only interested in those papers. Here's where you come in." And now his voice is rising. "When I see you at the site, you don't talk to me. I talk to you."

"Okay." My head drops in shame. I'm not going to challenge him on anything anymore. He has explained my options. He isn't going to explain them again.

"Good," he hands me his card. Without my eyes leaving the ground, I take it. Mario gets ready to open the door and walk out. "You have my number. If you find something you call me. You don't talk to me at the site unless I talk to you," he repeats.

I read his card. Mario is his real name. He is more than a cop. That's why he doesn't need foul language or gimmicks, like cops do.

Mario is the government, and he carries that big stick and says very little.

"I could arrest your friend. I could storm that church and turn it upside down. That doesn't mean I'll find those certificates."

Does he want me to thank him? I don't know.

"I'll let you in on a little secret. I stole those pipes. I did."

"You stole the pipes?" I quickly lift my head in surprise. "Why?"

"Because," he says, "as soon as that boss finds out, he'll have me arrested at the site. When that happens, it'll mean this sting is over. Hopefully," he says opening the door, "you or me will have something by then."

I'm angry. I'm guilty. I'm alone. And worst of all, there is nothing I can do about it. It's no longer just my building or Helen, but also my freedom. I need all the help I can get.

I've heard some of the dumbest ideas come to you when you're so backed up against the wall, so backed up you're past heaving up Hail Marys. So backed up the wall is getting dented in the shape of your back. These ideas are what religious people call apparitions, angels, or visions. Like putting armor on a girl and sending her to lead the troops, might as well. These acts of desperation come to us all. They happen to million-dollar ball players on slumps, to generals losing wars, and to regular people who live to get home and watch television. It's moments like these when people turn to their faith.

After school, I visit Papelito's botanica. He is about to lock up but I knock at the glass and he lets me inside.

"I need help, Papelito," I say, wanting to cry on his shoulder.

He understands.

Papelito sees and hears the urgency in my voice. He doesn't press me or anything. He takes my hand and guides me around his botanica. He kindly instructs me to purchase a statue of a Native American chief. It's a tall statue of a man with his arms spread out like he is calling the wind to form a twister. Papelito instructs me to light seven lavender candles and place them at the statue's feet.

"He shares a duality with Oshosi, the hunter," Papelito says.

Then he points at a statue of Saint Peter. Instructs me to purchase it and light seven black and green candles.

"This is Ogun," Papelito says. "And you already have an altar for Elegua. Together these three will eat anything. Feed them almost anything."

"Why?" I say.

"Because *mí amor*, these three are warriors. They eat anything," Papelito answers in that delicate voice of his as he places books filled with specific prayers for each Orisha. "And from the look in your eyes, you are going to need warriors."

18G

I walk inside the First People's Church of God in Spanish Harlem,
the greatest collection of misfits, sinners and freaks. Christ himself
couldn't have put together the motley crew Maritza has.

Getting the sound system ready for the service is Trompo Loco.
He sees me and waves. He takes his job seriously. He has his hard hat
under his arm, because I'm sure Maritza has told him he can't wear it
inside. Working alongside Trompo Loco is Sweet Suits Pacheco, an
ex-junkie of all trades. Pacheco is in his fifties and he can fix, assem-
ble or build anything. Sweets Suits Pacheco lived off others once,
and that's why he could get you anything you wanted. For a price.
And now he lives off lazy supers who hire him for odd jobs in their
buildings. He had fallen in love late in his life, and had gone clean—
"Yeah man shot the horse, pa'. Right through the head. Horse is
dead, pa'." He was proud of kicking his addiction, then his wife got
breast cancer and died, leaving him with three kids, and so he went

shooting up. It was Maritza who helped him through it. Even
ng him get his kids back from the state.

Distributing the pamphlets and books for the service is Minerva
"Three-Dollar Mindy" Vega. An ex–crack whore who got her name
after the other crack whores heard she was fucking up their prices by
charging three dollars instead of the usual five for a blow job. All the
johns would rather wait for her, and so the crack whores went on a
manhunt and beat the shit out of her. It was Maritza who found her
on the street, bloodied, and saved her.

I keep scanning the room and see someone I thought I'd never
see at Maritza's church. La Hermana Garcia comes up to me and extends her hand. I had always disliked her. When I was a kid and she
was a young woman, she claimed that she had never known a man. In
fact, she swore that no man had even seen what her bedroom looked
like. When brothers and sisters would visit her house she would shut
the door of her bedroom and lock it with a key. "No one can ever ac-
cuse me of loose conduct," she'd say, "my body is *pa'l Señor.*" And
then, for emphasis, she would lock the bedroom key in a little toy
safe for all the visiting brothers to see. I don't know why she thought
she was so hot. Who would sweat her? Who would want her fat
body? She had more rings around her stomach than Saturn. Even
when Sister Garcia was young she was nothing to look at. Maybe it
was her way of making herself attractive for the young ministers who
were always on the lookout for virgin sisters. Now, well into her for-
ties, she has become a bitter spinster.

La Hermana Garcia doesn't live alone though. Her sister and her
sister's husband both died of heart attacks, and she is taking care of
her two young nephews who she keeps in a tight, godly line. They
are about ten and twelve, and I know they will never have sweet-
hearts. They will never know what it's like to steal a kiss from a girl,

or the security and sense of belonging when hanging with the boys. I really feel sorry for them. When she extends her hand to me, I nervously shake it, only to be pulled into her huge body and given a kiss on the cheek.

Then there is Big Black, the fattest and most beautiful person in the neighborhood. When Big Black smiles, his whole face glows, like a little kid's. His big smile is radiant and, caught in that beautiful light, you smile back at him. He is an African American whose mom was Puerto Rican, the church's very own Arthur Schomburg.

Chuito, who is mute, Pabellon, who is blind, and Sandra, who is deaf, all sit together, helping each other along. Each one filling in the gaps for the others.

Most of Maritza's congregation is made up of undocumented people. New immigrants from Mexico or Central America who need a kind community that will take them in. They have nothing to offer the streets, and therefore the streets of Spanish Harlem have little use for them, so they network in church. Just like politicians who need voters, any voters, Maritza has taken in what other churches in the neighborhood had rejected or ignored. There are single mothers galore. They are wearing tight, short dresses, so tight that the only word for it is "scandalous." I spot the "new virgin." The girl that the women sheltered that day when they humiliated her father for what he had done to her. She is talking to her mother. They see me and turn away as if I'm going to hurt them. I leave them be.

The church space itself is nothing special, filled with folding chairs and a sound system that sounds worse than the MTA's. Except for a few pictures of landscapes and Bible texts, the walls are pretty bare. The place does have two flags, Old Glory and the Puerto Rican flag. They hang next to each other, with a few plastic flowers decorating the center of the platform.

Watching Maritza talk with Papelito before the service is about to begin only makes me feel shame. As much as Maritza called me names and pushed me around, truth is she has never done anything to hurt me or my family.

"*Mi amor*, nice surprise, wha-choo doin' here." Papelito weakly hugs me.

"*Que pasa* Papelito," then I point at Maritza, "You owe me money. You ain't paying Trompo."

Maritza can't believe it. She looks at me like I just asked her to die.

"This is church, Julio," she says, hands on her hips, her pastor gown on, ready and waiting to get on that pulpit. "Talk about that later."

"Give me a break? Please, I know what church is. This ain't church."

Maritza rolls her eyes. I steal a glance at her breasts, which, even with that baggy pastor's gown on, call for attention.

"Julio," Papelito smacks my hand weakly, "that's not nice, *chulo* face."

"Sorry Papelito, but you know, I'm broke," I say.

"A son of Chango broke, what else is new?" he says, fixing my shirt collar.

"Stop it," I say as Papelito begins to tuck in my shirt more neatly.

"*Mira papi*, it's for your own good. A lot of single sisters here, look good, *papi*, look good."

Antonio walks in. I see him looking around, and many of the people in the church greet him. He must be a regular. I knew he and Maritza have something going, but I would have never thought that a church like this one would attract him. Despite his infidelity, Antonio seems like the old-fashioned type. The ones that you see in those old black-and-white Spanish movies, where the peasants are dumb enough to give their hard-earned pesos to the church, all the while starving.

Trompo and Pacheco turn the music on. Everyone heads for their seat.

"You staying *feo*?" Papelito whispers to me.

"Imma stick around," I whisper back, because people are getting ready to sing. Maritza heads to the pulpit. "Nine hundred dollars is a lot of money, Papelito. And she hasn't paid Trompo Loco, like she said she would." I have no other legitimate excuse to be there. In truth, I am ashamed.

Papelito leaves me to go compliment three fat women.

"*Nenas*, you look so good. What you been doing?" I hear him say.

Then the music plays and the people start singing and I love it. Even though I'm not there to worship, never would worship again, it feels good and warm to listen and be around all these families. Because when you have been raised by the belief in God, one that loves and cares for you, that dream that He really exists stays with you. And when you hear the gospels being sung, or something that strikes up those young memories of when He was as real to you as your parents, it fills you with joy. I'm very happy to be here, to hear all these people sing and praise the Lord. Tears almost come to my eyes as I drift back to my childhood when I was told the earth would be a paradise and I could play with baby animals. Those religious days when my parents were young, in all their glory, and sang to God and to the angels for light and fire.

After the singing dies, I hear coughing and suddenly remember my real reasons for being here. God has nothing to do with it.

A brother opens the service with a prayer in Spanish. Pastor Maritza Sanabria walks up to the platform.

"If I speak in tongues of men and of angels but do not have love," Maritza says in Spanish, the service is all in Spanish, "I have become a sounding piece of brass or a clashing cymbal, *aha, así.*" I'm impressed, fixed in my chair. She knows her Bible well. "And if I give all my belongings to feed others and if I hand over my body, that I may boast but do not have love, I have not profited, *no asi, aha.*" She is quoting Corinthians, so now, like a good pastor, she is picking up speed. "Love is not jealous, *verdad?*" She has learned well from all those years attending our Pentecostal bake sales. The congregation is nodding after her pauses.

"It bears all things, *verdad?*"

They nod.

"Believes all things, *verdad?*"

They nod.

"Hopes all things, bears all things, *ah así, mismo.*"

They nod.

"And it accepts all things, all things, all people, healthy or sick, *no es verdad?*"

She is a piece of work. Now she is breaking away from Corinthians and taking her sermon somewhere else. Some social issue, I am sure.

"So should we shun, should we ignore, should we disfellowship people from our church when all they've done is follow what the Bible says? *Sí mis hermanos,* there are people who did the right things, followed the word of God, and were still punished."

The congregation is puzzled, no one is nodding. And as confused as they are, I feel that they know their pastor sets them up like this every week. I feel they know Maritza has a revelation to tell them.

"I want to call up to testify La Hermana Garcia, *alleluia.* You all know her, you all love her, now you all will hear from her. *Con el fuego de Dios ella va hablar.*"

Maritza steps aside and Sister Garcia nervously gets up from her seat. When she reaches the pulpit, she can't speak. Her lips move but no sounds escape. The congregation starts urging her on, murmuring, "Speak, speak, testify, testify." She tries again. It is very humbling for her, her days as a star saint are over. Some tragedy has befallen her that has made her see herself as a human and not as some perfect creature.

"Before becoming a member of this church, I was arrogant," La Hermana Garcia sobs a bit. "I thought the Lord would prevent anything evil happening to me or my family."

I listen as Sister Garcia recounts her experience.

"My sister's husband is positive. He didn't tell anybody." No one is murmuring, no one is shouting to the Lord, no one is doing anything that I can remember being associated with what church is supposed to be like. They are just listening. "At the hospital, when they first told my sister she was sick, my sister said, 'But my husband never looks at women. He always comes home to me and he only goes out with his friend Raymundo.'" In unison, the entire congregation moans. La Hermana looks at the ceiling as if she is looking for God's mercy, "*Ay Señor Santo.*" She is not crying or nervous, she is speaking from her heart and feels these things need to be said. "My sister died last year. I had to tell the brothers it was leukemia." She swallows hard but is not sobbing. "I needed to . . . tell the truth . . ." It is very brave of her to be up there, alone. Addressing strangers, whether they are your brothers or sisters in Christ, they are still not part of your immediate family.

Maritza comes to La Hermana Garcia's side along with another brother, and they walk her back to her seat. Maritza picks up the sermon again, she speaks about teaching women that marriage is the cure. Abstinence and marriage. And that yes, the Bible says God loves a good marriage and we shouldn't fornicate. She quotes some texts backing this statement up and then she throws that splitter, that curve her congregation is famous for. "La Hermana Garcia's sister did all these righteous things, she only had one man in her life and it was her husband, and the monster still found her."

The congregation is quiet and Maritza spews no prophecies. No yells or cries and shouts to God. She thanks the Lord once in a while, but her sermon is subtle and gentle. "The church is a place many of us turn to in times of sickness and death. But if we have to lie or keep silent, then there is no comfort," she says.

Then Pastor Maritza Sanabria invites an ex-pastor of a rival church to the pulpit. This pastor tells how he has lost his only son to the monster and how he, too, had to lie to keep his position as a pastor in good standing, until his conscience could no longer let him sleep and he had to tell the truth. He was then kicked out of his parish, "for a man who cannot tend to the needs of his family cannot tend to the needs of his congregation," he says.

After the ex-pastor gives his testimony, Maritza calls up to the pulpit two guest speakers from some public health agency to address the congregation on matters concerning HIV. They have with them charts, pamphlets, free condoms and needles for the brothers and sisters to pick up after the service. They speak in Spanish but say they are from an African American Baptist church in Harlem. They explain how their congregation is also dealing with high infection rates. Many ministers, they say, used to believe the monster was a punishment from God, and that many of their brothers were dying and no one did anything because it was all a part of His plan. Until someone important in their congregation died. A leading member died, and so they now fight the epidemic with the word of God along with educational pamphlets they pass out. But more important, they now speak about it, they've chosen to tackle the monster in the church.

After the somber service, some people go home in anger and shock, but most stay to socialize and gossip. Trompo Loco begins to put away the sound system and to put the songbooks back in order. The table where the brothers from the African American church had set their pamphlets is not approached. Those who stayed are very hesitant, and nobody wants to take any material.

Then a hesitant and shy Pacheco led by Maritza walks over to the table.

"*No pa'*," Pacheco says, "I don't do that anymore."

"I'm not saying anything, Pacheco," Maritza says, "I just want my brother to be alive that's all." She picks up those things that Pacheco is shy about and puts them in his pocket. Pacheco doesn't take them back out, he wipes his running nose and thanks the African American brothers at the table and walks away. Then Maritza takes a handful of condoms from the box and puts them in her purse. I roll my eyes, as if she's actually going to have that much sex. All show. Then I watch as everyone looks at each other not knowing exactly what to do. Papelito holds the hand of Minerva Vega, the ex-prostitute, and they both take some literature as well as condoms and even sign some petition or something.

Big Black walks over and he doesn't take anything but he shakes the hands of the African American brothers. Pabellon, who is blind, Sandra, who is deaf, and Chuito, who is mute, also go over, and although they don't take anything, they look around and, as a group, handle the goods. They do their best to describe to each other what the others can't see, hear or speak about.

The revirginized girl and her mother don't go near the table. Others do but slowly, as if the table bites, they begin approaching the table cautiously and ask questions. Antonio is at the table, as if he isn't afraid of anything. La Hermana Garcia and the ex-pastor, who had both given accounts of their experiences with the monster earlier, walk over to the table. "For the first time," she says, looking at some of the information that is scattered all over the table, "I was able to weep in my own church for the death of my sister." And the ex-pastor says, "Amen, *hermana*."

Just then Helen walks inside the church with Greg. It's not every day white people enter Maritza's church. Right away they size them up, worried that Helen and Greg might be INS. To ease the tension, Papelito walks over to Helen and Greg.

"*Sí?*" Papelito introduces himself, even though I'm sure they've seen each other before.

"I hope I'm not intruding," she says, "I live upstairs and always wanted to see this place from the inside. I mean I can hear it from my apartment upstairs."

"Just a church. But the service is over," Papelito answers.

Helen looks around, spots me.

With a happy, shy face Helen then says to me, "We have to talk, okay?"

"Yeah, soon," I tell her, and she blushes.

Helen goes over to the table where all the pamphlets are neatly displayed. She wants to see what they're about.

"Can you show me where the contribution box is, Julio?" Greg asks me like he can't see it for himself. I point at it, but he wants me to accompany him. The box is only a few feet away, but he wants me to show him where exactly. Then Greg drops a hundred-dollar bill in the box. His eyes hold mine for a second. He wanted me to see his generous act.

I notice Helen looks up to Maritza. Like she idolizes her. Maritza, on the other hand, brushes her away with a polite handshake and goes over to where Antonio is and holds his hand. No surprise there. It is Maritza at her best. Here is the most feminist of all feminists and she is dating a guy who complains that this is the only country where you go to jail if you hit your wife. Not only that, but he is married. Maritza, without even knowing, or maybe she does know it, has become like every other pastor. She can't practice what she preaches. I don't blame her. Who could follow all those fucking rules anyway. It's impossible to be that saintly, before you know it something will get blemished. Someone will find all these dead cheerleaders in your closet. I don't care who they are, how pious, they will be found out.

"Julio, what you been up to, my good man?" Greg says. "Given thought to working for the party? Come on, four years of that jerk from Texas is enough."

I just make a nice face and tilt my head. I let him talk, because I think he enjoys talking.

"Think about it. Wouldn't it be nice if you could start by organizing drives to get these people their documents and then straight to the voting booth?"

"Why? They love Mexico."

"Why? Why? Because now they're in America, they should become citizens and vote. Democrat, that is."

"Maybe they never came here to be Americans," I say, and Greg shakes his head as if he knows that I'm wrong even before I finish saying it. "Maybe they just came here to work."

"No, no, no. These people are just shooting themselves in the foot. The party has always sympathized with the poor."

"Has it?"

"Of course it has."

"Really?" I decide to throw something at him. "Listen Greg, I thought Carter was the sweetest of men, but my neighborhood was burning while he was in office."

"Carter?" he shouts, then sucks his teeth. "Carter? That's ancient history. Julio, this is the New Democratic Party."

"Greg, I'm not good at this stuff, you might want to talk to Maritza."

"All right, Julio," he says my name like he knows me, like we're friends. Like he has known me a long time. "It's too bad. You could have been a special liaison for the Democratic Party," he says, as if I had just turned down the job of my life. Like Special Liaison Stoned Joan.

I go outside to clear my head.

One of the mothers across the street had been with me in junior high school. Her kid is skipping rope, maybe about six or seven years old, and is as beautiful as her mother has been.

Greg and Helen follow me outside. Helen is shaking her head, a bit amused.

"What a church. Maritza is awesome. The woman is awesome. Where was this place when I was a kid? Did you know there was a transsexual in attendance?"

"Oh, that's Popcorn," I say, continuing to look at the girl I once knew, who is now a mother. I remember she used to call me Eskimo. And her family was the first family on my block to get cable.

"Popcorn is an old friend of Papelito," I tell Helen.

"I need a drink. Does anyone need a drink?" she says.

Then the girl I once knew, who is now a mother, picks up her daughter and takes her inside the projects, and I feel real jealousy. I want her life, her joy, single mother or not. I want to be like her. I want to point at the woman and say to Helen, that's what I want us to be. Like that. To complete that.

"Look, think about it," Greg says to me. "Here's my card."

Another card. I take it.

"How much does the job pay?" I ask him.

"Pay?" Greg looks at me incredulously, "it's volunteer work. But the work is so rewarding. Think about how many people's lives you'll be saving. Making them Americans so they can vote. Democrat, of course." Greg hugs Helen good-bye and hails a cab with no problem.

When we are alone, Helen kisses my cheek.

"Helen," I say, gently pushing her away.

"Let's get a drink, come on."

"Helen," I say, pushing her away again. "What's Greg doing in Harlem?"

"Why do you care?" she says, frustrated that I'm not paying attention to her. "I don't know, following Clinton. He loves that party."

"And you, Helen," I ask her, "what are you doing here?" As if I don't want her around. Which I do.

"Me? What am I doing here? You didn't ask me that the other night," she says. "I'm just trying to understand all of this. Get to know you." She gets close again.

"Helen," I say, brushing away that wonderful smell of almonds. Her hands are cold and soft. Her hair is straighter than I've ever seen it, and the artificial light pouring from a lamppost shines it to gold.

"So, it's not like we were intimate," she says. "It was just sex."

"You don't mean that," I say.

"Of course not," she erupts. "What is it with you guys. Hey I like you, I don't just sleep with anyone, okay?"

"Well it was a mistake," I say, and I wish I could tell her more.

"You didn't think so the other night," she repeats.

"I don't want to talk about it," I say and go back inside the building.

Helen follows me.

"No, you're going to talk to me," she says, following me up the stairs. She reaches for my shirt and pulls down on it. I stop walking up the stairs. "Hey are you embarrassed to be seen with me?" she says, her eyes squinting, showing tiny, tiny wrinkles. "Because this is New York City, us together is no big deal." Helen studies my face again, only this time like a jeweler does a newly bought diamond, looking for flaws. "Do you think that you're the first Latino guy or that I'm only into Latino men? Is that what you think?"

Silence ensues. Helen stands there, waiting to see if my face will tell her anything. She's a good actor, her face is almost unreadable and she knows how to hold the moment.

"The problem is—" I sigh.

"Yes, what is it?"

"The problem is," I pause and stare at her baby wrinkles, "poverty brings you shame and makes you do things." I catch myself, though I want to tell her I have done things and now I am paying for it. When I met her, I thought of Helen as an intruder in my neighborhood. And just when I was about to give that feeling a rest, to step back and reflect on what I had once thought of people like her moving into El Barrio, Elegua had to further complicate my situation.

I am so sure Mario was right. The service was all in good faith, but it was the faces of all those undocumented people that told me Maritza must have those forms. They were so appalled at her speaking about AIDS, and at church, no less. Their eyes were so filled with disdain and disgust, yet they held back, because they wanted something from her.

Helen has no idea what is happening. How can I tell her I am burning her house down, that I am in trouble with the law and that her idol is a fraud? It is too much happening at once, like listening to too many stations on the dial. All I get is static. I can't hear myself think.

"Like what? What does it make you do?"

Instead I choose to return to what we have already argued about.

"Like a man I knew who wrote poems and went crazy?"

"What man?" she crosses her arms impatiently, because she senses I am getting away from what happened between us the other night and into something else. Truth is, it is about us.

"He'd read his poems out loud. In the street, to anyone who listened, and when there was no one around he recited them to himself. He walked around the neighborhood with stacks, reams of his stuff. He was broke, always broke. When he got kicked out of his apartment, he lived on the street and still wrote. One day I found him stretched out on the curb, next to a manhole, writing. You know what he told me?"

"No, what?" she uncrosses her arms, lets them flap loose. She isn't into my story.

"He told me that he was writing poems from the gutter. True poems from the street—"

"Do you want to get something to drink?" Helen says, more lost than Columbus. My fault though, I should just come out and say it.

"He lived where you live. Right here. Right here, years before this shitty building went co-op. He survived fires, neglect, inflation, crime, all those things you did not, or will ever face."

"That is so unfair," she says in almost a faint whisper.

"Well, all this history, Helen," I say, "is alien to you and those like you."

"The people at the church tonight," she says, her eyes becoming slants of anger, "the new immigrants, don't have a history here either, Julio. You are just afraid."

"Of what?"

Helen quickly answers, "Afraid of change."

"Please."

"This is New York City, Julio. The city changes by nature. The world does."

"Well, Fifth Avenue never changes, Helen. It always stays rich and white. It hasn't changed. Fifth Avenue will only change when they want it to change. But neighborhoods like mine, though," I pause as I dig in my pocket for Greg's card, "they change all the fucking time." I crumble Greg's card and fly upstairs. Leaving Helen to stare up in disbelief at my rudeness.

19H

Dear Julio,

You are so unfair. Regardless of what I wrote to you about my
town, you have no idea that my town, like many of them across
America, shares certain universalities with Spanish Harlem.
There is a powerful feeling of kinship between us all in the
community, and this may be hard for you to believe, but my town
has a tolerance for human eccentricities, too. Just like your
Spanish Harlem gutter poet, there are people in my town who are
just as crazy. The Toad Lady, for instance, who every Sunday
during the summer months bakes cookies and leaves them at the
edge of the pond so frogs can have some sugar. Yes, it's true.
She is also so religious that she makes the justice of the peace
drive for miles over to her house so he could marry her farm
animals to each other. So even her animals won't fornicate

without approval from the Almighty. My town is a place where we
still vote with pencils on paper ballots, where the preschoolers
sing "Horse With No Name" for ecology lessons. Where, as a kid,
I would go and find the mayor at his house and ask him for the
keys so I could open the library and read all by myself.

Julio, I understand your anger (and fear maybe) toward your
neighborhood changing. If you could give me a few more lines,
I'd like to tell you about when the cows left town. How it broke
my heart. The sun didn't rise for me till I was much older. The
memory of Gregory Fallis's cows being marched up a metal ramp
and into a truck was frightening. It took four hours to gather up
the whole herd, and then the truck started its slow decline down
the hill and out to the auction block sixty miles away toward
Concourse. Seventy cows in that truck, it was a small herd by
Wisconsin standards, but it represented the last dairy farm in
Howard City. The next day, when my mother was driving me to
school, we passed by Gregory's land and I caught a glimpse of
him disassembling the feed carts. I knew the milking machines
would be next. In the back seat I cried and couldn't be consoled.
His barn was an auto graveyard in a vacant lot, like the ones you
played in as a kid in Spanish Harlem, his barn was its equal for
me. Julio, you should've heard how Gregory talked about his
cows. About his town, about how it was full and lush and
filled with farms. "Back then," he'd say, "everyone had a few
cows," and you could see the moisture in his eyes, the gravel
in his voice. "No sir, no one had to go to the general store
for milk, back then." Now that I think of it, he sounds
like you.

I guess by now, Julio, you know this is not a love letter. I hate
to fight. It's such a waste. Julio, the entire planet is changing.

For better or worse? I don't know. I'm only certain of two things.
I like you, a lot. And that the paintings at the Met dream in color
when the museum is closed on Mondays.

      Helen

P.S. Please come to the opening, at least to pick up your
watch. You left it that day. I would have slipped it under the door,
with this letter, but . . .

Pops sees me by the bookshelf. Just by the look on his face I
know he got to it before I did. It's the same smile he gave me when I
received the first letter. I don't get mad at him though. I should, but
I don't. He smiles a little smile and hopes that I talk to him about it.

"Hey," Pops says, with a trumpet and a cloth in his hand, "sorry I
read your letter but it's better than if it had been your mother."

"It's all right, Pops."

"I mean it was just lying there underneath the door." Pop shines
his instrument as if a genie will appear. "I thought it was a bill, you
know."

"Don't worry about it, Pops."

"I read 'Dear Julio,' and you know my name is Julio, too—"

"It's all right, Pops," I say.

"I didn't read all of it, I hope you know—"

"I said it's okay."

"What you going to do now?"

"I don't know."

"You did that altar, *pa'* Ochun. See what happens." Pop points a
finger at me, "I'm not like your mother, I respect that religion and I
know, because of Hector Lavoe, that that shit works!"

Pops makes me happy when he talks, at times. He can place salsa music heydays into any conversation.

"Your room now is starting to look like a botanica, Julio. Incense and all those altars. But that stuff is real, Hector knew it too. See, like that song," he sings, "*tu me hiciste brujeria, bruja, bruja.*"

"Okay, Pops," I say, "what would Hector Lavoe do?"

"Hector wouldn't care one bit. He was a genius but not one of the nicest of people—"

"Wow, you trashing Lavoe." This is a first.

"No what's true is true, *ese hombre no respetaba a nadie.*"

"Okay so what would you do?" I ask.

"I would first take that letter out of that book, because if your mother finds it, forget it. She'll have you married with children—"

"So what's wrong with that?"

"*Nada, mijo.* I just don't want your mother to get her hopes up. It kill her if this is nothing. Is this nothing, Julio?"

"I don't know, Pops."

"Well, you left your watch at her place, so it's something. *Mira que tu ma* is from a time when girls wouldn't give anything away unless they had a proposal. So just make sure that you and that girl don't have her making plans and then feeling stupid." He taps my shoulder, making sure I understand. "Your mother is the only person to consider. The rest is nothing. I just don't want your mother hurt."

"Really? Her being *blanquita* is not a factor—"

"What you talking about, Julio? *Mira,* you kids these days are more white than some of the white kids. For us, it was a big problem. I could never be with a white girl in my time, crazy. For you kids, it's not that bad. See what I mean, jelly bean."

"Pops," I say, "it's not just the *blanquita* that's been on my mind. I think we'll have to leave this place."

"What you mean?" His eyes get smaller.

"I don't think we can keep it afloat, that's all."

"But we are doing good. You even quit that other job of yours. Is it that? Is it that other job of yours coming back to get you?" Pops knows the score, unlike Mom who would be asking God the questions. Instead he asks me.

Still I can't seem to tell anyone what's really happening.

"No, it's just that we're going to need another loan, and I don't think we can get it. Maybe we should go to Puerto Rico—"

"I don't want to go back to Puerto Rico," he says, making this face like he just swallowed a lemon.

"Why? I thought all people your age wanted to go back?" I say, not that I want to go back but it's better than the alternative. Because to me the island is a myth. It's just something that, as a kid, I kept hearing about day and night. How things were beautiful there, and how wonderful the island was. How it was paradise, and I, as an asthmatic child, could not get sick there because I could run through the hills and the air was so clean. Green hills and freedom. I was told this not just by my parents but by everyone around me. When my mother finally took me there when I was nine, we landed in San Juan and I got sick. I got real sick.

"Not me, Julio. Your mother maybe? But I've stopped talking like that years ago. When I first came here, I hated the cold. *Un frio peluo.* But now, El Barrio is my home."

Mine, too. The last time I went back to Puerto Rico was when I was eighteen, and by then Spanish Harlem was what was real to me. I had grown up with people waving that flag up and down, right and left, parading every year in an avenue that wasn't even ours. On an avenue where none of us lived or could ever afford as a people. Fifth Avenue was the wealthy face of New York City, yet that afternoon we owned it. But by the next day, it was back to reality, and that's when it hit me. Being Puerto Rican is more than waving a flag on the second week of June.

"You know Julio, to go back to Puerto Rico would be to lose all that stuff that we recreated here in El Barrio. The sounds, the smells, the tastes of the island. Right here."

"But Pops," I say, "that barrio is gone. It's been gone for a few years now. There's only pockets left, and those are fading, too."

"Hey, *todo tiene su final; nada dura para siempre*," Pops quotes from a Hector Lavoe song, "*tenemos que recordar que no existe eternidad*. I know all things must stop, Hector Lavoe knew it too. I walk around here now, and there are blocks that are so safe and white, and then I turn the corner and I'm back in the seventies. I know that. But though this barrio is no longer what it used to be, I'm still alive, and to me, this is home." He walks over to the closet where his other musical instruments are stored. He places the newly polished trumpet in a case.

"But you always said you want to be buried in Puerto Rico—"

"I do. But I don't want to live there. Know the difference, Julio?"

"Whatever Pops. I don't want to go back either. But we have family there and maybe we can find another house," I say, and Kaiser comes out from under a sofa. "Or stay in New York and move to the Bronx or something. I just don't think we can stay here."

"But with my disability checks, your job and your mother's at the hospital we can keep this place. What we have to do is fix those rooms and rent them."

"Yeah Pops," I sigh and pick up the cat. "Yeah that's what we'll have to do." I leave it at that.

Kaiser loves to be petted. The cat is wonderful, and I know Mom loves him so much. Having him close to me makes me happy, because I think of Mom. I'm holding something that my mother loves. It's a bit silly, really, maybe I just like cats?

"*Seguro*, that's what we'll have to do. Let me tell you, me and your mother, we like it here. We ain't going nowhere."

"Okay, Pops," I say, looking at the cat's eyes. I hadn't noticed before that one eye is green and the other yellow.

"That's right. Now about the *blanquita*, if it's really nothing. Then it's nothing. But if it's something, you better tell her everything. I mean everything because she'll find out sooner or later. Now, you never told me or your mother how you got this place, but I trust that when you're ready you will. But a girlfriend is different, a girlfriend wants to know everything."

I let go of the cat.

He lands on his feet.

"I know," I say, as the cat moves over to Pops for affection.

"I know you know, Julio. You know what I mean—go away." The cat receives no affection from him. "Let me just tell you this Julio," Pops gets a little bit closer to my ear, "I didn't read all of your letter—"

"Oh yes you did, you knew I had left my watch there."

"I skipped to that part."

"Fine," I sigh.

"Let me just tell you this, Julio, from what I read, you blaming her for something—"

"If it was just her—"

"*No pera*, let me finish. I see all these *blanquitos* moving in and you know what, Julio, they can only experience El Barrio as El Barrio shows itself to them, *me entiende*? To think that they will see El Barrio for the first time, the same way we saw El Barrio for the first time, is stupid of us, *me entiende*? Julio, unless you can put that *blanquita* of yours on a plane and take her back to El Barrio of the sixties, the seventies or the eighties, and make her live that, you can't be angry at her for not understanding, *me entiende*?"

I do understand. Doesn't mean that it's all good. That no harm is done.

Pops walks to his favorite chair where he always sits as he looks at old salsa album covers. Sometimes he plays them in low volume. Drifting back to the past, his past when he saw his first snowflake or heard the word "spic." He was one of the many Puerto Rican casualties of Operation Bootstrap. Brought over to the United States for cheap labor. The labor ran out. Now he dreams of a time when he'd healed his back broken from pushing garment-district carts all day by playing in salsa bands all night. It was rough times, and though he fell prey to addiction, it was Mom and that music that saved him.

It was sweet of Pops to think of Mom. I do as told and take the letter out of the book. I don't know where to hide it, because Mom looks in my things. Pops knows it and I do, too. But I don't want to rip it up or anything. I see my altars and think that it would be a good hiding place. Mom would never touch that.

I go downstairs, next door, to find Papelito. I have always felt he was the wisest of men, and I am going to level with him. Tell him what a mess I'm in. Hopefully he'll give me good advice and maybe I'll take a consultation, being that the last one was right on target. Maybe the Orishas are singing to me? Maybe Helen was their way of telling me to take my time, that they will wait for my complete dedication. Papelito said stories are there to guide us. Maybe he'd have a story for me as well. A story where I can get lost in someone else's misfortunes or maybe just a story with a laugh.

As soon as I walk inside the botanica, I feel happy. All that darkness I sense when I see Eddie or Mario, is the exact opposite of the feeling I get when I walk inside Papelito's botanica. Like I'm hit with a spring day at the Central Park Zoo. I love Papelito's botanica. It always smells of jasmine, spearmint or some scented incense. I look behind the counter, where the valuable and dangerous items, like sulfur, frog eyes, cow hooves and other items used for the darker side of Santeria, are stored. And there, next to all these items, are stacks of San Lazaro. The statues are small, just a few inches taller than children's dolls.

Papelito is arguing with this dark man who's just as dark as Papelito is. Both men have such a dark complexion, they almost look blue. They stare at each other intensely. The man is wearing a blue-and-orange dresslike garment. He speaks in an African language that I don't understand. I think of Helen's letter and wonder, if I keep listening will I feel that overwhelming buzz? Helen had written how she likes to be surrounded by understanding. That's one reason she loves it here. But for me, witnessing this conversation, a conversation I can't understand, is not enjoyable at all.

In any language, I can tell it's a fight. I get ready to leave when, suddenly, Papelito and the man switch to English.

"Yes, yes, Akinkuato," Papelito interrupts the other *babalawo*. "It once protected the slaves from being punished, but no longer is the case. We live in a country where we have backing and religious freedom, Akinkuato." Papelito's delicate gestures are evident, but his speech is missing the usual flirtatious overtones. This is serious business between these two. "I'm going to do it," Papelito says, "I'm going to film it."

The other head priest doesn't like what he has heard. He snarls at Papelito.

"In Brazil," he tells Papelito in a loud, aggressive expression, "in Cuba, you can't just walk into an Ocha room and observe the rituals—"

"Yes, yes, Akinkuato," Papelito seems respectful but he is putting his foot down, "but seeing something is not the same as experiencing it. Anyone can see our rituals but will they understand them? Will they know how they work?"

The other *babalawo* says something in African, and his eyes bulge in their sockets. His head moves with such passion as if he is trying to make Papelito understand that this is a matter of life and death. Two women enter the botanica only to turn around and leave.

"No, no, Akinkuato," Papelito points at the street, "in Nigeria what we call Lukumi secrets are common knowledge to any kid walking the streets. It's about power, Akinkuato. I don't want any part of that. I don't want fear and secrecy because it just breeds power and badly trained priests."

The other *babalawo* is stunned. His face turns an even darker shade. They must have been arguing intensely for so long they don't care who hears them. It is such a heated debate that they must feel like they are the only two people who exist.

"Because of all this secrecy," Papelito kindly places a hand on the other man's shoulder, a sign of friendship, "corrupt and inept priests have swindled so much money from those who sincerely want to learn Lukumi. If the people know what it is about, then they can't be cheated."

The man takes Papelito's hand off his shoulder and throws it aside with force. If Papelito's hand wasn't connected to his body, it would have hit the wall.

"You don't know what you are doing," the man can speak good English when he wants to. "If these secrets get into the wrong hands, think of the bad things that can happen. I am your *oluwo*, you will listen to what I say. It is the way it's done in Cuba!"

"Please understand, my *oluwo*, that this is not Cuba," Papelito says. "You can throw me out," Papelito's eyes are watery, "expel me, take away your sponsorship. But I will film it. I will film the *Asiento* ceremony."

The man is about to say something, something angry. His arms are in the air and he is standing on his tiptoes, as if he was about to summon a lightning bolt and hurl it at Papelito. But the man short-circuits himself, and instead he storms out of San Lazaro y las Siete Vueltas, the fury of his energy still present in his absence.

I see Papelito's head hang low, his eyes staring intensely at the floor, as if he could count each molecule.

"Julio," Papelito doesn't take his eyes off the floor, "the bank called me."

I don't say a word.

"Your mother doesn't know," he says and looks at me. "Your mother doesn't know."

"She doesn't have to know."

"*Mira, papi,*" he seems a bit rattled. "I have enough problems, okay? I need good *ashe*. Please tell your mother what you're doing."

"I'm not nine years old," I say, but truth is I know my mother would never have agreed to have a *santero* do a favor for her family. It's like a Muslim letting a Kabbalist make him dinner. "I don't have to tell her anything."

"Well you better, *papi.*" Papelito then looks at me and brings out a letter from his pocket. He hands it to me and I see it's not the usual mortgage bank statement he hands over to me every month, but a real bank letter. I open the bank letter. It states that a woman came to ask for a loan claiming that her son owns the property. The bank was reminding Papelito to be aware of identity theft. Something along those lines. The letter ends, we are always looking out for the best interest of our clients, thank you for doing business, blah, blah, blah.

Papelito is angry and he doesn't want to get into another fight. I have come to ask for his advice but I don't feel like it's the right time.

"Papelito who was that man? I mean if you're in trouble I can maybe help you," I say.

Papelito is not himself. I have never seen him this disturbed.

"He is my senior *babalawo*," he starts arranging the scratch-off lottery-ticket shelf, "he is 'head,' he is my *oluwo*."

"Meaning?"

"Meaning," and Papelito walks behind the counter and brings out a copy of *El Diario/La Prensa*, opens it and places it on the counter for me to see, "that he has the power to see."

I begin reading it. That man's picture plus his readings are in bold. The captions say this year's strongest Orishas are Babaluaye and Ochosi. Sickness and war. A bad year for the country, it reads. Increase in cases of HIV and a nasty, long war are imminent. The man who was just here a second ago, this "head," predicted all this last January.

"Every year all the *babalawos* get together to find the *odu*," Papelito says, "the future and where we are headed. He is the one that speaks for all of us."

"So why is he mad at you?"

"I don't like all this fuss, all this secrecy, it just creates trouble. It was needed once, but not anymore. So *mira*, I informed my *olowu* that I am going to film an *Asiento*."

"An *Asiento*?"

"The ceremony when someone gets his Orisha placed on his

head. The two will be one for life. Possession and sacrifice will be part of it, and I'm inviting the local news shows, too. Of course he is against it. *Pero, pa'mi*, I think I'll break down the walls that have made people afraid of Lukumi. Secrecy creates trouble, Julio. That is why, *papi*," he says, "you have to tell your mother that it's your apartment and it's your money, but that it's under my name."

"I don't want to, Papelito. My mother, you know how she feels about you, and you know, I think she'll never change."

Papelito takes my hand.

He places me in front of Santa Barbara, the saint that shares her duality with Chango.

"Let me tell you a *pataki*." I look at Papelito, but he turns my face toward the saint.

"There was a time when the Yoruba Nation was plagued by war and internal conflict. Chango brought stability and united the country. But with all this peace he got bored and tricked his two brothers into fighting to the death. *Que zángano.* Anyway, the people were very unhappy about this and so Chango, because of his mistake and grief, hanged himself from a tree."

I look at Papelito.

"So?"

"So what that story teaches you?"

"Papelito, I have to go—"

"*No mira, papi*, if you want to walk in the way of the saints you have to interpret the stories to fit your life."

"It teaches me," I sigh, "to love peace?"

"Wow, I didn't see that one," Papelito squints, placing a finger on his chin, "yeah, I guess it teaches to love peace. But in your life, what does that story tell you about your life, Julio?"

"I don't have brothers, Papelito," I say, not interested right then.

Though I did like the story, I'm not in the mood to interpret any-thing.

"*Mira, hijo de* Chango, let me tell you what I see. What this story teaches me."

"Okay."

"That we all make mistakes Julio. Even the god of fire. But Chango owned up to his mistakes. I don't expect you to be that dras-tic, *mijo*," Papelito picks up a glass of water that was on a shelf, "but you have made some mistakes, and the sooner you own up to them the better." Papelito dips his fingers in the glass and starts to sprinkle water around his botanica. When he stops, he sprinkles some water on me.

"*Mira, mi amor,* I see great things in you. But none of it will pass if you don't live in truth. I see terrible consequences that we, we will all have to pay because of your mistakes."

"So I should tell my mother, is that what this is all about?"

"That," Papelito says, placing the glass down hard, and his hands on his hips, "is just a start."

Papelito stands there in one of his most graceful poses, expecting me to tell him things. To confess my errors. Mistakes he won't force out of me. He wants it to come from me and me alone. To free myself by telling the world what I've been hiding.

I turn around.

I leave him standing there. I leave with the hopes that when I see Papelito again, he won't be angry at me. I had heard what he could do when he got angry. How he could kill with prayers, but that didn't scare me, because I knew he would never hurt me like that. It's what he had said about people in my life paying for my errors that did.

At work I expect nothing. I get there, hopeless, angry. If I didn't have to I wouldn't have come at all. To go to that construction site is to be reminded of all that's wrong. A little overseas America at work in a bottle, right here in my neighborhood. These undocumented workers who supply everything and demand nothing. They just work and keep their mouths shut. They have no rights, they can't speak.

"Julio, how does he do it? How does the boss get away with it?" Antonio asks me in Spanish. I look at Mario, who is working more out of mechanical impulse than anything. Mario is smoking and getting ready to sledgehammer a wall down.

"The boss is a nobody," I tell him, knowing Mario is too far away to hear me.

"I knew it," Antonio takes a sip of his coffee, "I knew it, because the people who are really in charge never need to act like it."

"*Mira*," I say and he laughs at my Spanish. "I have to talk to you about Maritza."

"My woman?" he says, and I cringe at that, because if I or anybody else said that about her, she'd kill them.

Before I get a chance to say anything, Mario comes over. He smokes his cigarette, and Antonio notices my meekness. He looks at me like I'm another person, like I'm a child who has to shut up because his parents have entered the room. Mario asks me if I have any cigarettes for him. I know what he means. I say I don't. He answers that's too bad. Mario stares down at Antonio before he walks away. I ask Antonio if I can drop by tonight. It's important.

Mario calls me over.

I go.

"What did he tell you?"

"I was trying to get him to invite me over to his house."

"Did you go to that church?"

"Yeah, the other day. I saw nothing."

"Okay," he says, then points at Antonio. "After you see him, call me," he says and then hands me a cigarette. I take it and, when he walks away, it hits me. Mario isn't worried about the undocumented workers knowing who he is, he's worried about the boss and the owners of the names finding out. What if one of those people, someone like Eddie, knew about these blank forms? Then he'd have a real mess on his hands. It'd be a race, for sure, and I, for one, would put my money on guys like Eddie.

There are nine men in this apartment, counting Antonio, two know me from work. There is a sign by the door that states in Spanish that only three minutes is allowed in the bathroom.

"Hey Antonio," I say as I watch one man get skipped, another man just cut in front of him as if he was in the school lunch line. "Let's go out and get a beer somewhere else."

"Nah, nah, nah," he says, almost like a baby. "No I do not want to be caught by a policeman drunk. Too dangerous."

There is a television on top of the refrigerator. Pots and pans in a sink, unwashed dishes, and a plastic garbage can that needs to be emptied.

"Where do you sleep?" I ask him.

"Over there," Antonio points, "you just pick your spot and drop your mattress and that spot becomes yours. I do not like living with eight men. Nasty and the smell of sweat can kill you," he says, laughing.

Antonio lives in a commune of lonely men. A locker room of wifeless husbands who work all week and come home to eat, sleep and then go back to work the next day. Except tonight. Tonight is Friday night, and because they have this job, where we don't work on Saturday, they want to get drunk. I have come not really wanting to, because I told Helen I would meet her later tonight, but I need to ask Antonio about Maritza. If she has those certificates, why is Antonio still undocumented? Why hasn't he given the workers those papers like he promised them? Maybe Maritza doesn't have those forms after all. Maybe Mario is wrong. For a brief second I feel relieved, like my problems have been cut in half. If that's the case, then it's only me that's in a bind, and I don't have to snitch on anybody. But the mere fact that I'd rather face Antonio than Maritza pretty much indicates I know I'm lying to myself. I don't face Maritza because I fear the truth is real. That after she fights and argues with me, she'll tell me that yes, and what of it?

"So the boss is a nobody, Julio?" Antonio asks me, and soon I get used to the sound of men tapping on the bathroom door because someone is taking too long and with all this beer they need to pee.

"All those men that come to get that check that you worked for, they are nobodies too. They are the small favors being given to them by the most powerful people in this city, the builders. The builders raise large funds to elect an official, and then, when that official is elected, they can do as they please."

From Antonio's look, he doesn't think it's so bad. In Mexico it's probably ten times as corrupt. But we are the self-proclaimed land of the free, God's chosen country, the conscience of the world, what's our excuse? I don't try to explain it to him. He has a job and he'll call me spoiled.

"I have something to tell you, Julio." A man walks in the kitchen. There have been men walking in and out of the kitchen, opening the refrigerator and grabbing beers, all throughout our conversation. This one doesn't ignore us but places his index finger on his lips, telling us to shush. He then goes to where the plastic garbage can is and pulls out a bottle of tequila.

"To my wife," he says in Spanish, taking a swallow, "to the delicate flower that she is." And he hands Antonio the bottle, and I follow.

"I'm a poet," the man says to me.

"I see that," I say to the man who's probably, I'd say, twenty-five?

"My wife was the most beautiful woman in San Matias—"

"You are from San Matias," Antonio cuts him off, "you are more poor than me."

"Nothing there but farmers," the man strikes the pose of an intellectual, "so though I was not the most handsome or strongest, she loved me because I was a poet."

Another man walks in the kitchen and grabs a beer. He smiles at us behind the poet's back as he circles a finger next to his ear, telling us the poet is crazy.

"And did you feed your wife poems?" the man who just grabbed a beer asks in Spanish.

"No, I farmed but I was a farmer who wrote poems," he says, and the man with the beer, Antonio, and me laugh.

"Want me to recite a poem?"

"No," Antonio shouts. But I want to hear it.

The poet takes his bottle and leaves us alone in the kitchen.

"I wanted to tell you something," Antonio says, "it is about Maritza."

"Good," I say, "I wanted to talk to you about her too."

"You know I am married."

"I know."

Antonio pauses and weighs in his head what he is about to tell me. I can just see it in his eyes. He wonders if he should trust me.

"Maritza knows I am married too," he says, "if that is what you came to talk to me about."

"No, Antonio, I came to talk to you about something else—"

"Well it does not matter. Because I am leaving. I cannot stand it here. I am going back."

"Back to Mexico?" Nothing made sense here.

"I sometimes feel like she treats me like a project—"

A knock on the door interrupts us.

I hear the noise level drop like a car alarm just went off. All the men who were scattered around the apartment come out to see who it is. The men's eyes shift from side to side, fearing the worst. Finally Antonio leaves the eating table where we are sitting and goes over to the door and looks through the peephole.

"What you want?" he asks in Spanish.

"I have a woman," a male voice answers in Spanish.

The men calm down. Antonio looks back at the men.

"Well?" he asks them.

"Ask how much," one of them says.

Without opening the door, Antonio asks how much.

"Fifty dollars a man," the voice answers in Spanish and the men begin complaining. They ask Antonio what she looks like? Antonio makes it clear that she looks bad. They tell Antonio to say twenty-five. He does.

"Forty-five a man," the voice shouts back.

The men grumble that they don't have that kind of money. They tell Antonio thirty-five.

"For how many men?" the voice at the other side of the door asks.

"Eight," Antonio says, not counting himself.

I can hear the woman complaining in English. It's not enough for her, not for eight men. She wants at least forty. For that many she wants at least forty, she says.

The men want the woman. They discuss the situation and size it. They ask Antonio if she is really that used up. Antonio is fed up. He moves away from the door and tells them they can see for them-selves. One by one they go look through the peephole.

Only the poet is excited by her appearance.

"A man needs holes," the poet says in Spanish to the men, "and any woman can provide them."

Both sides then agree on forty and the poet opens the door. A Latino man with an old, haggard, bleached-blond, white woman walk inside. The man is polite and greets the men like he has done business with them before. The woman though lays down the law. She tells her companion to make sure he translates to the men that she is not their wife. There are things, she says, that they can't do to her, and they all better have their own rubbers. She then asks for a drink of water.

"Come on Antonio," I say, "let's go drink at my house. No policeman will find you there."

Antonio thinks it over for a second.

"It's early," I say.

"Yeah, but it is dark already. I am going to sleep."

"With all that racket," I say, "with all that's happening around you? How can you sleep?"

"You get used to it, Julio," he shrugs, bringing out his mattress.

I'm getting tired of all this. I crouch down toward Antonio who is about to lie down and go to sleep.

"Why hasn't Maritza," I whisper in Spanish, "given you a blank citizenship certificate?" I expect him to jump up. To deny their existence left and right. To tell me he knows nothing and that Maritza is just crazy. Instead he yawns like he's tired.

"I did not come here to be an American. I came to work," he says.

"Yeah, but with one of those you can travel back and forth to your country with no problems."

Antonio turns his body away from me. Like he could care less.

"I never asked her for one," he says. "I do not want it. I am Mexican."

I can't argue with that. I admire his pride.

"What about the guys at the site? They want to be Americans. Why haven't they received a certificate?"

"Because," he says, turning farther away to the edge of his mattress, "they don't have AIDS. Maritza is crazy. She will only give that document to sick immigrants."

Antonio wants to get some sleep.

I walk out and call Mario. I tell him that Antonio just wanted to booze it up. That nothing is happening. Nothing? he sounds surprised. I respectfully tell him he just recruited me the other day. Did he expect me to just add water and everything will fix itself? I need time. He reminds me that if my friend knows where those documents are and keeps quiet, it's a federal offense. Meaning serious time, and that I could be held accountable if I hold anything back. Then he hangs up.

I go meet up with Helen. It's a Friday night and the Met is open late. In Helen's last letter she said that the paintings there dream in color. I asked what she meant by that, and she said she had to show me. I want to see whatever it is she meant. Especially since my life as I know it seems about over. I am looking forward to seeing those paintings. Maybe, just maybe, they do dream, and, if so, would their dreams be in color? I can't remember if mine are in color or not.

21J

I have never had any difficulty falling asleep. No matter what problems I have. However terrible things are, I can sleep. It's like killing yourself and taking the easy way out.

It's waking up that I dread. Every morning, I go through the five stages of death. I wake up in denial that I have to go to work. Then I get angry. Then I bargain with God, or myself, and try to call in sick. Then I feel guilty and go into remission, until finally I accept that the day will suck and I get up.

From Helen's window, I look out at the projects and see it is raining in sheets. Though the projects look even more gloomy and doomy all wet, I feel happy. I can now postpone the inevitable some more. Mario is still there, hovering over me, but what does he really have on me? Unless he goes after Eddie, he can't prove that Papelito is a front for me. All we have to say is I'm his tenant and Papelito is my landlord. That we had an agreement for me to pay him in cash, and so, no trail. Then a shot of fear strikes my chest. Because the more I think about ways of getting myself out of this mess, the more lies I have to tell. It isn't stopping. In order for me to hear the song of the Orishas, I have to live in truth. I am so far from that truth that I feel taking baby steps won't get me anywhere.

I felt Helen get up before I did. I had stayed covered up, wallowing in my misery. If I had looked out the window, I would have known earlier I have at least one more day, one more excuse for happiness.

I get dressed. Helen has taken her little boom box back to the kitchen. I hear the lyrics of Silvio Rodriguez, *"Es una historia enterada, es sobre un ser de la nada,"* enter her bedroom.

Helen rushes in.

"I'm sorry," she picks up some makeup from her dresser, "I didn't make anything."

"It's all right."

"Aren't *you* late?" she says.

"Yeah," I lie, "I'm late, too."

She applies lipstick and, halfway through, stops and looks at me.

"You'll be at the opening? Right?"

"You know where I live. If I don't make it, write me a letter."

She kisses me, ruining her newly applied lipstick, and I notice for the first time that Helen's upper lip is almost a line. It barely exists, but her bottom lip is lush and therefore rescues the top one.

"The opening of my gallery is tonight, so I'll see you there, right?"

"I'll be there," I say, "don't worry."

"Good, I leave you with Silvio," she says, picking up an umbrella.

"No, I'm leaving with you," I say, and she shrugs like that's all right.

My only concern now is my mother. If she sees me leaving here I'll never get to work on time. She'll want to know everything— dates, times, kids.

I tell Helen I have to get some stuff at my place, and she kisses me again and continues to walk downstairs. I watch her go down, and when she reaches the last landing, she looks back at me and waves.

"Are you going to write me another letter?" I say.

"If you knit me a sweater," she says, winking. "Don't get wet, it's nasty out there. See you at the opening tonight." She opens her umbrella and walks out.

In my house the cat is asleep on the sofa. His belly lifts up and down gracefully, like someone blowing in and out of a paper bag. I pet him. Whisper that I'm sorry I yelled at him. He wakes up worried, but when he sees it's me, he lazily drops his head back and continues his slumber.

"Oh, no, you don't," I say to Kaiser, "if I have to work you're not sleeping."

Then I see the Bible open on top of the coffee table. Job, Chapter 9, Verse 8–9:

Stretching out the heavens by himself . . .
Making Osh, Kesil, and Kimah . . .

Mom is half right, Kaiser was in the Bible, only she was mispronouncing it. It's spelled K-E-S-I-L.

"You are in the Bible after all," I tell the cat and I realize, regardless of my misery, I must be happy because I'm talking like an idiot to a cat who licks my hand. I walk with the cat inside my bedroom. Trompo Loco is getting dressed. The bed is neat and he's made sure not to disturb any of my things.

"Your mother said I can stay," he says, cowering like I am going to be angry and throw him out.

"I'm sorry about that day, Trompo. I mean it," I say to him. "You wanna borrow my raincoat? It's pouring."

"I use trash bags," he says, putting on his shoes, "I make holes in them and make them suits."

"Here, just take my raincoat," I say, putting the cat down, making my way to the closet, "here, this will keep you dry."

Trompo looks at my raincoat.

"But it's plastic," he says, "the garbage bags are plastic, too."

"Yeah, but this," I say, knowing he'll then take it, "has pockets, see."

He smiles like I just gave him chocolate.

He puts it on and places his hands inside the pockets.

"Julio, you gonna talk to my father—"

"Trompo, we went through—" I stop myself when I see Kesil sniffing at what's left of my altar. "Trompo, did you mess up my altar?" My voice rises a notch.

"Nah, nah," he says, cowering again, "your mother did. Señora Santana did."

"Just now?"

"Yeah, she woke up mad, said stuff. Are you going to talk to my father?"

I leave Trompo hanging and head for my parents' bedroom.

I'm furious and don't knock. Pops is asleep like a rock, and Mom is nowhere to be found. I leave the apartment and find Mom outside, holding an umbrella that is so big she sometimes takes it with her to the beach. She is ready for work but she is arguing with Papelito who is also under an umbrella.

"*Pero señora,*" Papelito says in that delicate voice of his, "how can you say that."

"Ma'," I yell in the rain, "you had no right doing that!"

"*Mira qué demonio te han puesto,*" she yells back at me. "That's what he has done to you."

"Señora, please," Papelito shouts back.

"*Tu tienes un demonio,* Julio," she yells, "he did that so he can take your money. That's what *santeros* do, that's what they do, *yo sé.*"

Maritza arrives to open her church, which during the day doubles as a day care that nobody trusts. Nobody. But she opens it. And all the women that volunteer there are undocumented.

"*Qué pasa aquí?*" Maritza asks, concerned.

"I went to the bank," Mom yells even louder at me, "they told me you don't own this place. That he does."

"Let's all go inside," Papelito says, "we can all talk inside,"

"I'm not going inside no botanica!" Mom says with disdain, "with demons and you!"

"*'Ta bien,*" Maritza says, "let's go inside my church then. Talk there."

"I don't want to talk to her," I yell at my mother. "You went behind my back, Ma'—"

"You stole my son's money," Mom accuses Papelito, yelling so loud that even with this rain, even this early, people begin to peek out of their windows to see what's happening.

"No, *señora,*" Papelito defends himself, "I never took a penny from anybody."

"*Un hechizo,* and then took my son's money," she says.

"You think I'm that stupid!" I say, "Ma' give me more credit."

"Yes!" my mother yells at me again. "You can be like your father sometimes."

Trompo appears from the doorway. He senses arguing and doesn't like it. It scares him.

"*Dios,*" she says to Papelito, "*dios le va a castigar a usted. Por ser immoral y por ser un ladrón.*" Mom cries but I feel no pity for her. She turns to say something to me but I turn my head. She flares her nostrils; even in this heavy rain I can hear her molars grinding, her jaw a lock of anger. When I turn my head toward her, it's a mirror. She's as angry as I am. So angry at me, she walks away stepping in deep puddles like she can walk on water.

"You all right, Julio?" Maritza covers me with her umbrella.

"Yeah, I'm fine," I say, still angry at Mom.

I look at Papelito who can't stand the sight of me. He gives me those *brujo* stares of his. I know what he's thinking and I can't say he is wrong. Papelito turns around and noisily closes his umbrella and shakes the water out of it like he is getting rid of bad influences. As if it had rained bad spirits and he is shooing them all away. He then goes inside his botanica without saying a word to me.

"You want to come inside?" Maritza asks me, but I don't answer, because, pounded by the rain, next to a garbage pile, I see the items that once composed my altars. I see squashed fruit, nuts and shells, all scattered. My statue of Oshosi, the hunter, split in half. The decapitated statue of La Caridad de Cobre all bashed up. The goddess's scarf, her candles dark and wet and dirty in the rain. Then I see a piece of paper sticking out of her neck, like a Molotov cocktail inside her hollow body.

It's Helen's letter. I had hidden it inside the statue. Thinking my mother would never look there.

"Take my umbrella, stop being stupid," Maritza says. I don't take it.

Maritza takes one last reassuring look at me and then leaves me there.

"You gonna go talk to my father?" Trompo says as Maritza takes his arm and guides him inside the church to get stuff ready.

I just stand there getting wet. I stare at pieces of something my mother had no business touching. I feel like it was these pieces, this ritual, that had brought me some sort of happiness. I had awoken with some hope that something good was going to happen. The rain had led me to believe that I might be rescued at the last moment, because love does that. Last night, I had been fingered by grace, and I woke up ready to smile at every stranger in the street, at any animal, any soul. My life wasn't that shallow after all, my pockets were deep and full of hope. But anyone with the map of my terrible life could have pointed me in the right direction. The broken altar is an omen. I feel that everything I was after is already behind me, and everything I am running away from is still here.

I kick some of the items. They are useless now.

I go pull out Helen's letter. The paper is already turning soft, dissolving like a wafer. The ink is blurred. Helen's words are lost. Just as well. I let the letter fall from my hand. It doesn't float like a feather but sinks like stones thrown in a puddle.

I enter the church to face Maritza. Trompo Loco asks me if I am going to see his father. I say, yes I am, Trompo. Then I tell him to start cleaning the floors so I can speak with Maritza. Trompo Loco begins to get the floors ready. His smile is so radiant it shines. I have told him what he wants to hear and so he doesn't want to ruin anything.

I go talk to Maritza, who is checking her church's unopened mail. She is sitting on a folded chair with the letters spread over her lap.

"They are on to you," I softly say to her as I look around the empty church.

Maritza doesn't answer me, she continues to read a letter. She's probably already talked with her boyfriend and he's told her I dropped by.

"I'm not going to rat you out," I say, almost whispering. "Not that I have anything. They want those papers. And I can't help you. I have my own problems."

Maritza crushes some junk mail. She crumples it into a ball and flings it across the church. That's more like Maritza, always angry at something.

"I just wanted to tell you this."

Maritza doesn't open any more mail. Heavy in angry thoughts, Maritza stares at the walls.

Papelito enters the church. All wet, his hair is dripping water from being outside arguing with my mother. Yet he still sways his hips past Trompo Loco who is mopping the floors. He excuses himself for ruining Trompo's newly shined floors.

"Mari," he says to her, ignoring me, "you have to stop."

"Why," Maritza yells, "can't they just leave me alone!" The echo makes Trompo Loco stop mopping. I wave at him that it's all right.

"This is not the way, Mari," Papelito says to her, and the silence this church once held is gone. "It's not the way. They come because of what you can give them. Listen to me, Mari."

"I'm doing what's right," she finally looks at us. "I know that this is right."

"*Mija*, you can't force people," Papelito shakes his head, "you can't force them to embrace something that's right. You are buying them so they can agree with you, Mari."

"So what, I'm helping them—"

"Mari, who are you to choose who gets the help? You are doing exactly what you hate. You are playing God, Mari. You decide who."

I stand back and let them talk it out. I'm not going to interfere or add anything.

"Papelito," she says, "look at what we have accomplished. All the people we've helped."

There might be tears in Maritza's eyes, I don't know.

"Good, Mari," Papelito answers her, "good, then take that as your prize."

Maritza bows her head. I have never seen her like this. Her entire body is weighed down like gravity is pulling her down.

"And you," Papelito focuses at me, "that agent came to talk to me, way before he talked to you, Julio."

That's why Mario knew everything. He had gone to see Papelito.

"I didn't tell him anything, Papelito. About you, or her," I say pointing at Maritza, "he only wants those documents."

"I know that," Papelito gently places his hand on Maritza's hair. He delicately strokes it. Maritza welcomes it. "There's enough blame here to go around."

Trompo Loco is getting ready to dust the plastic flowers that decorate the platform. He has a bottle of Windex and he starts spraying and wiping. He seems to like spraying, because he sprays too much.

"I'm going to get those forms out of my botanica," Papelito gracefully retracts his hand away from Maritza's hair, "and give them up."

Maritza jumps up. The letters on her lap fall to the floor.

"No!" she defies him.

"Oh yes, I am," he says, angry that she has dared to confront him. After all he's done for her. "And then Julio," I straighten up in fear of him, "after the ceremony that I have to conduct tonight, you and me are going to the bank and we're going to set that right." He puts his foot down like he is my father. "I want your mother off my back, Julio. That woman is worse than the government." I want to at least smile but Papelito isn't joking. His lips are a straight line. "After that," he pauses to make sure we are listening, "I'm taking all the blame."

"No you can't—" Maritza protests. Papelito lifts a hand at her as if he is ready to slap her. She turns her face away, waiting for the blow.

"*Mira, que te doy un*—" he stops himself from striking her. It is the only time I have seen Papelito so enraged he almost harmed someone.

He swallows hard and orders me to follow him. I do as told and walk behind him. Trompo Loco asks to come along but Papelito shoots him a *brujo* stare. Trompo knows to leaves us alone. I whisper to Trompo that everything is all right, and he continues to clean.

Next door, inside San Lazaro y Las Siete Vueltas, Papelito takes a deep breath. He recites a small, quick prayer and calms down. Silently, Papelito walks behind the counter, where several small statues of San Lazaro, the saint for diseases, stand upright on a shelf. He takes one down and, underneath the small statue, like a piggy bank, is a small opening. Papelito digs his fingers inside and pulls out a thick paper, like the one Mario showed me.

I look at the shelf full of statues. Maybe twenty of them.

Papelito follows my eyes and knows what I was looking at.

"That's nothing Julio," and he points to a life-sized statue of a regal looking Santa Barbara. She stands upright, holding a golden goblet in one hand. I notice that underneath Santa Barbara, like a base or a foundation for the statue to stand on, is a thick metal box that resembles a large phone book made out of tin.

"That's the mother lode. Hundreds of them. That's what they want."

Papelito and I walk over to bring the statue down, getting the tin box from underneath it. It's a heavy statue, and when we do take it down and settle it on the floor, the cup that Santa Barbara holds in her hand breaks off and plaster shatters on the ground. Papelito stares intensely at the broken pieces. He sees things. Patterns, images or numbers in the white, chalky mess on the floor.

"Because of all this fear, Julio," he says, his eyes still intensely gazing at the floor, "we have given away all these rights. Gave the government the power to now come inside our bedrooms. But one day, Julio, this fear will die down. But the government will still have those powers and they won't want to give them back." He looks up from the floor and sucks his teeth. Papelito looks disgusted, as if a foul smell suddenly filled the air. "And now, Mari has given them just what they want. An excuse to call you or me a patriot, just for snitching on each other."

I realized then that Papelito had been in contact with Mario way longer than I had. I didn't know what Mario had on Papelito, but he had something. The same way Mario had something on me. The same way the government has something on everyone.

Maritza walks inside the botanica, seething. Nostrils flaring. She shakes her head in disbelief at Papelito as if he has betrayed her. She waits, stands there for Papelito to confront her. Instead, Papelito ignores her. Walks right by her and exits his botanica. I do the same.

Outside. In the rain.

Papelito looks at the curb. He looks for oil slicks, like someone trying to find peace with nature—at least his version of nature. There are leaves clogging a drain by the gutter. Different colored leaves bunch up from the heavy rain. Papelito is seeing something in the patterns they make. I watch him as I hear Maritza smashing statue after statue inside. I hear her yell in frustration at everyone and everything. It is only then that I realize that Papelito isn't looking for prophecies or philosophies in the leaves in the gutter. He is meditating so as to ignore Maritza's insults. They are both my friends and I want to stay, but I'm late for work. Papelito had already told me what I needed to do. It's all up to me now.

t's no surprise that the first thing I see when I get to work is Mario cuffed and being escorted into a squad car. The boss is talking to a detective.

"He stole the pipes," Antonio tells me in Spanish. "I always knew it was him."

"Great," I say, disgusted. "Are you going back to Mexico?" I ask Antonio.

"This will be my last pay," he says.

"Just like that. You won't say bye to Maritza?"

With all this rain around us, Antonio stays quiet. The cops drive off with Mario, and the boss tells everyone to get back to work. The boss approaches.

Antonio walks away. He doesn't want to deal with any of it—me, Maritza or the boss.

"Julio you're tainted," the boss says.

"Tainted?"

"Yeah."

"What the fuck is tainted," I say. "You mean I'm fired?" I say, not caring the slightest.

"Hey don't get sour with me, Julio," the boss says like he's an angel. Like he never does anything wrong. A perfect being who takes care of everyone. "Take it up with Eddie. He's in the trailer."

The trailer isn't that far away, just a few feet. But I drift to an incident that was.

It happened to me years back, when I was twelve. This fifteen-year-old Italian stallion of a kid kept picking on me. He was huge, already five feet eleven, and all those who didn't know him thought he was an adult. He picked on me every day, for months, and well into my thirteenth year. And there was no way I could take him. I could've cloned two more of myself, and he'd still beat all three of me, at the same time. This wasn't teasing, like Trompo Loco would get teased with verbal arrows, which hurt, too, but mine were real kicks and punches. And, of course, you're a sucker in the neighborhood if you tell your parents. In my case, my mother would have just said to pray to God. And I did, and that big kid was still beating the shit out of me. And so, after exhausting all my options, even praying to God, I lost it and just didn't care about the consequences.

Fuck it if you win.

Fuck it if you lose.

I swung.

I was about to do that now. All these bullies. I had nothing to lose.

enter the trailer and Eddie is sitting down, making adjustments to his books. He sees me and closes his ledger, like he doesn't want me to see how much he steals, takes or makes.

"What?" I say without a greeting. Eddie understands. He can see I'm angry.

"I got this kid," Eddie says, looking right at me, "from El Salvador taking your name."

"So he'll front for me? Is that it?" I ask and Eddie nods. I see what he's up to. "And you get most of his paycheck, right?"

"Of course," Eddie says. "Julio, you owe me a lot of money. This way, you can find another job and I don't lose another hand."

I start to hate him but it's a good deal. It's a good deal. It's a damn good deal. It cuts my problems in half. Now I only have to deal with Mario.

"Okay, thanks," I say. "I'll see you."

"Wait where you going?" he says, arms outstretched.

"You said you found a front for me?" I say.

"I did. So?"

"So, you're going to keep deducting what I owe you? I'm lending you my union membership?"

"I don't think you understand," Eddie says, bringing his swivel chair to an upright position, "that just takes care of the interest."

"Interest?"

"Listen Julio, I like you, I do. You never let me down. This is the best I can do. I'm giving you a chance to find work and to pay me back all at the same time."

I'm silent. I'm thinking about that kid who picked on me.

"But I've had it with you Julio."

I'm thinking about the day I got fed up with this bully and before this bully could even come over and beat me up, I went over to him. I had a glass bottle in my hand, and before he knew it I whacked him on the head. The bottle shattered above his left eye. There was blood all over his face, and I started kicking him while he was down.

"It's either do your own home or take that job in D.C."

The problem was, when that guy recovered, there was hell to pay. And that kid beat me up so bad he sent me to the hospital.

"So what's it gonna be?"

But when I got out of the hospital, he never fucked with me again. That beating we gave each other changed both our ways. We didn't become friends, far from it, but he respected me and I didn't fear him.

"So you now have a kid," I say to him, making sure I got it all straight, "who will take my name at this site."

"Correct."

"And you will take most of his check. Leaving me free to work for you in D.C.—"

"It's brilliant Julio, you'll pay me back and at the same time make money for yourself."

I feel that brutal feeling again. That same feeling I felt when I attacked that bully.

"Fuck you Eddie, fuck you and your job."

"What did you just say to me?" Eddie stands up. He is old, and like his son he's tall. Like a cornfield that towers over you, shadowing your view. A place where you can get lost and go in circles.

"After all I've done for you? You little shit."

"Keep all your jobs Eddie," I say, getting ready to head out, "I'll get you the money—"

"Yeah, well I need that money," Eddie holds my arm. "You hear me, right now!"

I whisk my arm away. I clench my hands into fists so hard my left arm cramps. It hurts but I don't want Eddie to see me massage it or to notice. So, I take quick breath after quick breath.

"You're going to go burn your building right now, this minute—"

"It's raining! You fuck!" I yell at him and he grabs me by the throat like a cop would a protester.

"Then you burn it tomorrow night, you hear me!"

He lets go of me. It wasn't a tight or vicious grip. My throat doesn't hurt the slightest bit. Not like my arm. Eddie grabbed me more out of frustration, like a bad parent slapping a child on the wrist. I am now sure that Eddie, like powerful men who back him, would never hurt anyone physically. Eddie is like a bomber pilot, who kills his enemies from a distance. He could never look his victims in the eye. If he did, they'd become too human for him to kill. That's left for the little people, like me.

"I never liked it, any of it." His eyes hold mine but there is no heart in them, it's just a job to him. A job where he will not see any faces. "You either set your house on fire or I'll send someone else to do it. And that someone won't send out any warnings to anyone living there."

22K

The *Asiento*, the ceremony where a person "makes the saint," when he or she will become one with the Orisha that chooses him or her, is taking place inside Maritza's church. The drumming can be heard a block away. It's a celebration, a sort of baptism, being born again but in Ocha, in Santeria. Papelito had not been kidding that he wants no secrets. There is a camera crew from Telemundo, the Spanish channel, reporting on the first ever public view of an Asiento. Papelito has been cautious as well, and has his lawyer present in case animal rights groups or other protesters show up.

Papelito has welcomed all progressive followers of Lukumi, as well as curious souls like myself. All he asks for is respect.

I walk into some heavy drumming. Sacred bata drums are being pounded by a group of men in a corner. There are a few fowls leashed to the legs of a chair and there are tables loaded with assorted symbols, all according to the Orisha that the table is set for. There is an artificial wall made up of white sheets, which hides a child's plastic wading pool that sits in the corner. Through the transparencies of the white sheets, I can make out a naked body standing, arms outstretched, being washed by other hands. The people surrounding the naked body dry it with towels and dress it.

"As a newborn can't do things for himself, so is one who is newborn into Santeria." A *babalawo* that I don't know is explaining every step to the Telemundo reporter. "The clothes are all white. Representing birth."

I look for Papelito. I want to apologize for what I was going to do. It would affect his botanica. Especially the water. The firemen will drench my building with so much water, it will overflow to his livelihood next door. His herbs, candles, and other items will be ruined. I need to tell him I have no choice, that if I don't burn the building, someone else will. That I hope he'd forgive me.

But it's hard finding him with the drumming so intense. With some people dancing, others praying, yet others eating and drinking.

I soon realize that Papelito, as the *padrino* of the initiate, must be one of the people behind the white sheet wall.

"We can't see it, but right now the *santero*," I get close to the *babalawo* who is explaining this to the reporter, "is now passing over the initiate's body two roosters whose blood will then be spilled over the items on the tables, making the items sacred."

That was what Papelito was doing. It's the worst time to talk to him. To say I'm sorry not for my mother but for other things, during a ceremony this sacred, is just plain stupid of me.

"And then the animals," the reporter asks, "will be eaten?"

"Yes," the *santero* says, "look around you, all these people have to be fed. The ceremony will last many hours and the guests will be hungry."

"So it's not cruelty to animals then, as some state?" the reporter asks, which gets Papelito's lawyer involved.

"Can I take that one, please." The reporter places the microphone in front of the lawyer. "The animals are sacrificed in a clean and humane way, then they will be served as the feast meal. The animals will be consumed as food. No different than when you go and get a burger at McDonald's. People don't understand that when they eat a steak that animal was killed in the same manner that the animals of this ceremony will be, and then, just like that steak, served as nourishment."

The drumming continues.

I see Papelito come from behind the wall of white sheets. He has two roosters in his hand. His face is serious, almost trancelike. I don't go over to him as the drums pound. Papelito disappears into the men's room, followed by other *babalawos*. When they reappear, Papelito has a jar in his hands. He goes over to the table and spills the rooster's blood over the items on the table.

"This is the first cleansing," the *babalawo* tells the reporter, "the animals passed over the initiate's body have taken away all past sins. A second cleansing with river water is next, before the—"

"One last word on animal sacrifice," the lawyer interrupts the explanation of the ceremony, "all this, what you see here, including the animal sacrifice, is protected under the First Amendment, freedom of religion."

Papelito is trancelike, as if he is praying inside all the time. I realize that is exactly what he is doing. Papelito wanted this filmed so people won't be afraid, so people won't be taken in by fake *santeros* who don't know what they are doing. It is important to him, so important that he is willing to get kicked out of his religion as a dissident.

I leave Papelito alone.

I can't talk to him while this most sacred and complex ceremony is taking place. I walk out of the church into traffic, and it feels like silence. The drums are now faint heartbeats. There's nothing more for me to do but wait until the ceremony is over. During that time, I go see Helen, because the same things I was going to say to Papelito, I have to say to her.

I walk toward Helen's gallery, passing by a Blockbuster Video, a couple of Duane Reades, a couple of Rite Aids, a couple of McDonald's, a KFC, a Starbucks, a Gap, and an Old Navy. I ask myself, "Whose streets are these?" There are a lot of Mexican *taquerias,* but they are offset by these chain stores that form an inner-city minimall. The only thing that hasn't changed are the churches. Some are above shops, others are in basements. Many don't even look like churches but more like sweatshops or warehouses. Churches don't go out of fashion in Spanish Harlem. If you have nothing to hope for, you are always going to be poor. And that's where Jesus comes in. He consoles you by stroking your hair. Whispering that every day is a gift, a miracle, your dreams are gold, and you are God's story. And many thrive on that, they believe it as if those words came straight from their parents.

I turn the corner and I see a crowd.

The protesters are at Helen's.

There is a large crowd of homesteaders and housing activists across the street from her gallery. The protesters are Latinos and they are chanting, "Renovate the buildings, not the people!" They carry signs that at night are a bit hard to read. I get closer, and make some of the words out. A man waves a banner that says RICANSTRUC-TION. One woman is lifting a board above her head, which reads CLINTON, I LOVE YOU. BUT GET OUT OF HARLEM.

One of the protesters is the skinny man with the mustache who had arrived at my house when Trompo Loco got kicked out. He recognizes me and hands me a flyer.

The real crime is taking away the people's art . . . I stop reading it right there. And cross the street.

"Hey," I hear him yell behind my back, "you're not going in there! Are you!"

"Damn right," I yell back, "it's not a picket line."

Across the street, it's a totally different story. Helen's gallery is jam-packed. The crowd overflows outside, near the entrance, where guests are ignoring the protesters and drinking wine and talking. There are a lot of kids who have come out of curiosity and for the free food. I walk inside, and the artist whose work is being displayed has let himself be tied like Christ, left arm to one beam, right arm to another. He looks Native American, with his hair long and lush, and his paintings are full of Southwestern colors. He never looks at anyone, just stands there tied with a blank expression on his face. He doesn't talk to anyone, either, and some people stare at him as if he is a painting and not a real person.

Helen's opening is a success, at least attendance-wise. Other artists from Spanish Harlem have come to support her. James de la Vega is here. "They didn't protest the Starbucks," I hear James de la Vega say, "Shit, now that's evil to the core." He has his big, blond, afro-looking wig on his head and is wearing a shirt that reads BECOME YOUR DREAM. Tanya Torres and her husband, Jose, who own the Mixta Gallery on 107th and Lexington, are here, too. Eliana Godoy, the owner of Carlito's Café, is here, so is Efrain Suarez of the Salsa Museum. Poets Prisionera, Yarisa Colon, and the Ecuadorian poet Veronica "de nadie" are in a corner talking with Professor Robert Waddle. Under better circumstances, I'd love to be part of all of this, just not now.

There are a lot of white people as well. I'm looking for Helen among the crowd.

Greg spots me and waves me to come over.

Events like these, where people are drinking wine and looking at art, force you to be somewhat prissy, even if you are here as the bearer of bad news.

I go over only out of politeness.

"This is Julio," he introduces me to an older white woman. "This is Ruby."

I say, "Nice meeting you" to Ruby, who's a bit on the heavy side, like a big baby seal.

"Ruby was just telling me how she doesn't understand why some people would want this place to remain only Latino, doesn't exposure change people, Julio?"

"Yeah, it does," I say, looking to see if I spot Helen.

"See, Julio agrees," Greg says.

"I didn't say I agree with you," I add.

"Well, regardless," Ruby says, "I've read that Alfred Stieglitz said he had seen at least," she says with emphasis, "at least, at least seven New York Cities from his window in ten years. Change is the nature of this city. These people—"

I walk away.

I keep looking for Helen, and it's hard finding her with so many people here. It's a sea of elbows and backs, bumps and swerving to avoid knocking drinks down. When I do see Helen, she has a glass of wine in her hand and is talking with a middle-aged man with white hair that's been shaved down to only tiny, white flare-ups. He is thin and good-looking. Next to him, I can tell, is his wife. A woman with wholly white hair and the presence of a Southern belle. And just by their small frames, I can tell they're Helen's parents.

Helen spots me, a big smile arises all of a sudden. She elbows her way through the crowd and comes over to grab me. She kisses me with no embarrassment at all.

"Isn't this awesome?" she says, tipsy, "look at all these people."

"Have you sold a picture?" I don't know what else to say.

"Only the ropes that Russell has tied himself with."

"The ropes are for sale?"

"Yes, isn't that clever." She is really having a good time. "Come." Helen takes me by the hand and steers me toward her parents.

"This is Julio," she says. "My father, Vic, and mother, Emily."

They are very nice people, standing like peacocks, proud of their daughter.

"Helen," I say, getting close to her ear, "can I talk to you in that little office of yours?"

"Sure," she says and excuses herself.

The office isn't that far away, yet we have to fight to get there, and people are always coming up to congratulate Helen. When we do reach the tiny office, it brings me back to the first time I made love to her.

"Helen I have something—"

Somebody walks in.

"Helen, the Armstrongs are asking about the mountain piece?"

"Julio," she says, "I'm busy, can this wait?"

I stare at her and want to tell her it can. But I know better. My expression must be one of desperation, because Helen senses something.

"Helen," the guy says, "the piece?"

Without taking her eyes off me, Helen answers, "Tell them I'll be right there."

The guy walks back out.

"What's wrong, Julio?" She puts her glass down and tenderly holds my face. Her hands are warm and smell of wine and almonds.

With all this chaos, why not just tell her?

So, I do. "Helen," I say, "I'm going to burn the building down."

"Great idea," she says, sipping some wine, "make sure the protesters are inside."

"No," I say, "I'm serious, I came here to tell you I'm burning the building."

"What building?"

"The building where we live, that building."

Helen drops her hands away from my face like they weigh a ton.

"Wait, did I hear that right?" she says, forcing a little smile.

"Tomorrow night, I'm burning it down."

"You're crazy," she says in total disbelief.

"Promise me you won't be there."

"You're crazy."

"Promise me on your parents," I say urgently, "promise me on Vic and Emily you won't be there."

"No this can't be you. This can't be right?" she says, focusing her eyes at something else, as if she's solving a mathematical equation. "No," she says to herself more than to me, "no that can't be right."

"You can call the police and have me arrested, but that will just delay it. If I don't burn it, someone else will. I know Eddie."

"Eddie? Who the fuck is Eddie?" I've never heard her curse. "Tell me if you're in trouble Julio? Just tell me, tell me."

"I tried telling you the other night," I say, raising my voice. The crowd outside murmurs louder, like more people have come. "I told you I set fire—"

"I thought you were kidding or were into some other stuff—"

"No, I set fires—"

"No, you don't. You do construction. I see you leave every morning—"

"No, I set fires." I hear the people laughing outside the office. They're having a good time out there. "Listen, keep your mouth shut, Helen, and I can promise you, seriously promise you fire insurance kickbacks. You can even have half of my share. Maritza will get the other—" I stop talking when Helen's eyes start to shine. The moisture in them is about to spill.

"I will not believe you." A heavy drop rolls down her cheek, "You can't be serious."

"I'm serious."

"I'm going to call the police," she says trancelike, as if she is one of the people in Papelito's ceremony. "I'm going to call the police."

"Weren't you listening to me?" Why do I expect Helen to believe me? This is something that only happens to other people, like getting struck by lightning or dying in a plane crash. You never think it can happen to you or to someone close to you, and so, when it does, it's like living in a dream world, and you have no idea what to make of it. "The police won't help us, Helen. The police will just make it worse, because then there'll be no warning and people will die—"

"I'm going to call the police," she says again and goes for the phone.

I grab the phone.

The murmuring outside the office is really loud, it feels like Yankee Stadium.

"Listen, Helen. Listen to me, were the police there that day when all those women humiliated that man? No, right? Were the police there when he molested his daughter? Are the police here

tonight with all those protesters? No, right? There's a new set of
rules here. You rely on your friends—"

"Friends!" she yells. "You're talking about burning my house!
Your house. A church? It's crazy. This sounds like you're crazy!"

It takes a while for betrayal to register. At first you deny it. Tell
yourself, it's just too much. It's not possible. Then there's the dead
zone, a silence, a processing of data and memories. After you've ex-
amined all the evidence against that terrible idea, you come to the re-
alization that you've just been lied to. Helen was going through that.

"Just don't be there, okay? I'm sorry," I say silently, because it's
all my fault.

I stop talking.

Then there's a gradual silence. As if some bad news had been an-
nounced on the radio and everyone has quieted down so they can
hear. It's that kind of silence. Something has happened outside that
has made this party quieter than a funeral.

I open the office door to find the crowd in horror. Trompo Loco
is bloodied, black-faced, his clothes charred. He is standing in the
middle of the floor space. Everyone has made way for him and he
sees me and starts to cry.

"He's got to talk to me now, Julio," Trompo says and starts to
spin. "He's got to talk to me." Trompo Loco spins with his arms outstretched. Trompo Loco spins, repeating the same words over and
over. Some people try to stop his twirling, but his skinny, tall body
makes it difficult to get a good hold of him. Trompo Loco's outstretched arms also inadvertently slap some people who try to get out
of his way. He spins and knocks paintings down. Some men try to
stop him and wrestle Trompo Loco down to the ground. Bad idea.
When he hits the ground, he just tightens his arms close together
and spins on the ground like Curly from *The Three Stooges*. Trompo

Loco is on the floor, spinning like a crazy top, crying out loud, "Talk to me!" A few people don't get out of Trompo Loco's way and his spinning body on the floor hits their feet, forcing them to tumble to the ground, too.

"Just leave him alone!" I yell, because I know if you try to stop him, you can hurt yourself or him.

Helen hides her face in her hands.

The paintings are ruined and on the floor.

The artist, who had tied himself near the wine table to make sure all could see him, is drenched, and someone is untying him.

Many people start to leave.

Trompo Loco is losing speed. Trompo is ready to pass out. When he does, his face is peaceful, like he is sleeping or dead. I get down on my knees to pick him up and take him home. Then his blank face makes me realize what he's angry about. He wants Eddie to talk to him. He wants his father to talk to him.

I run out of the gallery to my house.

Fire engines rush by me in the same direction. A block away from my building, neon lights of all colors shed light on everything around them. Red engines and police squad cars, ambulances and the news reporters fill the streets. A large crowd has gathered, watching in amazement at how a fire can pick up so much speed that even before the firemen's hoses can start denting it, it's pretty much a mouth of flames, eating everything up. I run, taking stock of the scene. When I make out that yes, that is my mother holding in her arms what looks like a baby, I know it's Kesil, and my heart's pounding lessens. Closer, I see my father is barefoot, holding a single album cover. I slow down after being assured that they are all right. I reach the scene to find my mother in tears. From across the street, where I used to admire my house, where I thought myself so smart and on my way, I now watch it burn. See the roof cave in. It all happens so fast.

A three-story building fire doesn't last very long. It gets consumed pretty quickly. The firemen put out what's left of the flames. Nothing but a shell of bricks and towering clouds of smoke snake up from the rubble, like a recently stubbed-out cigarette. Soon, the smell of burned wood, ash mostly, plastic, and paint will envelope the air.

I hold my father and mother. Kesil is afraid. He has seen this before.

"The man was a saint," my mother cries. "He saved me and my cat's life," she wails. Kesil digs his claws into the fabric of her blouse without hurting her flesh. He's so afraid of being homeless that he doesn't want to let loose from Mom ever again.

"All of us. He saved all of us." Pops is shaken, with tears in his voice, he is making an effort to explain what's happened. "We were passing out from the smoke, and he appeared from a wall of fire, like he could control it and feel nothing, just like that."

"He saved my life," Mom cries, *"Cristo lo bendiga."*

We stand there, and soon the smoke in the air brings out our neighbors. Women console my mother as their husbands place their hands on my father's shoulders. Most of our neighbors look stunned. My parents' friends hug each other and some cry, because the time when fires ran rampant is still vivid in everyone's memory. Some eyewitnesses who had been at the *Asiento*, tell me that Papelito had run out of the ceremony he was conducting that very minute, as if he had been tipped off by some spirit. That some spirit whispered in his ear to immediately rush everyone out of the botanica. That something evil was about to happen. How Papelito then rushed upstairs to my house and saved my parents and the cat. How a wall of fire got between him and the outside world, engulfing him until Papelito became a flame himself.

I look at the crowd, a circus of colorful gowns, dancers, drummers, maracas, bells and shakers, and the sacrificial animals. All outside, not having had a chance to continue their ceremony, they all begin to pray for *ifa padrino*. Then, all of a sudden, they begin drumming and dancing, as if they want to give Papelito a funeral right there on the street. They invoke many Orisha gods in their songs, and they dance in his name. *Belen, Belen, es el último Belen.* But I can't get into it. I look across the street at my building and at San Lazaro y Las Siete Vueltas, scorched, its glass window shattered into black pieces on the sidewalk. I feel as fractured as those pieces of glass. I didn't get a chance to thank him after all he'd done for me. To thank him and say I was sorry for disappointing him.

Many are celebrating his memory, but others are still wailing. I don't fall too far behind those who are crying. Papelito was my friend, and his saving my parents seems to have been his last gift to me.

Book III

FILL OUT AN APPLICATION. GET ON A WAITING LIST.

For this is your home, my friend, do not be driven from it;
great men have done great things here and will again—

JAMES BALDWIN,
THE FIRE NEXT TIME

Application #23

This application in no way reserves or assigns an apartment to you.
A nonrefundable fee of $100 must accompany this form
or it will not be processed.

My father has disability, and so, we're back in the projects. The deed was in Papelito's name, and now that he is no more, I have no records, no proof that the place had ever been mine. It didn't take that long, less than a year, for something else to be built at the site where we used to live. One day I was walking by that street. I saw these white guys walk out of the new building that used to be my home. I stopped and looked up at the windows. There was this anger that someone else was occupying my space. And later, when a Starbucks opened right in the space where the People's Church used to meet, I avoided the block altogether.

Helen now lives in a brownstone on 120th and First. Every time she sees me she crosses the street before I can get near her.

So I let her be.

. . .

never stopped hearing about Maritza. Or thinking about her. I
wasn't there, but I knew it was fact. Not long after the fire, Maritza
and Antonio had climbed to the roof of a tenement on 116th Street
and Second Avenue. The boulevard is named after a Puerto Rican
governor, Luis Muñoz Marin, responsible for the depopulation of
the island; but now so many Mexicans live on that avenue, there are so
many *taquerias*, that it's being labeled Little Puebla. It was during a
Mexican festival, I don't know which one, when everyone is out in the
street, when the Mexican flag fluttered, its green, white, and red taking over the avenue, when those documents that Mario was after
began raining on the people like confetti. Most knew what they were
and quickly snatched them up from midair, like they were wishes, and
swiftly left for their homes. Others stepped on them and continued
partying, enjoying their newfound neighborhood.

And then Maritza disappeared.

Regardless, El Barrio remains a place where rumors grow wild,
like trees do on the roofs of old, burned-out and abandoned buildings. Some say they have seen Maritza in Latin America, in some or-
phanage. Other rumors grew even wilder. In Mexico they mention
her name along with some saints. She had helped a whole bunch of
people's relatives when they had arrived, undocumented, here in the
States. They spoke about how if you could find "La Santa," she
would make you an American and you'd no longer live in fear. Like a
slave. Some say they have seen her in the Amazons. That she ate a sacred mushroom and became enlightened and now lives in caves,
where she preaches to jaguars on the nobility of eating grass and
plants. But I don't believe that one bit. I don't believe any of them.
My guess is she's somewhere in the United States, lying low and

helping out in some women's shelter or something like that. I do know she'll eventually show up. Whether Mario catches up with her or not. She'll be back, and when she does turn up at my door, she'll have no glamorous stories. No tales of heroism. Most likely she'll be cold and hungry and hit me up for money and demand favors, just like old times.

Maritza made her share of mistakes. She was an edgy, unpredictable creature who challenged American imperialism in a way in which no Puerto Rican or anyone could ever have imagined. That she failed is not surprising. That she even tried, that's the true miracle. The impact she created was enough to keep people dreaming. So, immigrants keep coming to Spanish Harlem. So do people like Greg. Maybe they'll balance each other in the future, who knows?

Maritza was always rude and mean to me, and I forget why, but I did love her. It was a long time ago, but I did.

got a job at a pizzeria. Pay is not so good but I can take some food home. One day a white man walked into the pizzeria and I knew he wasn't a yuppie prospector looking for cheap rent. I knew what he was. He asked me how much I made working at the pizza place and I told him. He then asked if I wanted to work in demolition. No experience necessary and that all I had to do was knock down walls and gut out tenements. He said he was going to do me a favor, I could work under his name, under his social security number, and when payday arrived we would swap checks for cash. I told him I was about to graduate and no thank you. School was the only bright spot in this whole mess. How I made all my classes and wrote all my papers during all this turmoil, I'll never know. I will have that degree by the end of the semester. The guy then said, nice talking to you, gave me a phone number, and said to "send your friends my way." I told him I was on parole, I had to fly straight. He said so was he.

One day I opened the mailbox to find an envelope with no return address. But by the smell of almonds I knew who it was from. The letter was short, more like a note. But it was a beginning, an opening of channels.

> The point is in the grand scheme of things, luxury vs. poverty is a secondary concern to the questions. How alive are you, Julio? How much do you really feel? How long does the memory of your touch last on another person's skin? Will you feel them in empty rooms where you've never been after they are dead? I mean, Julio, do you ever wake up in the middle of the night and feel you hear the voice of that gutter poet you told me about? Do you ever wake up and slide the curtains aside to see if the gutter poet's ghost is lying on the curb, reciting? What I'm trying to tell you, Julio, is that you are obsessed with the material: your building, demolition, and fire. What you have lost is the beauty and imagination your culture gave you as a child that made living in vacant lots and streets of fire bearable, even exciting and pleasurable. A nostalgia you confuse with anger. You go around talking all this history of your neighborhood and trying to fix everything partly because you are somewhat responsible for its demise. In your head, Julio, what you have romanticized the most are the days when everything was allowed to be broken.
>
> Finally, I feel that speaking of falling in love in any way but the abstract, speaking of you and me other than in the basics, is what got me in this mess.

I'm not so hopeful about *us*, but that doesn't mean, Julio, that there is no hope.

She didn't address it "Dear Julio" or sign it. Still, it was that last line that brought sunshine to my face. There are things that can't be written, said, or painted. I really think hope is one of those original things, like air or God, hope can't be successfully metaphored. And so, I hope Helen will eventually talk to me. And when she does, I will not explain anything, except shake hands with her and start from the beginning, again. Maybe I'll get it right this time.

My mother's anger toward me for not telling her everything has subsided. But she still holds me accountable for losing Helen.

Losing Helen? I was just getting to know her. But my mother already had us married. One night, as she watched her soaps on Telemundo, starring all these blond and blue-eyed Latin Americans crowding the screen, so many of them one would think there are no black or Indian people in Latin America, my mother kept sucking her teeth, "You could have married someone that looks like they do." My father, who was at her side, tightening a conga drum, just laughed.

"I didn't," he said, "I married you."

"*Hey que sangrón,*" my mother laughed back

The phone rang and I went to pick it up. Trompo Loco was being let out of the mental ward at Lincoln Hospital. We had counted the days for him to get out. I left to go pick him up. When I reached the hospital, I spoke with the doctor and collected his medicine. Then I went to the waiting room to see him. Trompo Loco was there, all ready and packed to come home. Seeing him anxiously awaiting my arrival made me feel ashamed that I never called him by his real name, Eduardo. So, I asked him if it was all right if I called him by his real name. He nodded and said that he likes both names and that he'd like to be called Eduardo only on weekends, because they are shorter, and Trompo Loco on weekdays, because there are more days there and he likes that name better. I said that was a great idea. I told him I was going to introduce him to his father by his real name.

E ddie?" I interrupted his reading.

As soon as he saw me, he knew what I was there for.

"Your son Eduardo is here."

I hadn't dropped by since the fire. Eddie didn't get paid, because everything of mine was in Papelito's name. None of us got any money. But it was his son who lit that fire, and he was held accountable. His inside people had cut him off. The site was being investigated, so even that was also on hold. He was ruined, and so was his secret that he tried so hard to protect. A secret everybody knew.

"He's not my son," Eddie said as if he was tired of saying it, like he had almost given up. Eddie must have denied the existence of Trompo to his friends at the insurance company left and right. Trying hard to make them believe Trompo was not his and therefore it was not his responsibility for the blunder. But it must have been no use. By now, Eddie had said it so many times that it only came out as a croak.

Eduardo was behind me.

"Hello, sir," Eduardo said, crouching, scared as if he was about to see God's face.

"Hello," Eddie said, uninterested.

"I did it for you," Eduardo said, licking his lips.

"I didn't ask you to," Eddie said, looking deeply in Eduardo's eyes, as if he was searching for traces of himself. But then he gave up, as if he had seen enough, and turned his face away.

"But I followed Julio that night and you wanted a fire, sir?" Eduardo had started to make fists with his hands, and his feet were shuffling.

"Well you screwed it all up."

"Thank you, sir."

"For what?" Eddie snapped a bit. "You screwed it all up."

"For talking, sir." Eduardo bowed, and he was so nervous at that point that he was ready to spin, so I held his hand.

"Eduardo," I almost whispered, "we gotta go."

"Okay Julio," he said and looked back at his father before walking out with me. And though Trompo was happy that his father had finally talked to him, it was Eddie's silence that spoke volumes to me. I was never one to judge anybody, not after the things I've done, but here was Eddie's last chance at finding some redemption. To finally acknowledge a part of his life that he was responsible for creating. Mistake or not, Eduardo was his son, and all he wanted was for Eddie to look him in the eye and tell him the truth. I could have said things. I could have said to Eddie that I knew he burned his own mistress's house. That Trompo Loco's mother became homeless because of him, and went crazy. How he could pray all he wanted, go to Rome and kiss the pope's ring, yet he could never take that back. But I saw how broken Eddie was, and it took all my strength not to say those things. To hold back and resist in not kicking him while he was down. Instead, we walked out on him. Leaving the old man to decay in that coffee shop.

Application #24

You will now be placed on a five-to-ten-year waiting list. Please note that your application will move further along as the units begin to vacate at their usual pace. Please note that this is due process. Thank you.

There was talk about this botanica out in Brooklyn run by a *babalawo* who was humble, good and real. So I went to check it out for myself. The botanica was very lively, and I did like it. Though it was nothing like San Lazaro y Las Siete Vueltas, the place did shine with its own resplendence. When I met the *santero*, I told him I wanted to walk in the "ways of the saints" and that I was sincere.

"Who the fuck do you think you are?" he said to me, and I was a bit surprised at a holy man with a potty mouth. "Why should I fucking teach you the ways of the saints? What have you done that proves you are worthy of knowing their stories?" I liked him right away.

He was real.

"I don't know, I just want to learn," I said.

"Well, Ocha is not like Christianity, we don't shove it down people's throats or give it away like government cheese to anyone who comes in here asking for it."

Now I really wanted him to be my *padrino*. I saw Papelito in his eyes. Only Papelito's delicateness, his feline moves, the way Papelito filled his space, were missing.

"I can pay," I said.

I insulted him. "Money? Who gives a shit about your money? In the East, there are temples that make you wait years before they let you in their fucking doors!"

He was a big man with huge hands. So big that I felt he could tear phone books in half.

"I just want to learn," I repeated.

"Oh, yeah. You want to learn. Well what have you done to prove you are worthy of the saints?"

I told him I have done nothing.

"Then you fucking see me when you have figured it out, and maybe I'll teach you the ways. Now get the fuck out of my botanica."

later that night, Trompo Loco was playing with his coin collection that my father had brought him and me, and my parents and me were playing Spanglish Scrabble. The rules were it had to be a word that didn't exist in either language. Not bullshit Spanglish of a bad pronunciation because of accent, like *grincar*, which is really "green card," or *soway*, which is "subway." Or code switching between English and Spanish. No, our rules are the Spanglish word had to be like words that my father continuously made up.

"*Tripiando!*" He spelled it proudly, placing his square letters down, "like tripping, you know, getting high?" Something he once knew a lot about.

"Sounds like eating *tripas*," Mom said to Kesil, who sat on her lap. Kesil always sits on her lap. "Like eating the intestines in your stomach. *Tripiando*?"

Our words were words that didn't exist altogether. They were hybrid sandwiches made of Spanish suffixes and prefixes while maintaining the healthy meat of the English word in between them.

Mom accepted the word, when a knock was heard at the door. I left the game to answer it and it was the *santero* from Brooklyn. He grabbed my neck and hugged me. "Why didn't you fucking tell me Felix Camillo was your ex-*padrino*?" he said, grinning. I don't know how he got my address, but it doesn't take long for things to travel in SpaHa. "Papelito was my teacher, too," he said, and when my mother heard Papelito's name, she got up from the table.

"You're a *santero*?" my mother asked him that night, and when he said yes, she invited him in. "Papelito," my mother said, about to pay Papelito her highest compliment, "was a true Christian." She said this to the *santero* from Brooklyn, whose name was Manny—his name in Ocha was Kimbuki—and he agreed.

"A friend of Papelito," my mother said, "is always welcome in my house."

Manny joined us at the kitchen table, and we explained the rules to him—and started the game from scratch.

It wasn't really that late, but my parents were getting ready to turn in. They said good night to the *santero*, who was getting ready to leave. I walked out with him and we talked by the hallway.

"Papelito once mentioned you to me," Manny said outside, as I waited with him till the elevator arrived. "Let me tell you Julio, that motherfucker was never wrong."

"Me? What he say about me?"

"That you, Julio Santana, was going to do great things. That he had seen a fire in you like no one he had ever met. That you were definitely a son of Chango. Do you know how fucking rare that shit is?"

"I did not know that."

"Well it's also fucking expensive, okay?" he said. Just like Papelito, Manny didn't deny that there was money involved. "He also mentioned another one. A woman."

"Maritza?"

"Yeah, that was it. If she wants to be my pupil I'll take her in."

"She's gone," I said.

"So, it's just you and me then. How far in the teachings did you get with my *padrino*? To the *collares*?"

"Nowhere near the necklaces," I said. "Not very far. I still have trouble remembering what color is attributed to what Orisha—"

"Shit, you're not even close to taking Lukumi 101. You're like in Remedial Lukumi."

I felt like I let him down. But he reassured me it was okay.

"Come see me in Brooklyn, and we'll talk about starting you on your way to saintliness." He hugged me. Told me he would lead me until I was ready for the ultimate ceremony of the *Asiento*, when, hopefully, if Papelito was right, I would become Chango. And, like in all intimate relationships, Chango would reveal to me the meaning of his stories, but only if I'd work in loving the Orisha. If I performed the rituals correctly, Chango would lead me to know the ways of a god. Chango would teach me how to love myself and all living things. My new *padrino* told me it would be a slow and painstaking process. But I would get there, and when I did, Chango's fire would no longer have to be lit, because the Orisha's candles would be inside me. His bata drums would be my heartbeats. Then I, too, would share a duality, like the one Chango shares with the Catholic saint Santa Barbara. Like her, I would be forever linked, become one and the same, with the African black god of natural forces—of lightning, thunder and fire.

The elevator arrived.

Helen shyly stepped out.

Manny hugged me one last time, got in and left.

Helen didn't kiss me or shake my hand. She was wearing a light blue overcoat, so I couldn't see what she was wearing underneath it, but her shoes were the same clunky ones she always wore. Seeing her appear like that made me feel like spring was just around the corner, when in fact it was still January.

Helen apologized for just dropping in like this and asked how I was doing. I said fine. She asked if I got her letter. I thanked her for it. Told her, her letters always reminded me of her hands. Delicate and beautiful, kinda mysterious, too.

"I can only see you in public places," she blurted out.

"Like this hallway?" I said, joking.

"Yes, like this hallway." She smiled just a bit. "I don't trust you, Julio. You or myself. So, can we only meet in public places?"

"Sure." It was no inconvenience to me.

"Okay," she said, punching the elevator button. "The Dalai Lama's in town. Are you interested?"

"Am I interested?" I said happily. "I can go stare at a wall with you."

"Right," she said, looking down, not sure if she had made the correct call by coming to see me. "Right, okay. I'll write you," she said, and the elevator arrived.

Helen said good-night. Then she got in and left.

Brother Malcolm ended his story by giving all the glory and credit to his God while pinning all the mistakes on himself. I'm nowhere near as noble as he was. But after all that's happened to me I feel . . . blessed.

So what? I got knocked back down a few notches. I've been in the projects before and I got out. And I'll get out again. This time, I'll do it right. This time, I'll do it for good. I thought of Helen's letter, the last line. It was authentic, genuine and true.

Papelito once told me that sometimes you play the right number and it never hits. Sometimes you play the wrong number by mistake, and that's the number that wins. When I think of Helen, I finally know what he meant.

And so, full of hope and light, I went back inside my apartment and closed the door behind me.

ACKNOWLEDGMENTS

Legend has it that one day, as he sat in front of a Midtown man-made waterfall, René Alegria had a vision, and this imprint, Rayo, was born. With that same uncanny ability to see beyond what's there my editor guided me toward the completion of this book. His assistant, Andrea Montejo, has been a doll in taking care of all the important little things. I'd be lost without my agent, Gloria Loomis, who was more than supportive during the many false starts I encountered before this novel began talking to me. I thank Katherine "Triple Threat" Fausett (Brains, Beauty, Benevolence); her encouragement was just as invaluable. Justin Allen always kept me up to date. I also thank my father, Silvio, my mother, Leonor, my sisters Frinee and Haydee, my brother James, and my cousin Rafael—their love is always comforting. As is Kendra Hurley's friendship and sound advice and Stefanie Schumacher's company. Cesar Rosado is the best "wing man" a guy could have (those days are over but the adventure continues). His mother, Juanita Lorenzo, is evidence that fictional kinship is possible. Silvana Paternostro practically gave me a chapter, her kind voice was always welcomed. Russell Contrera's humanity, Mat Stafford's nobility, Will Ross's intelligence, Susan D'Aloin's attitude, and Jeanne Flavin's brilliance all continue to contribute to my growth. And lastly, thanks to Brian Flannagan, proprietor of the Night Café; his Sunday-night trivia made a boring day just a tad more interesting.